Catlin

Catlin

Don Higgins

St. Martin's Press
New York

Library of Congress Cataloging in Publication Data

Higgins, Don.
  Catlin.

  I. Title.
PZ4.H6363Cat [PS3558.I3553] 813'.5'4   79-23241
ISBN 0-312-12471-6

For my sisters,
Marybelle and Ted

I

I don't play with girls much, but Catlin's different. She was born a girl but ever since she was born she's wanted to be a boy. She told me so, herself. She said she used to try to pee standing up like a boy. But she ain't got a peter so the pee ran down her leg. I told her I thought that was dumb. And she punched me and said she'd never tell me anything ever again. Catlin can punch doggone hard when she wants to, so I shut up about it.

Catlin's got short hair—a lot shorter than mine—and she wears pants all the time. Some grownups that don't know better call her "Sonny" because they think she's a boy. I don't know why they think she's a boy. She looks exactly like a girl to me. She's got these great big eyes that tell you right off she's a girl. They're blue and purple at the same time. And her eyelashes are long and black like a movie star's. Even her short hair looks like a girl to me. It's that light brown color like caramel candy. With light places in it where the sun hits. It's kind of pretty.

The very first time I saw Catlin I knew she was a girl. It was the day we got to Ruffins Inlet and I didn't know anybody here. So I didn't have anybody to play with. I was sitting on the front steps trying to get up nerve enough to go down the road to where some kids were playing basketball, when this girl with a white T-shirt on and old jeans with holes in the knees came across the yard and sat down on the bottom step. There was a big old gray dog along with her. And when she sat down on the step, the dog flopped down on the ground in front of her and rested his head on one of her bare feet. She took her other foot and scratched back of his head with her big toe.

"Don't never cut 'cross Mrs. McKenzie's yard," was the first thing she said to me. She nodded her head at the house next door so I'd know which yard she was talking about. It was the only house around with the grass mowed. "Mrs. McKenzie don't like people walkin' on her lawn. She'll get her shot-gun an' shoot your ass."

"For true?"

"See that window?" the girl asked me. She leaned over and pointed at an upstairs window that you could hardly see for a big sycamore tree in the way. "She shoots at you from up there."

"She shot a gun at you?" I was very surprised at what she was telling me. Nobody in Richmond shot guns at you for walking on their grass.

"Only once," the girl nodded. "Buckshot went all 'round me. She missed me. But it scared th' shit outa me all th' same."

I slid my eyeglasses back up my nose so I could look at her good, to see if she was telling me the truth. But I'd only just met her so I couldn't make out for sure whether she was faking or not.

"I always go 'round th' other way," the girl said, poking her thumb in the other direction. "Jus' so I don't have to pass by Mrs. McKenzie's house. I don't want that woman shootin' at me no more."

"I don't blame you," was all I could think of to say. I untied my new sneakers and took them off. They're green with blue stripes on the sides. Look just like Adidas only they're not. Mama bought them for me before we left Richmond. I thought the girl would say she liked them, but she didn't.

"What grade're you in?" she asked me.

"Fifth."

"You're gonna be in Miss James's class next year," she said. "She's a bitch on wheels. I had her last year."

If there was one thing I didn't want to talk about, it was school. We'd only just gotten out for summer vacation. And there wasn't no sense in messing up vacation time talking about school. So I picked something else to talk about.

"Who's that big girl down yonder playin' basketball with them two boys?" I asked the girl.

"Th' one with th' big boobs? That's Shirley Mae." She answered me without bothering to look and see who I was talking about. "She's retarded."

The big girl, Shirley Mae, and the boys were shooting baskets in a backyard where somebody had put up a pole and nailed a bushel basket onto it. They were all barefooted. One boy looked like he was eleven, like me. He had red hair and a lot of freckles and had on green shorts, but no shirt. The other boy was a lot taller and older, maybe fifteen. He was a little bit fat and had brown hair and he was only wearing shorts, too. His back was real brown from being out in the sun a lot.

Shirley Mae was about the same tall as the big boy. She had big boobs like the girl said, and light brown hair hanging straight down onto her shoulders. Her shorts had orange and yellow flowers on them and she had on a yellow shirt. She wasn't *real* pretty, but kind of. When she jumped around with the basketball her boobs bounced up and down like you wouldn't believe.

"She won't wear a brassiere," the girl on the steps with me said, like she was reading my mind. Then she looked at me and giggled, and said, "She's yo' cousin, you know."

"No such a thing. She ain't *my* cousin," I said. I was surprised that this girl I'd never seen before would say something like that, even funning.

"Like hell she ain't," the girl said back. "Miss Sissy's your aunt, ain't she?"

"I reckon," I halfway nodded my head, knowing by the way the girl said it that she was making me admit something I'd be sorry for. I didn't know which people in Ruffins Inlet were cousins and which ones weren't. I was born in Richmond and I hadn't ever been to the Inlet before. I remembered hearing Mama and Papa talking about Aunt Sissy because they talked about her a lot. I knew she was Papa's sister and that she was rich and owned an eating place. But the other Inlet people didn't get talked about much and their names kind of floated by me, not hitched to a face or anything that would make me remember who was who. I was sure about one thing, though. I'd never heard anything about a retarded cousin. If Shirley Mae got talked about in Mama's and Papa's talking, there wasn't nothing ever said about her being retarded.

"What's retarded?" I asked the girl.

"Oh, you know," she said, shrugging her shoulders a little bit.

"Shirley Mae ain't real smart. Couldn't pass th' third grade. But she's okay. You wouldn't hardly know she's retarded 'less somebody tells you. She can even read a little bit, like funny papers an' stuff."

"Is she really my cousin?" I asked the girl, hoping she'd say she'd just been fooling me.

"Sho is," the girl said. "Miss Sissy's her Mama an' Cap'n Will's her Daddy. An' that makes her your cousin, don't it?"

"I reckon so," I said slowly.

The girl grinned at me. "Tha's okay," she said. "I'm almos' kin."

"How you mean *almos'* kin?"

"Not blood kin. Jus' kinda kin. Me an' Shirley Mae sleep in th' same room."

"You live at Aunt Sissy's?"

The girl nodded.

"How come you don't live with yo' Mama?"

"My Mama's dead. She got run over by a Exxon truck when I was little."

"Tha's bad."

"I guess so." The girl spit through her two front teeth and sent the spit sailing through the air. It landed maybe ten feet off. That's real good spitting.

"I was real little when it happened," she said, "an' I don't remember Mama so good. 'Cept I remember that she was real pretty. Cap'n Will gimme a picture of her. I'll show you how pretty she was sometime."

We didn't talk for a while. Just listened to the basketball bouncing and the noises the birds and the crickets made. A little green lizard ran across the yard in front of us and left a wavy line in the sand where his tail dragged.

"Where's your Daddy?" I finally asked the girl.

"Ain't got no Daddy," she said.

I don't know what you say to somebody when they tell you they ain't got no Daddy. And when I didn't say anything for a minute the girl asked me, "Is it true what they tell 'bout yo' Daddy?"

"What about him?"

"That he's at . . . th' Funny Farm?"

That made me a little bit mad. "No, it ain't true," I told the girl. "It ain't a bit true. My Daddy's sick in the Hospital."

"Wha's he sick with?"

"He's got mental illness."

"Tha's bad, huh?"

"Yeah, it ain't good," I told her. "But he's gettin' better. And anyway, it *ain't* the Funny Farm."

"Okay."

I reached down and patted her dog on the head. I'm a little bit scared of dogs and I was glad when this one wagged his tail and acted friendly. The girl put her arms around the dog's neck and under his belly and pulled him up in her lap. He was so big he was half in her lap and half on the ground. "Ol' Booze," she said to him and gave him a kiss on top of his fuzzy head.

"That's his name? Booze?"

"Beautiful Booze," she said and gave the dog another kiss. Then all at once she stood straight up, dumping Booze off her lap. "Shit!" she said, and ran off down the road to where Shirley Mae and them were playing. Booze barked and took off after her. Only the two boys were playing basketball now. Shirley Mae was gone.

"Where'd she go, Bootsie?" the girl yelled at the biggest boy. He took one look at Catlin and Booze running toward him and he dropped the basketball and him and the other boy ran up on the back porch and locked the screen door. Booze scooted behind them up to the steps and then sat down, like he was guarding them.

"Call yo' damn dog, Catlin," the big boy said. But Catlin didn't hear him. "Where'd Shirley Mae go?" she asked him again. The red-headed boy said, "MacDonald," and pointed his finger at the next backyard.

"I tol' that pig-fucker not to come 'round here no more," the girl said. She was real mad and I couldn't figure out how come she'd get so mad at Shirley Mae going somewhere with somebody. But I didn't ask her how come. I just ran after her to see what was going to happen.

The girl went scooting off to where the red-headed boy had

pointed, looking behind every bush and garage that she passed. Two houses down there was a shed in the backyard. When she got there, she stopped dead still and hollered loud as she could, "Shirley Mae!" Then she cocked her head to one side and waited for an answer. But there wasn't no answer.

"Shirley Mae, damn you!" the girl called again. "I know you're here someplace."

When she said that, we heard a little giggle come from inside the shed. The minute she heard it, Catlin ran over and swung the shed door wide open.

I didn't see Shirley Mae right off. First thing I saw was this bare behind. Catlin saw it, too, and she grabbed a stick off the ground and gave the behind a hard smack. She smacked it so hard that it left a red mark across one side. She was getting ready to smack again, but the guy whose behind it was grabbed her arm before she could do it. He was holding her arm with one hand and pulling up his jeans with the other one. I thought he was a man, but when I looked at him good in the sunlight I saw he was only about seventeen, or maybe eighteen. As soon as he got his jeans pulled up he took off, walking fast, almost running across the backyard toward the highway, zipping up his pants at the same time.

"God damn you, MacDonald," Catlin yelled after him. "You stay 'way from Shirley Mae or else Cooter's gonna give your white ass a beatin'. You hear?" MacDonald didn't look back. He just kept on walking. When he got to the corner he turned around and grinned and gave Catlin the finger. Then he went around the bend and we couldn't see him no more.

Shirley Mae was sitting on a bench that ran along one wall inside the shed with her legs stretched out in front of her. She had on her yellow shirt, but her pants with the yellow flowers were lying on the cement floor of the shed.

"Leave him alone, Catlin," Shirley Mae said. "We didn't do it." She leaned over and picked up her shorts and started putting them on.

"Don't gimme that shit," Catlin said back to her. "Both of you bare-assed. Don't tell me you didn't do it."

"Well, we didn't," Shirley Mae said.

Catlin took Shirley Mae's arm and gave it a jerk. "Le's go," she said. Shirley Mae went right along without saying a word. It kind of surprised me because Shirley Mae's bigger than Catlin. But she did what Catlin told her to. They cut through somebody's yard and started off down the road. I didn't know what else to do, so I followed along with them.

"What were they doin'?" I asked Catlin. I kind of had an idea what they were doing, but I wasn't real sure because I didn't think kids could do that.

"You don't know what they were doin'?" Catlin asked me. I could tell by the way she said it she was still mad.

"I couldn't see so good," I lied.

"They were fuckin'," Catlin said. "Tha's what they were doin'." She spit in the road to show how mad she was. "You know what fuckin' is, don't you?"

"Yeah," I said. I felt funny talking about it in front of her and Shirley Mae. But it didn't seem to bother them none.

About that time somebody yelled, "Hey Catlin." It was that boy named Bootsie. Him and the red-headed boy were still on their back porch, holding onto the screen door. "Call yo' damn dog!" Booze was sitting at the bottom of the steps watching them.

Catlin called back to him, "S'pose I don't want to?"

The red-headed boy said, "Aw, c'mon, Catlin. We tol' you where Shirley Mae went, didn't we?"

Catlin said, "Le's go, Booze," and snapped her fingers. Booze gave the boys behind the screen door one last look and then trotted right over to Catlin. She leaned over and hugged him around the neck. And we headed down the road again.

"Catlin, we wuzn't fuckin'," Shirley Mae said. "Swear to God. Really we wuzn't."

"Okay, Shirley Mae," Catlin said. "I believe you. You say you wuzn't fuckin', so you wuzn't fuckin'. But you know damn well you would've been if I hadn't got there when I did." She was talking to Shirley Mae like a grown-up talks to a little child. "An' you remember what happened last time."

"Un-huh."

"An' you didn't like it."

"It was awful." Shirley Mae looked like she was almost ready to cry.

"We don't want that happenin' no more, do we?"

"Sho don't. Catlin, please don't be mad at me anymore. I don't like it when you're mad at me. I promise I'll be good. I promise I'll never do it with anybody ever again."

"I ain't mad at you," Catlin said. "But Lawdy, if Miss Sissy ever finds out, she'll chew my ass to a frazzle."

"How come?" I asked.

Catlin looked at me like I was asking a dumb question. "Cause I'm s'pose to look after Shirley Mae," she said. "To keep her out of trouble, an' that ain't easy. Shirley Mae's harder to keep up with than Frank Jenkins's ol' squirrel-huntin' bitch when she's in heat."

"Ain't, neither," Shirley Mae said.

Catlin paid her no mind. "Y'all be extra quiet when we get to th' Manor, now. I don't want Miss Sissy hearin' us."

I hadn't met Aunt Sissy, yet. When me and Mama got off the Greyhound bus from Richmond, Cooter had met us in the pickup truck. Aunt Sissy had sent him to meet us and drive us to our new home. He'd told us that Aunt Sissy wasn't feeling good and she wasn't up to seeing anybody. She'd send word over to us when she was up to a visit, Cooter said. That was okay with me and Mama. Seemed like we'd been riding on that old Greyhound forever, and we were tired. The bus had broke down in North Carolina someplace and we'd had to wait a long time for them to get another bus to pick us up. So we didn't feel much like seeing nobody, either.

II

That day riding on the Greyhound bus for such a long time, listening to Mama talking, and watching her when she wasn't talking, it came on me that something was different about her. When Mama talked, it was higher sounding than it was before. And when she laughed, it was real shrill and didn't sound like she thought what she was laughing at was funny. She was just making a laughing noise.

I figured maybe it was because Mama was worried about leaving Richmond. Richmond was the only place she knew about. That's where she'd been born and where she'd always lived. In the same house, even. Born there and grew up there. She'd be there right now only we had some bad luck and Papa got sick and had to go to the State Hospital. Mama had to sell the house to pay bills and to get money for her and me to live on.

For a while we took in boarders. But that didn't work out good. Them boarder people just fussed about everything until Mama said she thought she was going to have a nervous breakdown. But instead, she sold the house. The guy that bought the house was going to tear it down and build a filling station in the place of it, and that bothered Mama a lot. Mama said the house had a lot of history in it, that it'd be a shame to tear it down. Her Great-granddaddy had give a party there for Mr. Jefferson Davis one time when he was in Richmond. And when Granddaddy Ottway was in the legislature, the Vice President of the whole United States spent the night in the big bedroom with the bay window on the second floor.

And when Mama was twelve, the Governor of Virginia came to her birthday party. That was before Granddaddy Ottway died, and it was the biggest birthday party anybody in Richmond ever had. Granddaddy Ottway put up a big, red and white circus tent in the backyard and more than two hundred people came and ate ice cream and birthday cake. They had a band playing music and a magician doing tricks. Not just children came, grown-ups too.

And everybody brought Mama a present. She wore a long, white dress that Grandmother had to send all the way to London, England, for.

I think Grandaddy Ottway must have been pretty rich, but Mama said No, that he was just comfortably fixed. Anyway, after he died and Grandmother got sick, there wasn't hardly enough money for Mama to finish St. Catherine's and go to college on. She had to sell a great big painted picture of Great-Great-Grandmother Ottway in a fancy gold frame that hung in the front hall, and one of Great-Great-Granddaddy Ottway from over the mantlepiece in the front parlor. She'd kept the house then, but now she had to sell it to a guy who wanted to tear it down and build a filling station. He was the only guy that offered to buy the house and we needed the money. So Mama finally sold it to him.

That was when Aunt Sissy called on the telephone and said for Mama and me to come to Ruffins Inlet. She said that she had this little house nearby and we could come live in it. When she told me all about it Mama said how sweet it was of Aunt Sissy to do this. She said she didn't know exactly what her and me would have done if Aunt Sissy hadn't called.

But after that Mama started looking a little bit different. The white part of her eyeballs started showing all around her blue eyes. She never said a word or let on to me that anything was bothering her. And it didn't come over me till we were riding on the Greyhound bus down to Ruffins Inlet that maybe Mama was scared of something.

"Mama, you scared of something?" I asked her.

"Scared?" Mama asked, and laughed that new, different laugh. "Whatever would I be scared about?"

"I dunno," I told her. I knew that I was a little bit scared, going to a new place to live where I didn't know anybody. We didn't even know what kind of house we would be living in, or who lived next door, or anything. I tucked my hand snug in between Mama's arm and her side, and it helped my stomach not to feel so jumpy. Mama was reading the Hospital letter again—the one we'd got the day before, that said Papa was getting better. She looked at me and smiled and pushed some hair back under her hat that had slipped out.

Mama said she wasn't scared, but if she wasn't scared then what was she? She sure was a lot different from how she was back home in Richmond before she had to sell the house. In Richmond, Mama was always calm and easy. Even that time when Papa got mad and broke all the dishes on the supper table, she didn't get upset.

Maybe Mama was pretending not to be scared now because she didn't want me to know that she *was* scared. My stomach felt funny again when I thought that thought. So I tried hard to think about something else. I looked at the comic book spread open on my lap and tried to think what Batman was doing climbing up that brick wall.

Then I had to go to the bathroom and when I told Mama, she said it wouldn't be long till we got to the next town. But then we went through a bunch of towns without stopping, and I thought I was going to wet my pants. I was holding onto my peter because I was scared some pee would leak out. I had to do that sneaky and cover my hand with my comic book so that Mama wouldn't know what I was doing because she never likes me to put my hand down there. She says that's what common people do.

Anyway, I made it all the way to Ruffins Inlet. Because that was the very next town we stopped in. As soon as the driver started pulling off the road and said "Ruffins Inlet," I squeezed past Mama's legs and ran up to the front of the bus so I'd be the first one off. I left so fast, I forgot my comic books.

The Greyhound stops at the Texaco Filling Station in Ruffins Inlet. I was lucky. The toilet was the first thing I saw when I got off the bus. It was directly in front of me and the door was wide open. I didn't know till afterwards that I went in the Ladies' Room instead of the Men's. But nobody knew. Inside, the Ladies' Room stunk real bad. Maybe that's why they leave the door open. I had to hold my breath the whole time I was peeing. And the door wouldn't lock, so I was holding the door closed with one hand and peeing with the other one.

I got through as fast as I could so I could get back outside and get a big, deep breath of air. The Greyhound bus was gone, and

Mama was standing by the side of the road talking to a tall, skinny colored guy with one blue eye and one brown one. The blue eye didn't move from side to side like the brown one did. The guy was a lot older than me, but he wasn't a grownup, yet. His shoulders were real big—so big they made the blue-striped T-shirt he was wearing look like it was too little for him. And his arms had the biggest muscles I'd near-about ever seen. As big as the guy on the back of my comic book named Charles Atlas. The rest of him was skinny, especially his long bare feet sticking out the legs of his baggy jeans.

"Cooter, this is Chester, Junior," Mama was saying when I walked up to where they were standing. She put her hand on my shoulder.

"You don't need to tell me that, Miss Lucy," Cooter said, pulling my hand up from my side and shaking it and smiling big at me. "I could tell he's a St. Clair a mile away!"

"Chester," Mama said, turning away from Cooter even while he was still talking. "Aunt Sissy's not feelin' well today. I think it must be this heat that's got her. Anyway, Cooter's going to take us to our new home. It's just a little ways down the road from Manor House. And as soon as Sissy feels better, we'll run over and pay our respects."

While she was telling me that, Cooter got our suitcases that the Greyhound had set out on the side of the highway. And slung them up into the back of this old, beat-up, green, pickup truck that was parked nearby.

"Be careful with those bags, Cooter," Mama called to him as we walked over to the truck. "They're pretty old, and they're not very reliable."

"Don't you worry, Miss Lucy," Cooter said. "I'll take good care of 'em." He held the door of the pickup open for Mama and me to climb in, and then went around and got in under the wheel. And we started off down the highway. We went past a supermarket that said *Piggly Wiggly* and a store that said *Western Auto Supply* and another one that said *Henriette's Fashion Shoppe* all stuck together in one long, orange brick building, with a cement place out front to park cars in. Sort of like a piece of a shopping center, but not the whole thing. A little further down the highway, Cooter took a left-hand turn onto a sandy, dirt road that was like a street in a town, only it was dirt and not cement and there were no sidewalks. There were houses along each side, set back from the road and not so close together like in Richmond. They were little houses, all on one floor. Each one had a front porch, some screened and some not, and most all of them were white, except one gray one and one yellow one. They weren't spotted regular along the road. There'd be a couple of houses and then some woods and then two or three more houses. Then maybe a vegetable garden or some chicken coops. And there were lots of trees.

Most of the front yards were planted with grass that ran right down to the road. But some yards, like the one we turned into, were mostly sand with little patches of grass and weeds scattered around.

Cooter drove the pickup off the road and up into the front yard and stopped under a big, old tree with hairy stuff that Mama called Spanish Moss hanging down from every limb. A little off to one side was the house that was going to be our new home. It was a little house like all the others, with a front porch running across the front. On the porch was a swing and a rocking chair, but it wasn't a screened porch and there wasn't any bannister around it. Not even a rail running around it. The house had no upstairs, only downstairs. It was made out of wood and it didn't look like it had ever had a coat of paint on it. The wood was old and gray and you could see all the grain and knots.

The big twisted tree with the hairy moss icicles dripping off its branches shaded most of the front yard. But on one side where it didn't, there was a great big bush in the sunshine with lots of pretty, white flowers all over it that smelled real sweet. Everything was extra quiet. All you could hear were bugs flying around, and crickets and katydids making their racket. It was real peaceful. But it was a little bit spooky, too.

While we were standing there looking around us, Cooter unlocked the front door and put the two suitcases inside.

"I brought you some stuff over from the Manor, Miss Lucy," he said to Mama. "There's milk and eggs in the ice box. An' some salad fixin's. An' there's some flounder an' shrimps an' hush puppies for yo' supper. All you got to do is warm it up a little bit an' it'll be ready." He handed Mama some keys. "This one goes to th' front door. I don't know what them other ones go to." He smiled at Mama. "Miss Sissy said to give 'em to you, so they mus' go to somethin'."

Mama took the keys from Cooter and didn't say anything. She just looked at Cooter. I didn't know what to say, so I didn't say anything, either.

Then Cooter said, "It's a nice house, Miss Lucy. It ain't fancy, but it's nice." Mama smiled at him then, and told him "Thank you" and said we appreciated him meeting us at the bus. And we stood and watched while he got back into the old pickup and backed it up and drove off down the road. The truck wheels whirled up smokey-looking sand that hung in the air after it was gone.

Mama was crying. Not out loud, but tears were coming out of her eyes and slipping down her face and dripping off her chin onto her good pink and blue-flowered dress. I didn't know what to do. I wasn't used to seeing Mama cry. It made my stomach start quivering again like it did back there on the bus. I thought I might cry, too, but I couldn't make any tears come. I took hold of Mama's hand.

"Come on, Mama," I said. "Le's go inside an' see our new house." Mama just stood there and didn't say anything. I didn't know exactly what to do so I waited a minute, and then I started walking toward the front porch. She didn't hold back, but walked right along with me like she was blind and I was showing her which way to go. She still didn't say anything when we went up the front steps, and I was getting scareder and scareder and thinking maybe Mama wouldn't never talk anymore. Then she changed and started talking again.

"I'd forgotten how awfully hot it gets down here in the afternoons," she said. She stopped a minute in the middle of the porch and took her hand loose from mine so she could open up her pocketbook and search out a crumpled Kleenex to blow her nose on. Then she took a deep breath and took hold of my hand again. She pointed with her pocketbook at one of the windows that had a loose shutter that was hanging crooked. "We'll have to fix that shutter there right away," she said. "Looks like the whole place could stand a good coat of paint." Then she tucked her pocketbook under her arm, pulled the screen door open, and stepped inside, pulling me along with her.

The house was all dark inside except for streaks of bright sunshine coming through the closed shutters in the back that made yellow stripes across the floor.

"Well, wasn't that sweet," Mama said. "Cooter closed the shutters on the back to keep out the sun and the heat. It keeps the house cooler. But it makes it kind of spooky, doesn't it? I feel like there are plat-eyes in the corners, watching us."

"What are plat-eyes, Mama?" I asked her.

"Didn't I ever tell you about plat-eyes? They're scary things. But don't worry. They come out mostly at night."

"Are they some kind of ghosts or something?"

"Well, sort of. Oh, let's not talk about plat-eyes. They're kind of scary." Mama does that a lot. She'll start talking about something and when I get interested and want to know more about what she's telling me, she decides she doesn't want to talk about it anymore.

There wasn't much furniture in the living room. A couch with grey and green stripes and a black pillow in the middle that said "Souvenir of Washington, D.C." with little pictures of the Capitol and the White House and the Washington Monument on it. At one end of the couch there was a little wood table with a fat, blue lamp on it. On the other side of the room there was a wood chair with wide flat arms and a big red pillow on the seat and another one in the back. Down at the end, near the window that looked out at the big bush of white flowers, there was a rocking chair like the one on the front porch, only this one was painted white and the one on the front porch wasn't painted at all. I don't think I've ever seen a living room before that didn't have a fireplace, but this one didn't.

The floors were covered with that shiny stuff like they put on kitchen floors, with curly red flowers and green leaves all over it. Mama pulled back one side of the window curtain that had come undone and hitched it back where it was supposed to be. I heard her whisper "Plastic" to herself when she did it.

The dining room was about the same size as the living room.

Not real big and not real little, either. Middle sized. It had the biggest table in it I'd near-about ever seen, big as a Cadillac car, I reckon. There were two chairs down at the other end of the table. Over in one corner there was a tall, wood cabinet-thing with glass doors that had dishes and cups in it. That was all the furniture.

The room was all sweet smelling from a bowl of them sweet-smelling white flowers from the bush in the side yard that some-body had put in the middle of the table. It was sitting on a little, round, white, lacey, paper thing. Instead of making it seem nice, the sweet smell of the flowers kind of made it seem like it had gotten even hotter.

"Gardenias. Isn't that lovely?" Mama said, smiling at the flow-ers. "Ches, honey, see if you can open these windows any wider. There's not a breath of air in this place." While I was trying to open the windows wider and couldn't, Mama leaned way over the big table and pretended to smell the flowers. I knew she was pretending and not really smelling them because I watched her out the corner of my eye and she didn't breathe in. She was just doing something that went along with what she was saying. I'll tell you right now you didn't have to stick your nose down in them flowers to get a smell. The smell was all over the house.

Off one side of the dining room was a big kitchen with a table and two chairs and the usual kitchen stuff, a stove, and a re-frigerator, and cabinets. And off the other side, a hall went to the bathroom and the bedrooms. There was a bedroom for me and a bedroom for Mama. Each room had a two-people bed in it. And a dresser with a mirror over it. And one straight-up wood chair, like the ones in the dining room. The windows had green shades on them, but they didn't have curtains.

"That'll give me something to do," Mama said. "I'll borrow Sissy's sewing machine and run up some nice pink and yellow curtains. That'll brighten things up a lot."

We had looked over the whole house in no time flat. That shows you how big it is.

"Why don't you run outside and look around," Mama said. Then she changed her mind. "No. Before you do that, you'd better help me put the suitcases in the bedroom." So, together me and her dragged the big suitcases into one of the bedrooms. We couldn't lift the big suitcase up on the bed, so Mama just opened it on the floor and dug around till she found me some shorts and an old red T-shirt to put on so I wouldn't mess up my good clothes. I kept on my new sneakers, though.

Then I went outside and looked around the yard. I've said already what the front yard and the side yard looked like—a lot of weeds, a big tree with moss on it, and the big bush with the sweet-smelling flowers. In the backyard there was a garage with a falling-down shed leaning up against one side of it. In the garage there were three stacks of magazines in one corner on the dirt floor that said *Saturday Evening Post* and *Look*. And a rusted bicycle with no tires. In the shed there was only a big trunk with old, smelly clothes in it.

I'd seen all there was to see on the place in five minutes. I went back in the front yard and sat down on the front steps. That's when I saw Shirley Mae and them boys playing basketball in somebody's backyard down the road. And that's when Catlin and Booze came across the yard and sat down on the steps with me.

III

When I went with Catlin that day to take Shirley Mae home was the first time I saw Inlet Manor. There was a sign by the side of the road, a big white sign that was rounded off on the top and on the bottom. At the top it said: HISTORIC INLET MANOR in big black letters. Right underneath that, on a line all by itself, it said: 1790. And under that it said: Seafood—Steaks—Chops. Dinner 5PM–10PM. Closed Mondays. And at the bottom there was a crooked arrow pointing into the driveway.

When we went around the curve of the driveway I was expecting to see something big and fancy, like a castle or something. But it wasn't nothing like that. The house was big all right. But there wasn't no way you could call it fancy. It needed paint worse than our little house, even. You could see little pieces of paint along the sides where the house had one time been white. But now most all the paint was worn off, leaving the old grey boards underneath.

The Manor sat up pretty high off the ground on big, brick things, like posts. And it was turned around so that the front porch pointed the other way, toward the creek, and not toward the road. The back porch was closest to the road. The steps going up to the back porch didn't have backs on them, just the step-on part.

The roof was made out of tin. And that part looked brand new because it was all shiny and red. There were great, big chimneys. And a lot of windows, the kind that poke out of the roof. Most of the windows had shutters, but not all of them.

The Manor looked like the kind of house that poor people live in. But there was something nice about it, too. Sitting there all shaded in the big trees. With the smell of the creek. And the sound of the ocean coming from way off.

Pulled up under a tree near the back steps was the green pickup truck that Cooter had rode us home from the Greyhound bus in. And alongside it was an old, red jeep that this guy was taking cartons of groceries out of. The guy called back over his shoulder to us when he was going up the back steps "Who's your friend, Catlin?" And he grinned at me.

"Tha's yo' cousin, Chester," Catlin called to him.

"Hiya, Coz," the guy said to me. Then he went into the house.

"Tha's Sweetpea," Catlin said.

"Catlin loves Sweetpea," Shirley Mae sang like a song.

"Shut up, Shirley Mae." Catlin tried to punch Shirley Mae, but Shirley Mae jumped out of the way too fast. She said, "Catlin loves Sweetpea," two more times and then quit.

It was only four o'clock, but people were already piling into Inlet Manor to eat dinner, and Catlin said we should go in the back door so we wouldn't get in the way.

"Now remember what I said 'bout bein' real quiet," Catlin said, going in the back door. "I don't want to bother Miss Sissy even a little bit."

Inside the house was nicer than outside. The downstairs hall had wallpaper on the walls. It was old and faded, and peeling off in some places, but the little pink flowers and curling green vines all over made it look pretty. On the right hand side of the back hall there was one of those telephones hanging on the wall like you see in telephone booths—the ones you have to put money into. On the other side there were two doors with a long, skinny, wood cabinet in between them. The cabinet had blue and white dishes standing on their edges on the shelves. The door on the right hand side of the cabinet went into the dining room. You could see people sitting at tables spread with red-checkered tablecloths. Some of them were eating and some were waiting for the waitress ladies to bring their dinner to them. The walls were a kind of light yellow color and had big pictures of people in old-timey clothes like the pictures of Great-Great-Granddaddy and Grandmother Ottway that Mama sold. Through the other door you could see the kitchen. There were some colored women hustling around and the cousin they call Sweetpea was moving stacks of dishes from one place to another. Cooter was sitting on a stool leaning over a barrel on the floor in front of him. His arm was stuck down in the barrel all the way up to his shoulder.

Catlin walked over and closed the kitchen door. "That door's s'pose to stay closed at dinner time," she said. I followed them down the hall, Catlin holding onto Shirley Mae's hand, and Shirley Mae walking along beside her like a little girl walking with her mother. When we passed the dining room door we could feel the cool air leaking out into the hall from the dining room air conditioners.

"What was Cooter doin' back there in th' kitchen?" I asked in a whisper.

"Mixin' hush puppies," Catlin said.

"A whole barrel full?"

"Sho," Catlin said. She turned and headed up the winding stair steps going upstairs, pulling Shirley Mae along with her. "People are crazy 'bout Miss Sissy's hush puppies. You might think tha's a lot of hush puppies Cooter's mixin' up. But come 10:30 there won't be a one left. Ain't that right, Shirley Mae?"

"Tha's th' truth," Shirley Mae said softly. "Everybody's crazy 'bout Mama's hush puppies."

Instead of going on upstairs with Catlin and Shirley Mae, I stopped for a minute to look out the big, front door with the little window panes on each side of it. Everything was brand new to me and I didn't want to miss a thing.

There was a big porch on the right hand side—all unpainted, old, gray wood with wide boards on the floor. The railing of the porch made a back for benches that ran around the sides. The left side of the front porch was boarded up part the way all around, as high as the handle on the screen door. And from there on up it was covered over with screen wire, like a screen porch. But it was different from a regular screen porch because the screen wire was covered over with plastic, like Saran wrap, only thicker. You could almost see through it, but not quite. I looked real careful to be sure what it was, because I'd never seen a screen porch covered with plastic before.

Out beyond the front porch the front yard was mostly sand, with little patches of grass every now and then. It was all shaded over by five or six of them big, twisted trees. The ones with roots that run along the top of the ground for a while before they go down deep. And with them long limbs that hang way down low. They got that hairy moss stuff dripping off of them, too.

At the edge of the front yard the creek flowed by, twisting in from both sides and then cutting out through the marsh directly in front of the house, twisting a little bit to one side and then turning back the other way, and then bending around out of sight. Even after the creek went around the bend, you could see the pattern it made in the green, marsh grass, twisting one way and then the other, like a snake. Way off, the marsh came to an end and you could see little, white sand hills in the distance.

In front of the house there was a narrow boardwalk that ran a little ways out into the creek with a lookout house at the end. The lookout house had benches all around the sides and a roof that looked like it was ready to fall down. Under the lookout there was a rowboat tied up and some ducks swimming around in the water. Even with the noise of the dinner people clanking their spoons and forks on their dishes and talking loud, it seemed real peaceful and quiet. Not like any place I'd ever seen around Richmond.

I felt like I had only looked out the door a couple of minutes, but it must have been longer. Because when I looked back up the stair steps, Catlin and Shirley Mae were out of sight. "Catlin!" I called as softly as I could, and I chased up the stairs after them, two steps at a time. The stair steps were the creakiest ones I'd ever been on and made more racket than any steps I'd heard before in my life. When I got to the landing, Catlin stuck her head out over the bannisters at the top of the stairs. "Sh-h-h-h," she whispered. "If Miss Sissy hears you, I'm gonna kick yo' ass." She said it kind of funning, but I could tell she meant it. I tip-toed the rest of the way upstairs, but it didn't help much. The steps still made an awful racket.

The upstairs hall had a window in the front looking out at the creek, and one in the back over the stair steps. Underneath the front window was an old-timey curved wood sofa with a stuffed red seat. On the wall on each side was a big, dirty, gold frame with a picture in it. One was a lady's head and one was a man's, and they didn't look very happy. The wallpaper was pink with thin, blue stripes. And in between the stripes were chains of yellow and orange flowers. There were two doors on the left hand side of the hall and three on the right hand side.

Catlin opened the nearest door on the left side, the one with a red sweatshirt hanging on the doorknob, and pointed her finger for Shirley Mae to go inside.

"Do I gotta?" Shirley Mae asked, kind of sad.

"In you go," Catlin said, real firm. "It won't be for long. It's 'most supper time. You can watch yo' television or listen to yo' stereo. If you get tired of that, draw me a picture of a horse."

"I jus' drawed you a horse," Shirley Mae said, disgusted-like. "I drawed you a horse day befo' yesterday. A brown horse with white spots. Don't you remember?"

"Tha's right. You sho did," Catlin said. "So this time draw me a cow. A plain brown one." She gave Shirley Mae a little shove that pushed her the rest of the way into her room, and closed the door behind her. "Make th' cow's horns pink," she said through the door.

"Pink?" You could hardly hear Shirley Mae.

"Yeah, that'll be pretty with th' brown." Catlin hooked the latch on the outside of the door. "I'll bring your supper up in a little while," she said quietly, holding her head near the door. I thought Shirley Mae would let out a yell, but she didn't. We listened outside the door for a minute. Then we heard Olivia Newton-John singing "Have You Ever Been Mellow." Shirley Mae had put on a record and was singing along with it. She knew all the words.

"She's okay," Catlin said. She straightened one corner of the flowered rug that had flopped back on itself. And we walked over and started down the stairs.

"CATlin," a lady's voice called out from behind one of the other doors. It was the door in front of the bathroom door.

"Shit!" Catlin hissed. "We made too fuckin' much racket." Then she called "Yes'm" back to the lady, making her voice sound as sweet as she could.

"Who's that?" I whispered.

"That's yo' Aunt Sissy, damnit," Catlin took hold of the bannister and pulled herself back up the three steps she'd gone down. She dragged her bare feet across the hall like they weighed a ton. When she got over to the door, she opened it and stuck her head through to the other side and said, "Yes'm, Miss Sissy?"

"Who's that with you out there?" the voice demanded.

"It's Chester," Catlin said. She waited a second or two, and then she said, "From Richmond," like she needed to explain who I was.

"I *know* where he's from, damnit," said the voice. "Boy, come in here."

So I went in.

IV

"You're a *little* runt, ain't you," Aunt Sissy said to me when I walked into her room. I didn't say anything back because for a minute I was so busy looking I couldn't say anything. I pushed my glasses back up my nose so I could see better.

In front of me was a little, dressed-up, fat lady, sitting in the middle of a gigantic, shiny brass bed. I guess you'd call her very plump instead of fat. Her skin looked like a blown-up pink balloon, with no wrinkles anywhere. Her hair was yellow-colored curls and waves all over her head, like the hair you see on baby dolls. She had on a red dress made out of some kind of shiny cloth. And it had lots of ruffles all around the neck. She looked like a big, chubby doll. But when she talked it came out low and gruff like a man.

"Well, can't you talk, boy?"

"Uh, yes'm," I stammered. I walked over and poked my hand out to her like Mama taught me to do. "Pleased to meet you, Aunt Sissy."

She took my hand, but instead of shaking it she used it to turn me around so she could look at the back of me. It made me feel silly. I shrugged at Catlin, and Catlin shrugged back.

"Cooter tol' me you looked like a St. Clair," Aunt Sissy said. "That damn nigger's blind in one eye an' can't see out th' other. You look exactly like your Mama's family. Got bad eyes like all them Ottways."

"Yes'm."

"Kind of prissy, too. Jus' like yo' Mama."

That made me want to punch her in the nose, but I knew I couldn't do that. You don't punch ladies, and besides, Aunt Sissy had give us a house to live in.

"He don't seem prissy to me at all," Catlin took up for me. I liked her a lot for saying that.

"Nobody asked you, dear," Aunt Sissy sneered at Catlin. "Nobody asked you a damn thing. So do me a favor and keep your little cracker mouth shut." She leaned way over to the round table beside the bed, reaching for a package of cigarettes, grunting and snorting the whole time she was doing it. She pulled a long, brown cigarette out of the pack and sat back up. Then she went through the reaching and snorting again to get a box of kitchen matches that was on the table next to the pack of cigarettes. When she got herself back up straight again, she lit the cigarette with one of the kitchen matches and then shook the match out.

"Seems to me if yo' Mama taught you any manners at all you'd have run 'round and got the cigarette for me." The smoking cigarette bounced up and down in her mouth when she talked. "I know better than to expect anything like that from *this* one." She nodded her head at Catlin, squinting to keep the cigarette smoke from getting in her eyes. She took a long drag on the cigarette and took it out of her mouth with two fingers like cigarette smokers do. "But I *do* expect it from a St. Clair."

"Yes'm."

"Is that all you know how to say, boy—Yes'm?" She picked up a grey-colored book marked LEDGER from a pile on the bed, pulled a pencil from behind her ear, and commenced writing in the book. "Now get th' hell outa here," she mumbled. "I ain't got time to waste on you brats."

Me and Catlin turned around and started to go. That's when I saw the baby-pen on the other side of the room in front of the fireplace. It was a regular baby-pen, except that it had pink and red and yellow plastic flowers twisted up and down the side spokes like they were growing up a fence. And instead of a baby, there were two dogs in it. Two little, white poodle dogs with little, pink ribbons tied in the fluffy hair on top their heads. They were standing with their front feet on the top of the pen watching everything Catlin and me did. I started to go and pet one, but when I took a step toward the pen they both started growling, so I backed up.

"Wait a minute," Aunt Sissy said. She dropped the ledger book down in her lap. "Jus' one damn minute." Me and Catlin turned around to see what she wanted. "What were you doin' up here in th' firs' place? You jus' lookin' over th' place, or what? I tol' Cooter to tell yo' Mama that I'd send word over when I was ready to see you." She pointed her finger at me. "Lemme tell you somethin', boy. Nobody comes messin' 'round th' Manor less they've been invited. D'ya understand' that?"

"I jus' come over with Catlin," I explained to her. "I didn't have no idea you'd be mad, Aunt Sissy." The way she was looking at me made my stomach feel funny.

"Since when does Miss Catlin invite her friends over to Inlet Manor?"

"He jus' come with me to bring Shirley Mae home," Catlin said. "Don't getcha self all upset, Aunt Sissy." Catlin put her hand over her mouth. She'd said *Aunt* Sissy instead of *Miss* Sissy. That made Aunt Sissy extra mad.

"What'd you call me?" she screamed at Catlin.

"I'm *real* sorry, Miss Sissy," Catlin said. "I made a mistake. Chester, here, was callin' you Aunt Sissy an' when I said it I made a mistake. It jus' slipped out."

"You bet you made a mistake," Aunt Sissy said. Then she gave Catlin a lecture about how her and everybody treated Catlin like a member of the family, but that shouldn't give Catlin the idea she was a *real* member of the family. And just a whole bunch of stuff like that. On and on and on. All the time Aunt Sissy was talking, Catlin's back got straighter and straighter, till it was straight as a board. And her neck stretched out so she looked two feet taller. Her chin was stuck so high in the air till she was looking down her nose to see Aunt Sissy. And there was a little piece of a smile on her face.

"Wipe that damn grin off yo' face," Aunt Sissy said.

"Yes ma'am."

"I got a good mind to give you a smack."

"Yes ma'am."

"Get th' hell outa here. Both of you."

I hustled myself out of the room as fast as I could, but not Catlin. She took her own sweet time, walking real slow. And closing the door even slower.

We walked down the creaky stairs without saying anything. Just looking at each other and saying "Whew!" with our eyes. I couldn't hardly wait to get outside so I could ask Catlin something. "Is she *always* mean like that?" I asked as soon as we got out the back door.

Catlin sat down on the top step. "Most of th' time, I guess. I mean, she *sounds* mean. But she ain't really mean." Booze came out from under the house and climbed up the steps, wagging his tail.

"She evermore sounds mean," I said.

"Well, you gotta take my word for it. Miss Sissy *ain't* mean." Catlin was trying to talk while Booze was licking her in the face, moving her head from one side to the other to get away from Booze's tongue. "I mean, well. Miss Sissy has took care of me ever since my Mama died."

"Yeah?"

"Yes, she has. And she's took care of Cooter, too."

"She has?"

"She has. You know that blue eye Cooter's got? It's made out of glass."

"I'll be dogged."

"Cooter got a bad sickness in his eye. An' Miss Sissy took him up north to a big hospital, th' best in th' world. An' she spent a heap of money tryin' to get his eye fixed so it wouldn't go blind."

"Aunt Sissy did that?"

"Sho did. It didn't do no good. In th' end his eye went blind anyway. But Miss Sissy spent plenty of money tryin' to get Cooter's eye fixed, let me tell you."

"I'll tell you one thing," I said to Catlin. "When you poke yo' chin up in th' air like you did you really make that lady mad."

Catlin smiled. "Yeah," she said. "I guess I do." Then she said, "Lemme show you something," and she got up off the steps and ducked under the house. So I did too.

You know how houses usually are, close to the ground so that you have to crawl on your hands and knees to get under them. Inlet Manor ain't like that. The Manor sits high off the ground so you only have to stoop over a little bit to go under it. Afterwards, you have to walk bent over like an old man. But sitting down in the sand, or even on your knees, you can straighten up all the way without your head touching the floor above it.

Underneath Inlet Manor there's stuff lying around everywhere. Old beat-up furniture, a step ladder, some long wood boards, an empty trunk, three saw horses, and stacks and stacks of window shutters. And split wood for the fireplaces.

Catlin put her finger up to her lips and said, "Sh-h-h-h, don't make no racket or they'll hear you." I wasn't making any racket, but I nodded yes anyhow. Booze must've thought we were playing a game or something, because he started barking and wagging his tail.

"Hush up, Booze," Catlin whispered as loud as she could. Then Booze put his front paws on Catlin's chest and started licking her in the face, and we had to giggle because Catlin's head was butted up against the floor of the Manor so she couldn't get away from Booze's licking. There wasn't nothing to do but let him lick till he got tired of licking and quit.

Catlin wiped her face with the back of her hand. Then she went a little bit further toward the front of the house and dropped down on her knees. Directly over her head there was a square place in the floor that was different from the rest of the floor. What it was, was a hole in the floor with something over it, covering it up.

"Ain't nothing but a flat piece of iron," Catlin whispered. She took both hands and slowly slid it out of the way. When it was all the way to one side, she stuck her head up through the hole. The hole was about the same size as her head, so it looked like her head got chopped off. In a minute she stooped and pulled her head back out of the hole.

"Ain't nobody there, yet," she said.

"Who's s'pose to be there?"

"I'll tell you later. C'mon."

"But I wanta look through the hole," I told her.

"Ain't nothing to see, now. You can look later."

She took hold of my arm and pulled me over to where one of the big chimneys came down to the ground. There were window shutters leaning against it and Catlin, after looking all around to be sure nobody was watching us, opened back the shutter on one end. Behind it was a big hollowed-out place in the chimney, like a fireplace.

"Go on in," Catlin said, giving me a little nudge. I crawled in and Catlin came in behind me. It was a real big fireplace, and after you got inside and pulled the shutter closed, it was like a little room. Catlin lit a candle and held it up so I could see everything. You had to sort of squat down or else you'd bump your head, but it was really *neat*. Catlin had some pillows to sit on. And a little green wood stool for a table, with a yellow napkin for a tablecloth, and a teapot full of Coca-Cola in the middle of it. Down at the other end of the little brick room there was a shelf-thing that Catlin had made out of driftwood. That was where she kept glasses and cups and spoons and things. After giving me a minute to look around, she set the candle down on the stool-table and poured us each a glass of Coke. It was warm and didn't have any bubbles, but it still tasted good. All around on the walls were seashells that Catlin had glued to the bricks. Periwinkles, and wing shells, and sea biscuits, and little conchs. It was really neat.

"Shirley Mae don't even know 'bout this place," Catlin whispered.

"How come?"

"Well, she don't mean to, but Shirley Mae tells everybody everything she knows."

"Oh."

"You ever tell anybody 'bout this place I'll beat yo' ass good and proper," Catlin whispered real gruff, to let me know she meant business.

"I won't tell nobody," I whispered back. "Why are we whispering?"

She pointed to a hole in the chimney up over our heads. " 'Cause everything we say goes right up there, to th' kitchen," she said. "Don'tcha hear 'em talkin' up there?"

I listened. Yeah, you could hear it pretty plain. Cooter was talking to the kitchen women. I could hear dishes and pans clanking and making racket. Cooter and the women were laughing and having a good time. They'd be talking along and then they'd stop, and a different voice would say, "Three regular seafoods," or, "One flounder," or something like that. Then there'd be some quiet and then the women and Cooter would start laughing and talking again. The only thing was that I couldn't

understand a word they were saying. The only part I could understand was when the different voice would come in and say, "Two
soft-shell crabs," or whatever it was she was saying.

I looked at Catlin. "Are they talkin' English?"

"Sho," Catlin nodded her head.

I listened a little bit more. Every now and then I'd think I
understood a word but I wasn't sure. I shook my head. "Don't
sound like English to me."

Catlin looked at me funny and said, "It's gullah. It's th' way
niggers talk. Don't they talk that-a-way in Richmond?"

"I never heard *nobody* talk that way before." I listened some
more while I was finishing my Coke. But it didn't do any good. I
plain couldn't understand them. "What'd you say it was they were
talkin'?"

"Gullah," Catlin said. "It's jus' a different way of talkin'. It's th'
same words. They jus' say 'em a different way." She pushed the
shutter open and we crawled out and sat down in the sand. Catlin
was careful to push the shutter closed after we got out. With the
shutter closed you wouldn't guess that there was a little room
behind it.

"You don't have no trouble understandin' what they were
sayin'?" I asked Catlin.

"Nope."

I didn't believe her. "Then what were they sayin'?" I asked her.

Catlin giggled. "Same thing they always talk about when they
don't know anybody's listenin'."

"Wha's that?"

Catlin giggled again. "They're teasin' Cooter 'bout his big
thing."

"What kinda thing?"

"Oh, you know. His *thing*. His . . .peter."

"Oh," I looked down at the sand. I felt funny. I'd never heard a
girl say that before. It took me a minute before I could look at her
again. When I did she had a little stick in her hand about as big as a
pencil, and she was stirring it round and round in the sand.

"How d'they know Cooter's got a big . . . thing?"

"Don't ask me," Catlin shook her head. She kept stirring the sand with the stick. "I guess they've seen it." Then she started saying a rhyme. I mean, it sounded like a rhyme the way she sort of sang it, only it didn't rhyme.

She said, "Doodle-bug, doodle-bug come to supper. What you got but bread an' butter." It sounded dumb but she kept saying it. Over and over.

All at once she said, "Got 'im!" She pinched up some sand from where she'd been stirring and put it in her hand. Then she held her hand out for me to see.

"What is it?"

"It's a doodle-bug, dummy." There was a tiny little gray bug in her hand about as big as a grain of rice. On one end he had little pinchers, like open scissors.

"That ain't no doodle-bug," I said.

"Th' hell it ain't," Catlin said. She frowned at me. "I bin catchin' doodle-bugs ever since I was born an' I know a fuckin' doodle-bug when I see one."

She sounded real sure about it so I just said, "Well, it ain't like no doodle-bugs we got in Richmond."

"What do they know 'bout doodle-bugs in Richmond?"

Catlin tilted her hand and let the bug roll back on the sand. As soon as it hit the sand it started digging. "Them yankees!" Catlin spit in the sand by her right knee.

"Ain't yankees, neither," I said, hard as I could.

"Well, *you* sho Gawd sound like one. Comin' down here tellin' me what *is* a doodle-bug and what *ain't* a doodle-bug."

"Th' doodle-bugs in Richmond are white an' look like a little worm with all his feet on one end with his pinchers. They dig little round holes in th' ground, an' when you stick a piece of grass down th' hole they push it back out with their pinchers. So you jus' pull th' grass out an' they're hanging on th' other end."

"I don't know nothin' 'bout *them* bugs," Catlin said. "*Our* doodle-bugs make little cups in th' sand. See all them little cups over there?" She pointed at a bunch of little holes that looked like the inside of a pointed ice cream cone. "Th' doodle-bug stays down at th' bottom with his pinchers ready. Watch." She picked up an ant that was crawling by her left big toe and dropped it into one of the little cups. The ant tried to crawl up the side and get out. But he couldn't make it up the side and kept slipping back down to the bottom of the ice cream cone. You could see the doodle-bug's pinchers snipping around, this way and that way, at the bottom of the cone, trying to catch the ant. Then all at once he caught him and pulled him down under the sand.

"See?" Catlin said. "Now he'll suck th' guts outa th' ant."

"How you know that?"

"Cap'n Will tol' me."

"I don't believe it."

"Suit yourself," Catlin said. "All I can do is tell you th' truth an' if you don't wanta believe it, then jus' don't. Ain't no skin off *my* ass."

I didn't say anything for a while, and Catlin didn't either.

"Were them people upstairs sayin' what you said they were sayin'?" I asked her finally.

"Sho were," Catlin nodded and grinned. "They tease ol' Cooter 'bout that all th' time. He mus' have a real big one. All th' colored people 'round here know 'bout it."

I was going to ask more about it. Maybe ask her if she'd ever seen a boy naked. But before I could ask her anything else she got up off the sand and hobbled hunchback over to where the hole was in the floor, and stuck her head up through it. Right away she pulled her head back out and signaled me to hurry over. When I did, she motioned for me to poke my head up through the hole.

It was crazy. One minute I'm under the house and the next minute I'm in the Inlet Manor dining room with my chin resting on the floor, underneath a big table. The red and white checkerboard tablecloth hangs low all around the table so nobody can see my head. The tablecloth keeps me from seeing good, too. All I can see are legs and feet. There's only two people sitting at this big table, a man and a lady. He's got on brown pants and deck shoes, and she's got on a white dress and red sandals. I can see that much. And I can see that he's got his hand on her knee.

You can't see much else around the dining room. Only men's and ladies' legs and feet, and some children's. There's a lot of racket going on. Dishes rattling and people talking.

"How come you won't let me put my hand on your knee?" the guy asks the lady over my head. His hand ain't on her knee anymore. She's holding it down by her side in between them. They're talking softly so nobody can hear them. Only I can hear them easy. I have to work hard to keep from laughing out loud. What would they say if they knew I was watching their feet and hands and listening to them talk?

"Silly," the lady whispered back to the guy. "Linda almost saw us that time. An' you know if Linda sees us everybody in Ruffins Inlet will know 'bout it before seven o'clock tonight. Now you be a good boy and maybe later. . . ."

I ducked my head back under the house. "Some guy wants to put his hand on this lady's knee an' she won't let him do it, " I told Catlin. I could hardly say the words for giggling so much.

"Y'know who that is?" Catlin asked me. She was giggling, too. "Tha's yo' Uncle Will."

"It is?"

"Tha's SueAnne with him," Catlin said. "You know which one she is? She waits tables an' she's got long blonde curley hair."

"We jus' got to Ruffins Inlet this afternoon," I said. "I don't know nobody."

"Well, tha's who SueAnne is. She waits tables an' her an' Cap'n Will eat supper together every evenin'."

"How come Uncle Will don't eat with Aunt Sissy?"

"Miss Sissy eats supper upstairs in her bedroom."

"D'you think she knows 'bout Uncle Will an' SueAnne eatin' together."

"Course she knows," Catlin said, looking at me like I'd said something dumb. "Don't nothing' go on 'round here that Miss Sissy don't know 'bout. Besides, everybody knows 'bout Cap'n Will an' SueAnne. Everybody knows that Miss Sissy slips Sue-Anne ten bucks a week extra so she'll eat supper with Cap'n Will an' keep him company. 'Bout th' only one that don't know is Cap'n Will."

"Yeah, but he's feelin' that lady's knee. Does Aunt Sissy know 'bout that, you think?"

Catlin laughed. "Most of th' time it ain't jus' her knee he's after. Most of th' time he's tryin' to slide his hand up under her dress. Every now an' then he'll get his hand all th' way up to her crotch." Catlin giggled. "Man, you oughta see ol' SueAnne jump then!"

I had to think about that for a little while. After you get married aren't you supposed to eat supper with the person you're married to? Before Papa went off to the State Hospital, him and Mama and me always ate supper together every day. Even after he started having those times when he'd get real mad and break things.

"C'mon, le's go," Catlin said. "I gotta get Shirley Mae her supper."

Before we left she made me promise again not to tell anybody about her secret place. I had to hold up my hand and swear to God.

V

Ruffins Inlet ain't much of a place. I mean, it ain't very big. In fact it's very little. It's not even a town. You call it a village. Catlin showed me the whole place in an hour.

There's one main road that cuts off of the Charleston Highway and goes curving this way and that down to Inlet Manor. Then it goes on by Uncle Will's Deep-Sea Fishing dock and curves back and runs into the Charleston Highway again. Mama says it's what used to be the old road to Charleston, before they made the big Highway. Now it's called Manor Road.

There are some roads that cut off of Manor Road and go straight back to the Highway. Everybody calls them "streets", but they really ain't nothing but roads. They're different from Manor Road because they go straight and Manor Road curves all over the place. There are four of them, I think. At least that's all I can think of right now. Willow Street and Church Street and Oak Street and King Street.

Near-about everybody in Ruffins Inlet is named St. Clair, or else they're kin to St. Clairs. Course, the summer people ain't kin. Neither are the Mercers or the McKenzies or the Jenkins or the Lazenbys. But just about everybody else is, I think.

Some are more kin than others, and some are just a little bit kin. Take Bootsie and Eugene. They call Aunt Sissy, Aunt Sissy, but they call Mama, Miss Lucille. Mama explained it to me one time, but I don't remember exactly why she said they do that.

And Mama explained to me that there used to be lots of Ruffins in Ruffins Inlet, but now Uncle Will's the only one left. I asked Mama where'd they all go to, and Mama explained that they hadn't gone anywhere, that Ruffin babies were all sickly and died young, except for Uncle Will. He's the only one left living, and him and Aunt Sissy don't have a boy-baby to carry on the Ruffin name. Uncle Will and Aunt Sissy have been trying to get Sweetpea to change his name from St. Clair to Ruffin, else when Uncle Will dies that's the end of the Ruffins in Ruffins Inlet. I asked Mama was Sweetpea going to do it, and she said she didn't know.

I got plenty of cousins. Jo-Jo and Shirley Mae and Mary Margaret and Sweetpea. Cousin Martha and Cousin Teresa are old like Mama, maybe older. And Millie and Herbert and Chico and Bernadette. And there's more of them that I don't remember right now.

Catlin's not a cousin. She's no kin at all. Her last name is Flanigan (I think that's the way you spell it.)

Manor House is the oldest house in Ruffins Inlet. I can't think exactly how old Mama told me it is, but it was built a real long time ago. Like before the Yankee War, even.

This guy that built it was named Ruffin, and when he built the Manor there wasn't nothing else around here. No houses, no nothing. That's why the Inlet got named after him. When he built the Manor it was just for summertime living, because in the wintertime this guy lived on a big plantation back yonder up Santee River. Him and his family would just come down to the Inlet in the summertime when the mosquitoes got so bad up the Santee they couldn't stand it. I'll tell you one thing right now. If they got more mosquitoes, or bigger ones, up the Santee than we got right here in Ruffins Inlet I feel sorry for them. I think maybe they got different mosquitoes up there from the ones we got here. Mama says there's a bad sickness people get from some mosquito bites. Mary-something.

All the plantations got names and this one has got a name, too. Greenleigh Hall. The first time I heard anybody say it, I thought they were saying Greenleaf. (I think that would be a better name.) Aunt Caroline and Cousin Martha and Cousin Teresa talk about it all the time, and from the way they talk you'd think Greenleigh Hall is this big, fancy plantation with a hundred rooms in it. Only it ain't. Catlin told me all about it. She said that the fanciest thing Greenleigh Hall's got are the front steps. They're real wide, she says, and it takes a lot of them to reach up to the front porch because the first floor is high off the ground. The front porch is big and fancy, too, with big posts called columns that, Catlin says, need painting. Inside the house ain't so hot, Catlin says. Two rooms downstairs and then two on top of them, upstairs. That makes four rooms in all. The rooms are great big, but they ought to be when you ain't got but four of them. There's a big hall or something in between the rooms where the stairsteps go up and down.

That's what Catlin told me about Greenleigh Hall. So now, when Aunt Caroline and them carry on like they do about how "beautiful" and "gracious" Greenleigh Hall is, I just think about what Catlin told me. But I don't say nothing, not even to Mama. I just listen, and when they start lying I know they're lying. Catlin says it ain't lying, it's bullshitting.

There's an old, colored lady that lives at Greenleigh Hall now. I don't mean *now* like she just moved in. I think she's been living there a long time, only now she's the only one that lives there. I forget what her name is, but she's ninety-two years old and she lives all by herself. It's a wonder that old lady don't freeze to death. Because you know what? There ain't no furnace in the house. Only fireplaces and a wood stove in the kitchen to cook on. To keep herself warm that old lady's got to make fires in them fireplaces all the time. That ain't easy. I can still remember Papa building a fire in the living room fireplace in Richmond. It would keep going out and he would get mad and say a lot of cuss words.

Something else about Greenleigh Hall. They ain't got no bathroom in the house, either. I don't know how the old lady handles that.

About the only time anybody ever goes up to Greenleigh Hall is on Grandpa St. Clair's Funeral Day. That's when they have this gigantic picnic, and everybody named St. Clair shows up. They used to have a picnic on Thanksgiving, too. Only one year it got freezing cold and nobody went. And nobody's thought about going up there on Thanksgiving since.

There's one thing Ruffins Inlet ain't got. One *big* thing. They ain't got a Picture Show. If you want to go to the Picture Show, you got to drive all the way up to Ocean City. Or else down to Charleston. That's a long ways to go for a Picture Show. When me and Mama lived in Richmond, we went to the Picture Show almost every week. Sometimes twice.

VI

Let me tell you about Sweetpea. His real name is Allison, and he's almost nineteen. At Inlet Manor they call him the bus boy. It ain't got nothing to do with the buses. What it means is that he clears away dirty dishes off the tables at the Manor when people get through eating. And he brushes the crumbs off the tablecloth if it ain't too dirty to use again. Or if it's too dirty, he puts a clean tablecloth on the table and napkins and silver around for the next bunch of eaters.

Sweetpea's pretty tall and he's skinny. But he's got plenty of muscles all over his arms and legs, and his back and stomach. You can see them real good when he lifts them red plastic tubs full of dirty dishes to take back to the kitchen. He wears tight jeans and tight shirts just so you can see his muscles. His hair is real light-colored from staying out in the sun so much, and it hangs down over his ears and down the back of his neck kind of like mine, only my hair's a lot darker.

The red jeep that's parked in back of Inlet Manor belongs to him. It's a very old jeep. It's so old Sweetpea says that it was in the World's War. He showed me two holes in the side that he said bullets made. He said that the soldier that was driving the jeep got both his legs shot off and had to get around in a wheelchair all the rest of his life. I don't know whether I believe that or not. I mean, how could two little bullets shoot a guy's legs off? But Sweetpea told me, and it's his jeep so I reckon he ought to know. The whole back seat is gone out the jeep so maybe a bomb hit it, and that's what shot off the guy's legs.

In the back of the jeep where the back seat used to be there's a wood floor, kind of like a shelf, that Sweetpea built. And on top of the wood floor he nailed two of them shiny steel kitchen chairs, the ones with them blue plastic seats and backs. It looks real cool with them blue seats sitting up in the air like that. And it's fun riding back there, only you have to hold on tight as you can, else you'll bounce out.

Sweetpea smokes grass. The reason I know he does is because one time, when me and Catlin went up to his room to get his new television to show Ramona (it's the littlest, teeniest TV you ever saw), I smelled this real sweet smell in his room. I asked Catlin what was making that sweet smell, and she showed me some stuff named incense that was burning in a funny-looking brass bowl and putting out this sweet smell. Catlin told me that Sweetpea burns incense because the smell of it burning covers up the smell of the grass he's been smoking. You never can tell by the way Sweetpea acts whether he's been smoking grass or not, because he cuts up and acts crazy all the time, anyhow.

Don't ask me why Sweetpea lives with Aunt Sissy, but that's what he does. Aunt Adelaide is his Mama and Uncle Benny is his Daddy, but Sweetpea lives at Inlet Manor with Aunt Sissy and Uncle Will. He started living there when he was six years old and Aunt Adelaide was real sick with pneumonia. Aunt Sissy took Sweetpea over to the Manor so she could look out for him, and so he wouldn't be bothering his Mama. Sweetpea just never went home after that. When you ask him about it, he jokes and says Aunt Sissy's holding him till Uncle Benny pays her the money he owes her.

Sweetpea goes to college up in the North to a place called Harvey or something like that. Then in the summertime he comes home and works at the Manor. He really works, too. You should see him hustling around the dining rooms, setting up tables, clearing them off, washing dishes. Anything needs to be done, Sweetpea does it. Things get broke, Sweetpea fixes them. He drives the pickup up to Ocean City every day to get groceries, because Aunt Sissy won't pay to get stuff delivered to the Inlet.

Aunt Sissy thinks Sweetpea's near-about perfect and she can't hardly talk about nothing else. She's *always* talking about how good-looking he is, and how smart he is. She thinks everything he says is funny, which it mostly is. And there ain't a thing in the world he wants but what Aunt Sissy don't buy it for him. Like Cooter said, "If Sweetpea ain't got it, it's 'cause Sweetpea don't want it." She bought him that little teeny TV he just got. And that red jeep with the two bullet holes in it. She bought that for him. Aunt Sissy didn't want to buy that old, beat-up jeep for him. She said that was a little trashy for him to be riding around in. She wanted to buy him a brand new Ford car instead. But Sweetpea wanted that red jeep, and that's what he got.

Him and Mary Ellen like each other a whole lot. Me and Catlin saw them kissing one time, and Catlin says they're in love. Mary Ellen is that girl that waits tables, the one with long, black hair that hangs down her back when she's not waiting tables. When she waits on tables, she pulls her hair up in the back and puts a net over top of it so hair don't get in people's seafood.

I asked Catlin wasn't she jealous of Mary Ellen and Catlin said, "Naw". She says Mary Ellen ain't going to last long at Inlet Manor. Catlin says Aunt Sissy don't like it when Sweetpea goes off to the movies and takes Mary Ellen with him. There was this girl at the Manor last summer, Catlin says, that Sweetpea took to Ocean City to the movies twice and to Charleston once. Her name was Veronica and she was pretty like Mary Ellen, and Aunt Sissy fired her.

VII

It was after supper and the moon was fat and round the night that Sweetpea took us to Greenleigh Hall to see Laura's grave. Sweetpea said it had to be a full moon otherwise there wasn't no sense in going. Because Laura only shows up when the moon is full.

I'll tell you who all went. It was Sweetpea and Cooter and me and Catlin and Shirley Mae and Mary Ellen. All of us got in the red jeep. First, Mary Ellen and Shirley Mae got in the front seat with Sweetpea, and me and Catlin and Cooter got in the back. Catlin and Cooter sat up in the kitchen chairs and I sat down on the wood floor in between them, because I'm littler. Then Shirley Mae said that she didn't like sitting up front and she wanted to sit in the back with Cooter. Sweetpea said No, that she had to sit up front with him and Mary Ellen.

Then Shirley Mae whined and pouted and carried on so about how the seat wasn't big enough for her and Mary Ellen both to sit on. So finally Sweetpea stopped the jeep and got Catlin to change seats with Shirley Mae, just to make Shirley Mae hush up her fuss.

Sweetpea said it only took fifteen minutes to get to Greenleigh Hall, but it felt like a lot longer than that to me, on account of the road was so bumpy and what I was sitting on was so hard. Every time we hit a bump, everybody would bounce up in the air off their seats and then come back down hard, bam-a-lam! Them boards was really giving my tail a hard time. Mary Ellen was giggling and laughing a lot and that made Sweetpea search out more bumps to go over so Mary Ellen would laugh some more. Catlin was laughing, too, and so was Shirley Mae.

Shirley Mae kept bouncing out of her kitchen chair and landing on Cooter and grabbing him around the neck. But you could tell by the way she did it that she was doing it on purpose. Once she landed square in the middle of his lap and put both her arms around his neck, all the time laughing a high laugh I'd never heard her do before. Cooter didn't seem to like that so good. He kept shoving Shirley Mae back over in her chair, but she kept bouncing back into his lap.

It was a crazy ride, and I was glad when somebody said "We're there!" and Sweetpea stopped the jeep. As soon as he stopped, Cooter and Catlin got out and opened these big, iron gates in front of us. Sweetpea drove through and waited a minute for Cooter and Catlin to close the gates and get back in the jeep. Then he cut off the headlights and drove real slow down this straight road with rows of big twisted trees on each side, drooping long, spooky branches with Spanish Moss all around us. The moonlight sneaking through the branches and leaves made eyes and mouths and scary faces with the shadows. Sweetpea laughed that crazy laugh like the guy does in scary movies, and Mary Ellen screamed. Catlin laughed and said, "Do it again, Sweetpea," but he didn't. I got as close to Cooter as I could and put my arms around his legs. I was pretty scared. I didn't want to giggle, but I was giggling anyway and couldn't stop it.

There was a big house at the end of the road and when Mary Ellen saw it, she screamed again. The moonlight was coming from behind the house and made it look black and ghosty, like a haunted house. Everything was black except at one window there was a face looking out. Over the top of the face was a kerosene lamp. The lamp light made ugly shadows on the face, making the eyes look like holes instead of eyes. It looked like a mummy with dead skin all around the face. I couldn't hardly breathe, my heart was beating so fast. All I could do was hang on to Cooter's leg. Everybody was screaming and squeeling.

"Hey, don't make so much racket," Sweetpea said. "You're gonna scare M'um Janey." He stopped the jeep and left the motor running while he walked over to underneath the window, and called up to the face looking out. "It's jus' me, M'um Janey. Sweetpea. We goin' over to th' cemetery, okay?" The mummy face looked down at him and didn't make a move. So he said it again, "M'um Janey, we goin' over to th' cemetery, okay?" This time the mummy face nodded slowly and then went away from the window. Didn't say anything. Just went away.

Sweetpea got back in the jeep and drove around the side of the house and part of the way down a little hill and stopped again. "All out," he said. "We gotta walk th' rest of th' way."

"How come?" I asked him.

"Laura don't like cars," he said.

When we got out of the jeep Catlin said, "Watch out for th' billy goats."

"Where?" I asked her. I was ready to get back in the jeep. I didn't want to get butted by no billy goat.

"Don't worry. They ain't gonna bother you," Sweetpea said. "They're in th' shed this time of night."

"Whew," I said. And Mary Ellen said, "Whew is right." She's scared of billy goats, too.

We walked the rest of the way down the hill to a graveyard near the bottom. Everybody was holding on to somebody else. I want to tell you that's a very spooky feeling, walking into a graveyard at night, even with a lot of people holding onto each other. I don't know who was holding onto who, but I was holding onto Cooter, and I wasn't going to let go.

"Don't hol' on so tight, man," Cooter said. "You cuttin' off th' blood."

Then we *really* got the fool scared out of us.

All at once there were a bunch of flashlights shining in our faces, blinding us for a minute. It made my heart go ninety-miles-an-hour. Everybody let out a yell or a scream and I peed in my pants a little bit. Then a guy's voice from behind the flashlights said, "Hey, y'all, it's Sweetpea."

"Who's that?" Sweetpea said back. "Hey, cut th' lights. I can't see who it is." The flashlights cut off and when our eyes got used to the dark again we could make out the shadows of a bunch of people sitting in the grass, under a tree, beside a big tombstone with a ghostly looking angel on top of it. The same guy's voice said, "It's Mabel and Jack and Butter and Jo-David and Sam." There were two ladies and three guys. You couldn't see what they looked like in the dark, but one of the guys had a big mustache and one had a beard. They all started talking, saying "Hey, man" and "How ya doin', Sweetpea?" And things like that.

Sweetpea sounded glad to see them. "Y'all say 'Hey' to Mary

Ellen an' Cooter an' Shirley Mae an' Catlin an' Chester," he told them. We said "Hey" and they said "Hey" back and we sat down on the grass beside them.

"Y'all come all th' way from Charleston to see Laura?" Sweetpea asked, slapping a mosquito on his elbow at the same time.

"Yeah," they said.

Cooter leaned over to me. "You can turn loose my arm any time," he said in a quiet voice. It was still scary, even with all them people around. But I figured I ought to turn him loose. Anyway, I needed both hands to swat mosquitoes. I was glad Mama had made me wear long pants so the mosquitoes couldn't get my legs. Shirley Mae was still hanging onto Cooter's other arm like she was glued to him. Cooter had to pull and twist his arm before he could get loose from her. She was really acting crazy, trying to get Cooter to put his arm around her and stuff like that. One time when Sweetpea handed a lit cigarette over to Cooter, Shirley Mae grabbed it out of his hand.

"Oh, no you don't Shirley Mae," Sweetpea said. He grabbed her wrist and twisted it the wrong way a little bit so she'd know he meant business. But not enough to hurt her.

"Jus' *one* little puff?" Shirley Mae begged him. "Please? Jus' one?"

"Okay, jus' one," Sweetpea said. Then he turned loose her arm and held out his hand, waiting for her to take a puff and give him back the cigarette. "If you say one word to Aunt Sissy 'bout this, I'll break yo' leg in three places. You hear?"

Shirley Mae didn't answer him back. She put the cigarette up to her mouth and took a long draw on it. But she didn't blow the smoke out.

"It's maryjane," Catlin whispered in my ear.

"I *know* it," I said back to her. "I smelt it."

Mabel and Jack and all them other names were passing around a maryjane, too.

"Can I have a puff, Sweetpea?" Catlin asked.

"Are you kiddin'?"

"You let Shirley Mae."

"But I *ain't* lettin' you," Sweetpea said.

One of the shadow people passed over a big bottle to Sweetpea. "Sip of Burgundy, Sweetpea?" he asked.

"Don't mind if I do," Sweetpea said. He put the big bottle up to his mouth and tilted his head back to take a drink. Then he wiped his mouth with the back of his hand. "Very tasty," he said. Mary Ellen and Cooter each got to take a swallow. Shirley Mae wanted one, too.

"Forget it," Sweetpea told her and passed the bottle back over to his friends. "Aunt Sissy would smell yo' breath and I'd catch hell."

One of the shadows asked, "When does Laura show up?"

"You might've scared her off with them flashlights," Sweetpea told him. "Laura don't like flashlights."

"That ain't so," a girl shadow said. "We tried shining a flashlight on her one night when she showed up. It scared her off for a little while but she came back."

"You swear?" Sweetpea asked her, like he didn't believe her.

"Cross my heart and spit," the girl said and spit.

"Then le's go, everybody," Sweetpea laughed. "Butter don't lie."

"Yeah," another voice said. "Le's get started before these damn bugs eat me alive."

Everybody got up off the grass and followed Sweetpea over to where there was a long flat gravestone, like a white marble door, lying on the ground off by itself. In the moonlight you could read the big, worn letters, L A U R A, at the top. That was all it said. Not Laura-who or when she was born or anything.

"How come she ain't got a last name?" I asked, not asking any special person.

"Don't nobody knoooooooow," Cooter said, making his voice sound like a ghost.

"Laura was a St. Clair," Catlin said. "Cap'n Will says his grandmother tol' him that."

"If her name was St. Clair, how come they left it off th' gravestone?" the girl named Mabel wanted to know.

"Who cares?" said the guy with the mustache. "Le's get started. I'm bein' eaten alive."

"Hush-up, Jo-David," Mabel said. "I wanta hear this."

"Aunt Sissy says don't nobody really know what her name was," Sweetpea said, like he knew more about it than anybody.

"Well, Cap'n Will says different," Catlin said, not backing up a bit.

"What's he say?" Mabel wanted to know.

"Cap'n Will says that Laura's last name was St. Clair," Catlin said. "An' there was this Ruffin guy that was gonna marry her. Only Laura died before they could get married. And th' guy wanted her to get buried in th' Ruffin cemetery. But she wasn't a Ruffin, yet, and the Ruffins didn't want no St. Clairs in their cemetery. Th' Ruffins didn't much like th' St. Clairs. So, they jus' left her last name off the tombstone when they buried her so nobody would know there was a St. Clair in th' cemetery."

"I be damned," Mabel said.

"Uncle Will tol' you that?" Sweetpea asked Catlin.

"Sho did."

"Wonder how come he never tol' me?"

"Beats me."

"Hey, c'mon. Le's get goin'," said the mustache guy, jumping up off the grass and swatting his hands all over his arms and legs. "I got more mosquitoes eatin' on me than I can handle."

"Me, too!" Sweetpea said, getting up and pulling on Mary Ellen's hand to help her up off the ground. "Who all's gonna take their clothes off?"

"Not me," Catlin said, before anybody else.

"Me, neither," I said, quick as I could.

"I will if Cooter will," Shirley Mae said.

"No you won't, Shirley Mae," Sweetpea said. "You keep yo' clothes on, you hear?" Shirley Mae didn't say anything.

"Me," giggled the one named Butter. She got up and moved away from the rest of us, out of the shadows into the moonlight. Didn't take hardly a minute for her to slip her shirt over her head and slide off her pants. In the moonlight she didn't hardly look naked at all. I mean, you could see her boobs and her behind, but the moonlight smoothed it all over so she looked like she had on a skin-tight suit.

"If Butter can do it, I can too," Sweetpea said. He put his hands in back of his shoulders and pulled his striped shirt over his head and flipped it into the grass. And unzipped his jeans and slid them down his legs and pushed them off with his feet. He didn't have on any underwear, so when he got his pants off he was all-the-way naked. It didn't seem to bother him whether anybody looked or not. He reached over and pulled on the shoulder of Mary Ellen's shirt. "C'mon, Mary Ellen."

"Not me," Mary Ellen giggled, pulling her shirt back straight. "I'm shy."

"Cooter? C'mon."

"Naw, Man."

"Me, Sweetpea," Shirley Mae said. "I want to take my clothes off, too."

"No. Not you," Sweetpea told her. "Hell, we got enough, anyway. Don't take but one an' we got two. Le's get goin' before th' mosquitoes carry us off."

We all made a ring around Laura's flat gravestone. The moonlight made it look glowy white and spooky. Sweetpea was telling everybody what to do. "Leave a place beside me on my left side, an' one beside Butter on her left side for Miss Laura, in case she wants to join us." Everybody started holding hands and connecting up the ring, except Shirley Mae.

"Shirley Mae, dammit," Catlin yelled. "Didn't Sweetpea tell you to keep yo' clothes on?" Shirley Mae was standing a little ways off from the rest of us. She'd took off her shirt and was in the middle of taking off her pants.

"Shirley Mae, pull yo' pants up and get over here," Sweetpea called to her, mean sounding. "Before I warm yo' tail. You gonna mess up everything if you don't behave."

Shirley Mae pulled up her pants like Sweetpea told her to, but she didn't put her shirt back on. And when she walked back over to the circle and took Cooter's hand, she held her boobs up real high, showing them off. Catlin grabbed her other hand before Jack or Jo-David or whatever the beard one's name is could get it.

Then we all took hands again. Cooter and Shirley Mae and Catlin and then me, next, and Mary Ellen and Sweetpea and then a hole for Laura, and then all the shadow people and the naked one named Butter. Everybody was holding hands and being pretty quiet, except for giggling a little bit, and swatting mosquitoes.

"Now," Sweetpea said, "Everybody move easy to the right side, thirteen steps. Real slow. One—two—three—" When he got up to thirteen everybody stopped. "Now Butter an' me'll hold out our hands for Miss Laura to join up...," he said softly. Sweetpea and Butter held out their left hands. "Everybody keep their eyes on th' gravestone."

I kept my eyes on the gravestone without blinking. Then it started looking funny. Swelling up and then shrinking, almost like it was breathing.

"I'm scared," I whispered to Catlin.

"Ain't no need to be," Catlin whispered back. "Laura ain't gonna hurt you."

About that time the moon went behind a cloud and it got so black you could hardly see a thing. Somebody said, "Ooooo-o-o-," and it made a shiver run up my backbone.

"Hold on a minute," Sweetpea whispered. "I think she's here." One of the shadow people asked him how he knew, but he didn't answer. All at once I had to go to the bathroom so bad I couldn't hold back, and my pants got a little more wet. "Everybody that's got on a ring hold your hand out and let Miss Laura see your ring," Sweetpea sang softly like it was a song. I didn't have a ring on, because the only ring I got is the one with the black stone and gold letter on it that Papa gave me, and Mama keeps it locked in her wood jewelry box. But I held my hand out anyway.

One girl, I don't know which one, squealed and said her ring was moving. "It's goin' roun' and roun' my finger," she squealed softly.

"Mine, too." Shirley Mae yelled. "Mine's goin' roun' and roun', too!" When she said it, she turned loose of Cooter's and Catlin's hands and started doing a dance all by herself, throwing her arms in the air, dancing around the grave like it was a Maypole. In and out of all of us standing in the circle, skipping under arms that got held up for her and ducking low under the ones that didn't. Her boobs were bouncing around like big, jelly cantelopes. One of the guys, the one with the mustache—named Jack, I think—started dancing with her. They danced around for a couple of minutes and then Sweetpea made them stop. He said. "Okay, Shirley Mae. Time to put yo' shirt on."

Shirley Mae stopped dancing. "I don't know where it's at."

"S'right over yonder," Catlin said. "I'll get it." She ran over and snatched the shirt up off the ground where Shirley Mae had dropped it. She walked back part the way and threw the shirt the rest of the way to Shirley Mae. "There. Put it on."

Sweetpea put his pants back on, too. "Come on, gang," he said to us. "We gotta head for home." He threw his shirt over his shoulder instead of putting it on, and walked back to where we'd been sitting in the grass, by the big tombstone with the angel on top of it. "First, I gotta have another taste of this stuff." He leaned over and picked up the big bottle of wine.

"Help yourself," one of the guys said.

Butter put her clothes back on, too.

"Y'all leavin', too?" Sweetpea asked.

"Naw," Butter said. "I put my clothes on to keep th' bugs from eatin' me."

"May as well split," the guy with the beard said. "I had enough ring-around-the-gravestone for tonight."

And the others said they reckoned they had, too, so everybody headed back up the hill to where the jeep was parked. The moon was straight up overhead. Sweetpea held his wrist watch up to see if he could tell time by moonlight. But he couldn't see good enough. Cooter struck a match.

"God-a-mighty! It's 'most one o'clock," Sweetpea said. "We gotta hustle. I'm gonna catch hell for keepin' y'all up so late." He jogged over and climbed into the jeep. "Pile in, everybody," he said. While we were piling in, he asked them other people where they'd parked their car.

"Got th' Hondas over yonder," the one named Jack said. Over where he was pointing, you could make out some bikes leaning against one of the big oak trees. Three of them. Sweetpea got the jeep started and turned around, and we headed down the long driveway back to the gate. We heard them Hondas going hudnnn, hudnnn, and before you know it them Charleston people zipped past us like we were standing still. They stopped and held the gates open for us to go through. Then they zipped by again, yelling "So long" and "Bye" and "Take it easy." We watched their tail lights ahead of us for a few minutes, but then there was a curve in the road and they were gone.

"Catch 'em, Sweetpea!" Catlin called out.

"No, don't," I yelled. "It's too bumpy!" Thank goodness, Sweetpea didn't try and catch them. I don't think he much wanted to anyhow.

Riding back, sitting there on that hard floor, hanging onto Cooter's leg, I got to thinking. "How come Miss Laura twists yo' ring aroun'?" I asked. I had to yell it out for anybody to hear me. It's hard hearing from the front seat to the back seat riding in the jeep because the wind blows the words away.

Catlin said something back, but I couldn't make out what she said. "What?" I called out. She said it over again and this time I heard. She said, "Miss Laura's lookin' for her weddin' ring." But I didn't know what that meant so I yelled "What?" again. Sweetpea answered this time, turning his head around and talking over his shoulder so I could hear him better. "She died on th' day she was s'pose to get married." He'd say a few words and then turn his head back to check the road so we wouldn't go in the ditch, then he'd turn his head back my way and say a few more words. " So they buried her in her weddin' dress. But somebody stole her weddin' ring before they could put her in th' ground. She can't sleep easy till she finds her ring."

Shirley Mae was trying to get herself bounced into Cooter's lap again, but she quit when Sweetpea told her she'd have to get up in the front seat if she didn't behave herself. Nobody was talking very much. It seemed like everybody wanted to do some thinking. I was thinking about Laura looking for her ring, maybe forever and forever. Or maybe one night she'll find it on somebody's finger, and steal it back and then go back to her grave and finish dying.

Then I thought about what Catlin said about Laura getting buried in the Ruffin Cemetery, and her being a St. Clair.

"Catlin," I called out, "If Laura's name was St. Clair, how come they didn't bury her in th' St. Clair Cemetery?"

Catlin turned her head around and looked at me and laughed. "St. Clairs didn't have no cemetery. They were po' white trash."

That made Sweetpea laugh, too. "Cat, you'd better not let Aunt Sissy hear you say that."

There was something else I didn't understand. "How come you take your clothes off when you go 'round th' gravestone?" I yelled.

"Damn if I know," Sweetpea yelled back. "Makes it more fun, I guess." And then he laughed and Mary Ellen made like she was hitting him. They sort of teased each other back and forth and it made me think that maybe Sweetpea liked taking his clothes off and letting Mary Ellen see him naked. Then I thought about the old lady with her wrinkled face staring out the window. I was thinking some more about somebody stealing a ring off a dead lady when a police car stopped us. It was just after we turned off the dirt road back onto the Highway. This police car came up beside us and blew the siren for Sweetpea to stop.

"Y'all got a boy named Chester St. Clair there?" this policeman stuck his head out the window and asked. What happened was that Mama had got worried about me being out so late and called the police. So I got to ride the rest of the way home in a police car. A *State* police car. The seat felt a lot better than them boards in the jeep.

VIII

The day that Cooter drove over in the pickup and said Aunt Sissy wanted us to come see her, Mama dressed up like it was Sunday, with a hat and gloves and everything. And she made me put on long pants and a clean shirt and wear shoes and comb my hair. It was a hot day, too, so putting on all them clothes was no fun. Cooter couldn't wait for us to get dressed and give us a ride over, because he had to drive to Ocean City on account of they'd run out of corn meal at the Manor and needed some in a hurry. So Mama and me walked over. It's not but a little ways. But in that heat it don't take much walking to make you sweat. And get your clothes to sticking to you.

When we got to the Manor, I started to show Mama the way in through the back door because it's shorter than going all the way around to the front. But Mama said No, that we were making a social call. And when you make a social call you *don't* go in through the back door.

Up till then I hadn't been around to the front of Inlet Manor before. I'd only seen it from the inside looking out. Through the front screen door. The house looks real different when you see it the other way—from the outside. For one thing, the front porch is a whole lot bigger than I thought it was. Especially the side that's screened in and covered with that plastic stuff like they put on clothes at the dry cleaners. That's the dining porch side and it takes up half the front and then runs way around the side almost to the back of the house. Inside, behind the plastic, all the people eating dinner looked like they were moving around in a bad fog. I thought I saw Sweetpea one time, but I wasn't sure. They got four big air conditioners humming away at full speed to keep that dining porch cooled off. That's how big it is.

It was just five o'clock when we got there, and already the dining room and the dining porch were both full up. There were twenty-five cars, or maybe thirty even, parked all over the big front yard in the shade under the trees. One car had a golden retriever closed up in the back seat with the windows rolled down enough so the dog could get some air, but not enough so he could jump out. I was sure glad he couldn't jump out, because the way he barked when Mama and me passed by sounded like he wanted to bite us. Up on the open side of the front porch there were people sitting on the benches around the sides waiting to get into the dining porch. They were families mostly, with little children and big children, all brown from being out in the sun, and all dressed up in white and yellow and red and blue clothes. One baby was crying up a storm and its Mama was walking it all around the front yard trying to hush it up. That didn't seem to do much good until she walked it down by the dock and showed it the ducks swimming around in the creek, and that made it hush up.

"Lordy, Mama," I said. "I haven't seen so many people since the Greyhound Depot in Richmond. Where'd all them people come from?"

"From all around," Mama said. She smiled at me for being so surprised. "From your Aunt Caroline's Boarding House. And from Ocean City. And from all the beaches between here and there. From Charleston. And Columbia. From all around."

"I'll be durned. From all those places?"

"Most of them are on their vacations, you know. And they don't want to cook on their vacations. So they come over to Inlet Manor for dinner." Mama took her glasses off and folded them up and put them in her pocketbook. "Then a lot of people drive up from Charleston, or down from Columbia, just to get some of your Aunt Sissy's seafood. It's awful good, you know. Just about everybody in this part of the country knows about Inlet Manor, and how good the food is. They tell me that when Sissy's got softshell crab on the menu that the crowd is backed up all the way out to the highway."

"You're kiddin'."

"That's what they tell me." Mama fanned a fly away that was buzzing around her face, and we climbed the steps up to the crowded front porch.

At the top of the steps there was a lady blocking the way. She had on a nice, yellow dress, with green dots all over it. Gold eyeglasses hung on a chain around her neck. Her hair was brown with lots of gray hairs in it. Part of it had come loose and was hanging down in her face. She kept pushing it out of the way with the back of her wrist.

"Have you put your name on our list?" she asked Mama.

"What list do you mean?" Mama asked her back.

"Our reservation list," the lady said. She smiled and pointed at a clipboard hanging on the porch rail. Mama looked at the lady for a minute and then she smiled and took the lady by the arm. "Adelaide, don't you remember me?" she asked the lady.

The lady stared at Mama for a minute. Her mouth dropped open and then the ends turned up into a smile. "Lucille, is that you? I do declare, it *is* you!" She put both her arms around Mama and kissed her on her cheek. And Mama kissed the lady on her cheek. Everybody on the porch smiled. "It's so *good* to see you," the lady told Mama. "I should have recognized you right off 'cause I knew you were in Ruffins Inlet. But, you know," she cut her eye around at all the people sitting on the porch and giggled, "you get so you don't hardly look at people when you see 'em a porchful at a time." She whispered the last part. Then she turned around and looked down at me. "An' this is dear, little Chester, Junior, isn't it?" She leaned over and kissed me on the cheek, too. "I'm your Aunt Adelaide."

"Yes'm," I said and tried to smile.

A man leaned over from behind me. "Could we put our name on the list, please ma'am?" he asked Aunt Adelaide. "Ferguson, party of six." There was a lady and four kids standing on the steps with him. Three girls and a boy.

"Yessir, Mr. Ferguson." Aunt Adelaide smiled a big smile at him. "I got so interested in talking to my cousin, here, that I jus' plum forgot to do my job. And I *do* apologize." She took her glasses off her big bosom and put them on her nose, and picked up the clipboard off the porch rail and wrote on the paper. "Ferguson, party of—let's see—six, right?" She wrote it down on the clipboard list.

"That's right," Mr. Ferguson said.

"Well, come on up here on the porch and find yourselves seats." Aunt Adelaide took the glasses off her nose and used them to point to the benches on the front porch. "It's goin' to be 'bout fifteen minutes 'fore we can get you a table. So make yourselves comfortable." Aunt Adelaide seemed to talk a lot. "That's a lovely family you have there, Mr. Ferguson."

"Thank you kindly," Mr. Ferguson said and him and his family (didn't look so lovely to me) came up on the porch and the people on the benches smiled and slipped over to make room for them.

"Adelaide," Mama said, when she could get a word in, "we'll just go on up and see Sissy. We're here to say 'Hello'."

When Mama said "Sissy" Aunt Adelaide got all flustered and dropped her glasses back on her bosom. "Wait a minute, Lucille honey," she said, taking Mama by the arm. "I better run up ahead an' ask Sissy if it's all right for you to come up. She hasn't been feelin' so good lately."

"She's feeling much better today," Mama told her. "Cooter came over this morning to tell us. That's why we're here."

"Sissy knows you're coming?"

Mama nodded.

"Oh, that's nice," Aunt Adelaide said, turning Mama's arm loose. She sounded relieved. "D'you know where her room is?" She held open the door for Mama and me to go in.

"Yes, ma'am. I do," I said. It came out louder than I meant it to.

Aunt Adelaide laughed. "Good," she said and patted me on top of my head. I hate it when ladies do that. It's like they're patting a little dog.

"Thank you, Adelaide," Mama said when we got in the front hall and Aunt Adelaide let the screen door slam shut behind us. "We'll see you in a little while."

"Wilson. Party of four," called a little fat lady from the front steps.

"Got you!" Aunt Adelaide waved to her and hurried over to write the lady's name down on the clipboard list.

Mama looked around the front hall for a minute or two before we started up the creaking stair steps. I think maybe she was looking around to see what was the same and what was different from when she was there before I was born, because she said, "Nothing changes," sort of to herself.

The door to the kitchen was open like it had been the day I came over with Catlin and Shirley Mae. The colored ladies were back there working hard. One was washing stacks of dishes at the big sink, and the others were hustling around doing other things. Sweetpea rushed in with a red plastic tub full of dirty dishes that he put beside the sink. Then he rushed out again. I waved to him, but he must have been going too fast to see me because he didn't wave back.

Through the other doorway, into the dining room, we could see people eating at all five tables in that room. And beyond them, through the big door onto the front porch, we could see tables and tables of lots more people eating. The place was really full up.

Some of the cool air from the air conditioners was slipping out into the hall and felt good on us, coming in from the hot outside. And the smells of all the good things cooking in the kitchen made my stomach growl and feel empty. Mama smiled when she heard my stomach growl.

"Smells good, doesn't it?" she said. "Maybe we'll have supper here tonight. How'd you like that?" She walked slowly up the creaky stairs, letting her hand slide up the bannister as she went.

"We got enough money?" I asked her. I was walking very slowly up the stair steps so I wouldn't get too far ahead of her.

"I think we can manage it."

"Three-fifty apiece?"

Mama laughed. "We're family, Ches. We can sit at the family table. That costs less."

"Only a dollar less," I said. "That's still two-fifty apiece."

"Well, I'll tell you what. Let's get *one* dinner and take it home and divide it."

I nodded. "Okay." We were at the top of the stairs now. Mama stopped and glanced around, looking over everything in the upstairs hall like she'd done in the downstairs one, and nodding to herself. "It's that door there," I said and walked over to show her which door I meant. "This one's Aunt Sissy's room."

Mama took a deep breath and blew it out. She had that same funny look in her eyes like on the Greyhound bus, and I got the feeling again that she was scared. She knocked on Aunt Sissy's door and the knock sounded scared, even. After she knocked, she straightened her hat and hung her pocketbook over her arm and put on a smile.

"I don't think she heard it," I said.

Mama knocked again, a little bit harder, but not much.

"Come on in," Aunt Sissy called out in her husky voice.

Mama pushed the door open, easy, talking at the same time. "Sissy, dear, how *are* you?" She walked over to the bed and leaned way over to give Aunt Sissy a kiss. Aunt Sissy was sitting in the middle of the big, brass bed like before, taking up her side of the bed and Uncle Will's side, too. She was leaning back on a bunch of big, white, bed pillows made out of some shiny cloth that Mama told me later you call satin. The same cloth her red dress with ruffles was made out of when I saw her the first time. Today she had on a rosy-colored dress made of thin cloth you could almost see through. With plenty of ruffles, but not as many as before.

"Don't kiss me," Aunt Sissy ordered, holding up one hand in between her and Mama to keep Mama from getting any closer to her. "I'm loaded with germs."

"Oh, poor Sissy," Mama said, wrinkling up her face like she hurt somewhere. "Cooter said you were feeling better."

"I *am* feeling better," Aunt Sissy said. And the way she said it made you know she was through talking about it. "Sit down, Lucille. Down there." She pointed to an old-timey chair at the foot end of the bed with a curved wood back and a stuffed red-cloth seat—like the sofa in the hall. Then she pointed at the baby-pen in front of the fireplace and looked at me. "Boy, reach me Flossie," she said. I went over to the pen with the colored plastic flowers twisted up and down the sides and looked down at the little white dogs. Which one was Flossie? They looked exactly alike to me. I reached over the side of the pen and grabbed for the nearest one. When I did, they both made a jump for me and tried to bite my arm. And they started barking and yelping up a storm. I jerked my hand back just in time.

"Don't you know *anything* about dogs?" Aunt Sissy yelled at me. She sounded exactly like old man Sutherland, the principal at school in Richmond. "You don't go sticking yo' hand in with strange dogs like that. You scare 'em, dummy. They'll chew yo' arm off." Mama came over to the baby-pen saying, "Nice puppy, sweet puppy," talking baby talk to the dogs. She leaned over like she was going to pick one up. "Lucille," Aunt Sissy yelled at her. "Let th' *boy* do it." Mama straightened herself up and went back and sat down in the chair at the foot of the bed, and fiddled with the mended strap on her pocketbook.

"Now, boy," Aunt Sissy said to me, "put yo' hand in nice an' easy. An' let 'em smell it an' get used to th' way you smell. Take it *easy*." So I reached my hand down in the baby-pen real slow and easy, like she said. But it didn't make any difference. Every time I got my hand near one of the dogs, they'd both start yelping and try and bite me. I'll tell you right now, they sounded so mean I was scared of them.

"Oh, never mind," Aunt Sissy said. "Leave 'em alone." She looked over at the bedroom door and yelled, "Catlin!" waited a second and yelled it again. "Catlin!" While she was waiting for Catlin to answer, she said to Mama, "Lucille, you know what you're gonna do with that big front room you got now? You're gonna open up a Laundrymat."

Mama was surprised. "A Laundromat? Whatever for?"

Catlin stuck her head in the door. "Yes'm, Miss Sissy. You want me?"

Aunt Sissy pointed at the baby-pen. "Fetch me Flossie," she said to Catlin. Then she turned her head back to Mama. "Lucille, that boy of yours don't know beans about how to handle a dog. You oughta get him one so's he won't be so scared of 'em. Don't get too big a dog, though. He's such a runt, th' dog might eat him up. Ha, ha, ha, ha, ha." She sounded like a chicken clucking when she laughed.

"Here's Flossie, Miss Sissy," Catlin said. She dropped the dog into the giggling lady's lap. Aunt Sissy quit giggling. "Don't be so rough," she snapped at Catlin. She picked the dog up and put it alongside her face and started kissing it. "You'll hurt Sissy's sweet little Flossie."

"Sissy," Mama said, leaning way over to get Aunt Sissy to look at her. "I've never heard of anything like that before. Why would I want to turn our *living room* into a Laundromat?" She got up out of her chair and walked up to the head of the bed to get closer to Aunt Sissy. "Why would I ever want to do a thing like that?"

"You gotta eat, don'tcha?" Aunt Sissy didn't even look at Mama when she answered her. She went right on kissing Flossie and making baby-talk noises.

"You need me for anything else, Miss Sissy?" Catlin asked.

Aunt Sissy stopped fussing over Flossie for a minute to look over at Catlin. "Shirley Mae had her dinner, yet?"

"I jus' brung it up to 'er," Catlin said. "She's eatin' it right now."

"Well, get on back there and be sure she eats her vegetables," Aunt Sissy said. "Last week when Ramona was cleaning up, she found a pile of string beans an' collard greens under Shirley Mae's bed, all dried up. She stuck 'em under there when you weren't lookin', an' made you think she'd eaten 'em."

"Yes'm," Catlin said. "I'll be sure she don't do that no more." And then she scooted out the door before Aunt Sissy could tell her anything else to do.

"Sissy," Mama said. Her voice sounded like she had a frog in her throat. I could tell she was real upset. "I don't want a dirty, old, noisy Laudromat in my living room. That's no way to bring up a child."

"No way to bring up a chile?" Aunt Sissy asked. "Well, maybe we ain't quite as fancy down here as you are up there in Richmond, Virginia, Miss F.F.V. Down here we put firs' things firs'." She set Flossie down on the bed beside her next to the stack of gray ledger books. "Jus' tell me, if you would please, exactly how you expect to eat?" She hadn't been looking straight at Mama before, but now she was. "You think I've got so much money I can let Cooter run free meals over from the Manor every day?" Aunt Sissy shook her head and made a funny racket, blowing her breath through her lips with her mouth closed. "You're jus' like th' rest of this damn family. You think there ain't no need to hit a lick at a snake as long as Sissy's pilin' 'em in at th' Manor Restaurant, don't you?"

"That's not true, Sissy," Mama said, straightening up her shoulders. "I don't think that way at all. We certainly appreciate all you've done for us. But I fully intend to support Ches-Junior and me. Just as soon as the truck delivers my piano from Richmond, I'm gonna give music lessons. Piano and voice."

"Lord help us," Aunt Sissy said. She smacked her hand down on her ledger books. The noise made Flossie's head pop up and look around. "Lucille Ottway St. Clair, you ain't gonna make no money with music lessons." She gave a little laugh that sounded like a pig snorting. "Don't you know that everybody in Ruffins Inlet is kin to you? You know what *that* means? It means everybody will send their chil'ren to you for piano lessons, and absolutely nobody will pay you for them." Flossie put her head back down and closed her eyes. "If you make five bucks a week offa this crowd you'll be lucky. An' you'll hafta work yo' tail off to make even that much. An' you know what you can buy with five bucks these days, don'tcha? Not much."

Mama's shoulders sort of slumped over, and she walked slowly back to the chair at the end of the bed and dropped down into it. Her hat had slipped off to one side of her head, but she didn't seem to notice.

"My mind's made up," Aunt Sissy said. "Boy," she said to me, "reach me that nail file over there." I ran around the bed and got the nail file off the round table on the other side and handed it to Aunt Sissy. She said, "Thanks," and started filing her fingernails and talking. "There ain't much you can do 'round here to make a livin', Lucille. Maybe you think I can give you a job at the Manor. Forget it. I got Adelaide on th' door an' Bernadette on th' cash register already. An' Sweetpea in th' dining room." She filed on her fingernails some more. "I thought 'bout you waitin' on tables. But you're gettin' a little ol' to hustle tables like them college girls. An' even if you had enough muscle to work in th' kitchen, I ain't about to let them girls go. Christine an' Blossom been with me for years. An' Ramona's been with me all my life." She filed some more on her nails. "Caroline don't need nobody at th' Gif' Shoppe. So what's left? Makin' beds at the Boardin' House? Does that appeal to ya? Or workin' at th' Fillin' Station?"

Mama didn't say anything.

"I tol' you my mind's made up," Aunt Sissy said. She slapped her hand down hard again on the gray ledgers. It made such a loud noise this time that Flossie jumped up and started yapping and making a terrible racket. Aunt Sissy picked up the dog and snuggled it up under her chin, and talked coochy-coo baby talk to it.

"No, my mind's made up," she said again. "We need a Laundrymat here at th' Inlet. Everybody's been driving all th' way to Ocean City to get their clothes washed. Now, we'll have our own Laundrymat right here at Ruffins Inlet." Flossie had quit yapping so Aunt Sissy put the dog back down on the bed again. "I called Frank Jenkins at th' Western Auto las' week. An' he's ordered th' machines. As soon as they get here he'll bring 'em over and hitch 'em up. There'll be six washin' machines an' two dryers. You can put three washin' machines on each side of th' livin' room. An' stick th' dryers down at th' end. . . . Lucille, what in hell are you cryin' about?"

I'd been busy watching Aunt Sissy and I hadn't seen that Mama was crying. She wasn't making a sound or moving a muscle. Just sitting there looking at Aunt Sissy with the tears pouring out of her eyes and sliding down her face. She was letting them drip on her good dress again.

"God A'mighty!" Aunt Sissy said. "You try an' do somethin' nice for somebody, help 'em make some money so they can stay alive, an' what do they do? Cry, for Christ's sake."

"C'mon Mama," I said, pulling on her arm to help her get up out of the chair. "Le's go home."

"Home?" Aunt Sissy laughed a not-funny laugh. "Whose home you goin' to? Lemme ask ya that." She rolled and shifted herself over to the edge of the bed and swung her feet down over the side. She had little bitty white feet. "Tha's *my* little house you're livin' in over there. Don'tcha remember?" Aunt Sissy shook her head slowly back and forth. "Maybe you led th' high life up there in Richmond, but you gotta know that down here in Ruffins Inlet we work for a livin'."

Aunt Sissy stretched her legs straight out in front of her and wiggled her toes. "Son," she said to me, "open up that armoire over there." I looked down at Mama to see if it was all right for me to do it, but Mama didn't make any motion one way or the other. I didn't know what else to do but open Aunt Sissy's armoire for her. But I don't know what an armoire is, so I opened the first thing I came to. "Tha's not an armoire, dummy," Aunt Sissy said, disgusted-like. "Don't you know a dresser when you see one? Now look over there in the corner by the window." She pointed to show me which corner. "See that tall thing there with th' big doors?" I nodded. "*Tha's* an armoire, boy. Now open it up."

I opened the big door on the cabinet-thing in the corner like she told me to. The whole inside was full of shoes. Black shoes, and blue shoes, and white shoes, and every color shoes. More shoes than I'd ever seen outside a shoe store. Shelf on top of shelf, all full of nothing but shoes. Shoes with bows, and shoes with buckles, and shoes with ruffles, and then just plain shoes.

Aunt Sissy laughed at the way I was looking at all her shoes. "Tha's a hell of a lot of shoes, ain't it, son?"

"Yes'm."

"Well, a person's got to have some enjoyment in this life. An' shoes are what I enjoy. Bring me them pink mules there on th' second shelf. Th' ones with th' feather pom-poms. No. Down at th' other end, dummy."

I picked up a pair of shoes that were pink and had big balls of pink feathers on the toes and held them up for Aunt Sissy to see. "These th' ones, Aunt Sissy?"

She nodded her head. "Bring 'em over here an' slip 'em on my feet," she said. She wiggled her toes again and said, "Don't you think I've got pretty feet?"

Now I've got to tell you that feet just plain all look alike to me—toes and things. Aunt Sissy's feet were real little ones with red shiny toenails, but they just looked like feet to me. But I didn't tell her that. I said, "Yes'm."

I held out the shoes and she wiggled her feet back and forth in them till they were on good. Then she gave a little jump with her behind and slipped herself down off the bed and was standing straight up on the floor next to me. I was surprised. "You can walk?" I asked her in a whisper.

Aunt Sissy threw her head back and laughed, "Haw, haw, haw. You thought I couldn't walk?" When she stood on the floor she wasn't any taller than me, so where'd *she* get off calling *me* a runt? She turned and picked Flossie up off the bed and walked, kind of big-shot, over to the baby-pen, and dropped Flossie into it. "You damn right I can walk," she said. "What'd you think I was, a cripple?" She looked at Mama and winked, but Mama didn't wink back because she hadn't got through crying.

"Yes'm, Aunt Sissy," I said. "I guess I did. I mean—well—both times I seen you you been sittin' there in bed, so I figured maybe you couldn't walk."

"Well, I ain't crippled," she said. "Not in my legs an' not in my head, either. An' you'd better be damn glad I ain't. Else you an' your Mama'd be sittin' over there in my little house starvin' to death."

She walked back—kind of strutted, like a fat drum majorette—and stood in front of Mama, looking down at her in the chair. "Y'hear what I said, Lucille? Starvin' to death. You an' th' boy would be over there with nothin' to eat."

Mama didn't look at Aunt Sissy, but slowly she got up out of the chair, kind of stumbling over her own feet doing it. She wasn't crying anymore, and I was glad of that. But now there wasn't any kind of look on her face at all. Her eyebrows didn't go up or down, just straight across. And her mouth didn't smile or make a frown, just went straight across, too. My stomach started feeling funny again, like there was a little mouse or something in there chewing away on my insides.

I took hold of Mama's hand. "Mama, le's go," I said, pulling her across the room toward the door. Halfway across the room, Mama changed again. She straightened herself up and took a deep breath. And then she smiled at me and said, "Yes, we'll go now." It made my stomach feel better when she smiled.

"Before you go, son," Aunt Sissy stopped me, "run downstairs an' tell Adelaide that your Aunt Sissy wants a double." I looked at Mama and Mama nodded her head that it was okay.

"A double what?" I asked Aunt Sissy.

"Jus' tell her I want a double. She'll know what you're talkin' about. I got somethin' else to talk over with your Mama. She'll be ready to go when you get back."

When I went out of the door to Aunt Sissy's bedroom, Catlin was there in the hall. She was standing a good ways away from Aunt Sissy's door, but I could tell she'd been listening to everything.

"Did you hear 'bout th' Laundrymat?" I asked her.

"Yeah," Catlin said. "Man, y'never know what Miss Sissy's got goin' on in her head. Tha's th' last thing I'd have thought about—a Laundrymat."

I started going down the steps to downstairs. "She wants a double," I said, turning my head back to Catlin.

"She usually does 'bout this time of day," Catlin said. "Sometimes two." She shrugged her shoulders and started back into her's and Shirley Mae's room.

I called to her softly as I could, "Wha's a double?" Catlin came back and leaned over the bannister to get closer to my ear. "Whiskey," she whispered. "A double is two drinks of whiskey at one time. Get it?"

"Yep," I said and I went downstairs and told Aunt Adelaide that Aunt Sissy wanted a double. But I didn't really have to tell her anything. The double was already poured and sitting on a round silver tray with a fancy lace napkin beside it. And another big glass that looked like water and smelled like water.

I took the tray back upstairs to Aunt Sissy and when I got there she was saying something to Mama about money and washing machines, but I couldn't understand what it was they were saying. I set the tray down on the table beside Aunt Sissy's bed and by that time Mama was over by the door, straightening her hat and saying "Goodbye" and "Glad you're feeling better." All at once Mama stopped and said "Oh, Sissy!" that she'd forgot her best news. She took out the Hospital letter and held it up while she told Aunt Sissy what it said, about Papa being better. Aunt Sissy said that *was* good news and she was glad to hear it. And then we left.

Going downstairs I thought Mama might say something about us eating supper at the Manor. But she didn't, so I didn't bring it up either. When we turned the corner at the landing, there was an old guy standing at the bottom of the stair steps with a cigar in his mouth, looking up and smiling at us. He was tall and had skinny arms but was a little bit fat around the middle. His face was so brown from being in the sun a lot that it made his short gray hair look white. He looked like an old-timey movie star—I can't remember his name. He had on one of them white shirts, the kind you pull over your head, that's sometimes got a little alligator on one side. Instead of an alligator, this guy's shirt had a name sewed there.

When we got almost to the bottom of the stairs, he took the cigar out of his mouth and spread his arms apart and said, "Welcome to Ruffins Inlet." The way he said it even sounded like a movie star. We were close enough so I could read the name on his shirt now—"Captain Will." It was my Uncle Will. (I didn't know his face because I'd only seen the bottom part of him. The under-the-table part I'd seen when I watched through the hole in the dining porch floor when he was feeling SueAnne's leg.) Uncle Will put the cigar back in his mouth and took both of Mama's hands in his big, brown hands as she stepped down off the last step.

"Lucille," he said, "it's good to have you here with us." The cigar was taking up one side of his mouth, so he was talking out the other side. "It's a pleasure to know that a lovely Virginia lady and her son are going to make the Inlet their home." His voice sounded a whole lot different than it did when I was under the house listening to him talking to SueAnne. You wouldn't even know it was the same person.

Mama gave Uncle Will a hug and smiled a big smile like I hadn't seen her do at anybody in a long time. Her eyes crinkled so you couldn't hardly tell she'd been crying. "Will Ruffin," she said, "you look more like Spencer Tracy every time I see you." (That was the name of the movie star I couldn't remember.) "And look on your shirt. 'Captain Will.' Very impressive!" Uncle Will smiled a smile like he was a little bit ashamed. "It's a little affectation," he said. "Sissy has them sent down from that Saks Fifth Avenue store in New York."

"It befits a man of your stature," Mama said and smiled that good smile again. Then she turned my way and said, "Ches-Junior, this is your Uncle Will." Uncle Will smiled at me and shook my hand just like I was a man. "How are you, son?" he said. "I see you've been taking good care of your mother, here." But before I could say "How do you do" back to him, Uncle Will had taken hold of Mama's elbow and was kind of pushing her in front of him across the hall and out the front door.

"Le's sit out on th' porch," he said, holding the screen door open behind him for me to get out.

"Only for a minute, Will," Mama told him. "We've got to get home and get supper started." There were people sitting on the benches near the front door waiting for Aunt Adelaide to call them into the dining porch. Uncle Will smiled and nodded "Hello" and "How're you?" to them and led Mama on past them to a bench down near the end of the porch. She sat down and he sat down beside her.

"You can sit on th' jogglin' board, there, son," he said to me, nodding his head at a bench-looking thing at the end of the porch. It was higher than a bench, so that I had to almost climb to get up on top of it and sit down. It was just one long, wide board about as long as a car, bent way down in the middle, with each end running through a stand-thing. When I sat down on it it was bouncy like a trampoline.

"You don't see many of *those* around anymore, Will," Mama said.

"No, you don't," Uncle Will said, crossing his legs and getting himself comfortable on the bench. "That one's been sittin' there for God knows how long. Belonged to my Great-Grandmother Singleton." He got a match out of his pants pocket and lit his cigar again.

They were talking about the joggling board like it was something special and it just looked like an old gray bent board to me. "What's it for?" I asked.

"Lucille," Uncle Will chuckled and puffed on his cigar, "you've neglected that chile's education." He stopped smiling and looked at me. "A jogglin' board performs a very important function, son. You joggle on it. Bounce on it. No home should be without one." Then he smiled to show me he was kidding me.

"It's very good for putting babies to sleep, too," Mama said. "Doesn't take any time to joggle a baby to sleep. It's better than a rocking chair."

I stood up on the sagging gray board and did a few test bounces. Then some harder jumps with most all my weight. The joggling board gave a nice springy jump like a diving board. But it made an awful clackety-clack racket because the ends are loose in the stands, not nailed to them. So both ends were knocking around in the stands and making a lot of racket.

"Chester!" Mama called out over the noise.

"Son, would you bounce it easy, please?" Uncle Will asked. "SueAnne is tryin' to tell me somethin' an' I can't hear a word she's sayin'." He was laughing, but I could tell he didn't want me to joggle anymore. I sat down on the board and looked at the light-haired lady standing in front of Mama and Uncle Will. She was wearing a white waitress dress and had on a real lot of lipstick and a lot of that black stuff over her eyes. You couldn't tell whether she was pretty or not. She handed Uncle Will a drink that looked like one of Aunt Sissy's doubles.

"Cap'n Will, honey," she said. "I been lookin' all over th' place for you. See? I been lookin' so long th' ice is all melted. You want me to fix you another one?"

Uncle Will shook his head and took the glass from SueAnne. He said "Thank you" and then he told SueAnne that Mama was his sister-in-law and she came from a fine, old Virginia family, and that I was her son. SueAnne smiled and said she was pleased to meet us and wouldn't we like something cool to drink. While she was doing that, Uncle Will drank his drink straight down.

Mama told SueAnne "Thank you very much" but that her and me had to be getting along home because it was supper time. I said I'd like a Coke but nobody heard me, or if they heard me they didn't let on that they did. Uncle Will said for SueAnne to please get him another drink while he talked his sister-in-law into staying for supper. SueAnne went off to get Uncle Will's drink and Mama told him again that we really couldn't stay for supper.

"Will," she said, "we've imposed on you and Sissy too much already." Uncle Will said they just had so much to talk about he really wished she'd stay. But I could tell by the way Mama was talking that we were not going to eat supper at the Manor that night. Mama and Uncle Will talked a little bit longer, mostly about our trip down on the Greyhound bus. Mama said it was "ghastly," and Uncle Will said there was really no good way to get to Ruffins Inlet except if you drove a car. Even if we had a car, Mama can't drive.

Then SueAnne came out on the porch with Uncle Will's drink and told him that his supper was ready. So Mama and me said "Good night" to Uncle Will and SueAnne and we went home and ate cornflakes for supper.

IX

Catlin likes to go places at night. I think it must be because she doesn't have a TV of her own. The TV in their room belongs to Shirley Mae, so Shirley Mae gets to pick the shows.

And most times Catlin doesn't like to watch what Shirley Mae likes to watch. So she goes out.

Me and Mama don't have a TV either. At night after supper, Mama reads to me out of a book she brought from Richmond about Greek gods. Apollo and Heracles and Jason and them people. She calls them "myths" and reads me one every night. Then at nine o'clock I go to bed, because Mama says that I ought to get plenty of sleep. If there's something special to do, I can stay up later than that. Special doesn't mean playing hide-and-go-seek with everybody after dark. And it doesn't mean playing Monopoly or Rummy with Bootsie and Eugene. Special means when grown-ups come visiting.

Like the only special night since we've been in Ruffins Inlet was the night Mr. Jenkins from the Western Auto and Mrs. Jenkins brought us some shad roe. They said somebody from Georgetown had sent it to them and it was more than they could eat, so they brought us some. Mama said, Oh, what a treat it was to have some shad roe, and she put it in the refrigerator. And she poured Coca-Cola in glasses for everybody and brought it all in on a tray. Mr. Jenkins sat in the red chair with the wood arms and Mama and Mrs. Jenkins sat on the couch, and I sat in the rocking chair. The way Mrs. Jenkins was sitting I could see right up her dress.

As soon as everybody had took a sip of Coke and got comfortable, Mrs. Jenkins said to Mama that the first thing she wanted to know was how Papa was. Mr. Frank said Now, Ethel. Mama smiled and said It was all right. And she pulled the Hospital letter out of her pocket and read them the part about Papa being better. About them using a new kind of shock drug and it looked like it was doing him some good. Mrs. Jenkins said that was wonderful news and Mr. Frank said Yes, it certainly was. Then Mrs. Jenkins said wasn't it lucky Mama had got Papa put away in the State Hospital back in Virginia, because that way the State paid for everything, wasn't that right? Mama didn't say anything and Mr. Frank cleared his throat and shook his head at Mrs. Jenkins.

For a minute it looked like nobody was going to talk any more, then Mama said that it surely had been hot the last few days and Mrs. Jenkins said My hadn't it?, that she couldn't remember when it had been any hotter. Mrs. Jenkins has brown curly hair with bangs and is a little bit pudgy. I like her because she laughs a lot. She said that all of us should move in with Aunt Sissy at the Inlet Manor and get some of that good air conditioning they've got over there. She said her and Mr. Jenkins couldn't afford but one air conditioner and they kept that one in the bedroom so they could get a good night's sleep. Mama said that the nights didn't bother her like the days did because we usually got a good breeze from the south side at night that blew right into the bedrooms. And besides, she said, we'd done enough moving in on Aunt Sissy already.

Mr. Jenkins laughed and said there wasn't no need to worry about that, that Aunt Sissy wasn't going to run out of money any time soon. Then he started telling about how Aunt Sissy had been making money all her life. How she started the Basket Shop when she was only fourteen. She got all the colored people that were making them marshgrass baskets and selling them off them skinny pine-branch racks along the Charleston Highway to let her sell all their baskets at the Basket Shop. Aunt Sissy charged more money for the baskets and kept the extra for herself. The colored people made just as much money as they had before. And they liked sitting inside the shop out of the weather, especially in the winter-time when it got cold.

Mrs. Jenkins said Don't forget to tell about the toilet dolls. Mr. Jenkins said Yes, that he was just getting ready to tell that part. He said that when Aunt Sissy was little her Mama used to buy little plastic dolls from the ten-cent store in Ocean City—Ku-pee dolls, he said—and she'd make old-fashioned dresses for them with big skirts. Mrs. Jenkins said You know the ones, don't you, that they were what you put on the back of your toilet to cover up a spare roll of toilet paper with the doll's big skirts. Mama said that she thought she'd seen one at Aunt Adelaide's house. Mrs. Jenkins said that Mr. Jenkins should get on with the story. Mr. Jenkins said that there wasn't no story, that Mrs. St. Clair made toilet dolls and when Aunt Sissy and Aunt Caroline were little they had to go to Ocean City every day in the summertime to sell toilet dolls. They'd hitch a ride over and back with old man Simmons when he was working at the post office in Ocean City. Mr. Jenkins said that was all there was to the story, except that when Aunt Sissy started the Basket Shop they didn't have to go over to Ocean City anymore to sell the toilet dolls. They sold them at the Basket Shop, along with all the baskets. Then they started selling pecan candy, and candles, and pictures of the creek when the sun sets, and all kinds of things, until it wasn't just a Basket Shop anymore, it was a Gift Shop. Mr. Jenkins said that Aunt Sissy had been making money hand over fist all her life. Mrs. Jenkins said Ain't it so, that everything Aunt Sissy touched turned to money.

I was sitting in the rocking chair listening and rocking. Mr. Jenkins said to me, "Son would you hold up on your rockin' for a little bit?" Mrs. Jenkins laughed and said, "Frank, th' chile's gotta work off his energy somehow." I quit rocking the chair like Mr. Jenkins asked me to, but right after that he said that they had to be leaving. When they were going out the door Mama asked Mrs. Jenkins did she play bridge and Mrs. Jenkins said she surely did. Mama said that she'd have to get the girls together and play bridge. Mrs. Jenkins said that sounded like fun, and they left.

That's been the only special night when Mama let me stay up later. Every other night I've had to go to bed at nine o'clock.

That first night Catlin came by, I'd gone to bed on time and was almost asleep. And she scared the devil out of me. I thought she was a robber or somebody like that. She scratched her fingernails up and down the window screen and the noise made me jump almost out of my skin. Then she poked her head against the screen and said, "Getcha pants on."

I didn't say nothing for a minute because my heart was pounding so fast. Then I saw it was Catlin and my voice came back to me and I said, "What for?"

"I'm gonna show you somethin'."

"What?" I fumbled under the bed for my glasses.

"Getcha ass out here," she whispered. It only took a minute to take off my pajamas and put on my shorts. I started to go out the door the regular way, but then I figured Mama would want to know what I was doing up and tell me to go back to bed. So I climbed out the window. Catlin held the window screen open for me.

Outside it was real dark because there wasn't no moon out. But the Texaco Filling Station on the Highway was putting out plenty of light so that we didn't need a moon. We were walking toward the Filling Station so the light came down the road in front of us and we could see good. When we got to the Highway we stayed in the shadows so nobody at the Filling Station would see us. And when we were sure nobody was looking, we raced across the Highway and down a dirt road on the other side. Now, the light from the Filling Station was coming from behind us, but we could still see good. A little ways down the road we came to this old shack of a house. There was one big light bulb hanging down over the front door and that was all the light outside. There were a whole bunch of cars parked all over the front yard and around the sides. I didn't know where we were or where we were going, but I didn't ask. I just followed Catlin. The way she was walking and acting you could tell she'd been here a few times before.

We stayed in the shadows and sneaked around behind cars until we got around the house and were in the backyard. There was a kind of lean-to shed against the back of the house and Catlin shinnied up the side, easy, putting her feet in places and catching her hands onto things that she knew by heart. It wasn't as easy as Catlin made it look, but I managed to make it up without too much trouble. When I got up on the roof, Catlin was over the other side of the shed, next the house, looking in a little window there. I slipped over and took a look.

Inside, the house was all one big room with a bunch of people walking around and lots and lots of cigarette smoke.

"Wha's goin' on?" I asked Catlin.

"Jus' watch."

I looked back through the window and saw some things I hadn't seen the first time I looked. All of the people on the inside were looking at a low, square, wood pen that was in the middle of the big room. You couldn't hardly see the sides of the pen for all the people leaning on it. We were up high so we could see good, right down in the middle of the pen. Inside the pen there were these two guys squatting down on the dirt floor in corners across from each other. Each guy was holding a chicken.

"What're they doin'?"

"Jus' watch," Catlin said again.

I looked back again. The squatting guys were holding the chickens out in front of themselves, pointing them at each other. Then the next thing I know the guys turn the chickens loose. And the chickens sail through the air at each other and start fighting like they were madder than hell. I couldn't hardly take my eyes off them at first. They would fight a while and then back off and circle around and look at each other. Then they'd be at it again, kicking at each other with their feet. All at once there was blood flying all over the place. I put my hands in front of my face. I couldn't look.

Catlin laughed. "Wha's th' matter?"

"Them chickens are killin' each other."

"Ain't chickens. They're cocks. They're s'pose to fight like that."

"An' kill each other?"

"Yeah."

"Wha's happenin' now?" I still had my eyes covered.

"Ain't gonna be much longer. That one looks in a bad way."

I waited and listened, with my hands over my eyes. All I could hear was the racket, the talking and yelling of the people inside. They were cheering like it was something great going on, like the World Series or something. I kept my eyes closed for a long time. Then Catlin said "It's over" and I opened them. One of the chickens was lying in the middle of the pen and he looked like he was dead to me.

"Is he dead?"

"Dead as a doornail."

"Tha's awful. How come they do it?" I was a little bit sick in my stomach.

"For money, dummy. All them people down there are bettin' money on which chicken'll kill th' other one first." She pointed over at one side of the room. "See that guy yonder, over in that corner, th' one in th' yellow shirt with all th' dollar bills in his hand?"

"Th' one with th' mustache an' sunglasses?"

"Yeah." Catlin turned her face to me like she was going to say something important. "Tha's yo' cousin Chico."

I pushed my glasses up on my nose and squinted to see better. There was a guy down one end of the pen with a handful of dollars.

He was taking money from some people and giving money to some others. He had black hair and a little thin black mustache and aviator sunglasses. And black and white shoes.

"An' see that guy down th' other end? Th' one with th' cigar. Th' bald-headed one. Tha's yo' Uncle Benny."

I shifted my eyes down the other way and spotted Uncle Benny. He was a short guy, a little bit too fat and had sort of brown hair running around the sides of his head but not on top. He was smoking a long cigar and walking around patting people on the back and smiling and laughing.

Catlin was talking again. "He don't look a thing like Miss Sissy, does he? But he's her brother an' he's married to Miss Adelaide. Sweetpea an' Bernadette b'long to them. Bernadette was in th' Peace Corps in South America or someplace, an' met Chico an' brought him home an' married him."

"Is Uncle Benny th' owner of this?" I asked Catlin.

"Sho looks like it," Catlin said. "But I wouldn't swear to it. Mr. Benny don't hardly own anything, you know, not even th' Fillin' Station. He runs it, but Miss Sissy's th' one owns it."

"Boy, tha's a lot of people down there."

"You think tha's a lot of people down there now, you should've seen 'em last week th' first night it opened up. You couldn't hardly get near th' damn place there were so many people. Twice as many as're here tonight."

"Wow! Uncle Benny mus' be gettin' rich."

"I don't know 'bout that," Catlin said. "Mr. Benny starts a lot of things, but don't none of 'em seem to work out too good."

"But look at all that money Chico's got in his hand."

"Yeah," Catlin agreed with me. "Looks like they doin' all right, don't it?"

Down in the pen two more guys were squatting there with two more chickens. There was going to be another chicken fight. My stomach started feeling funny again.

"Le's go," I said. "I don't wanta see no more chicken fights. I gotta go home."

"Ain't nothin' but chickens," Catlin laughed at me. "Ramona chops th' heads off a dozen of 'em every day."

But she followed me across the shed roof and down the side. I felt a lot better when we got away from the chicken-fight house and were back on the Highway again. We could see better, too, back where the Texaco Station had everything all lit up.

"See over yonder?" Catlin asked me. I looked down the Highway where she was pointing. "Tha's where my Mama got run over by th' Exxon truck."

"Near that ol' house?"

"Right in front of it. Tha's what Ramona said."

There was an old shack of a house down the Highway. Didn't have much upstairs, but the downstairs spread out over a lot of ground. The windows were all boarded up. It looked real spooky with just the little bit of light from the Filling Station hitting it.

"Was that where you lived?"

"Naw, that ain't a place to live in. It's a eatin' place. A res-taurant."

"What was your Mama doin' there?"

"Ramona didn't tell me that." Catlin shook her head. "She jus' said that Mama was there an' went walkin' 'cross th' road an' didn't see th' Exxon truck comin'."

Me and Catlin were real careful crossing the Highway. We waited until there weren't no lights coming from either way. Then we ran across the Highway as fast as we could.

After I got home and got in bed my stomach still felt a little bit funny. But I didn't throw up.

X

The week after me and Mama went to see Aunt Sissy, Mr. Frank Jenkins backed his Western Auto truck up to the front door of our house and unloaded six washing machines and two drying machines, and changed our living room into a Laundrymat. It took him and another guy almost all day to hitch up the machines. They put them just where Aunt Sissy said to. Three washing machines on each side of the room and the two dryers down at the end. And they moved the couch and other stuff out the living room and put them in the dining room for us.

Right away people started coming to our house to wash their clothes. Mama would wake me up at seven o'clock every morning and I'd put on my glasses and shorts and go unlock the front door. Mama would fix breakfast while I was sweeping out the Laundry-mat. I wouldn't hardly be through sweeping before somebody would drive up and start unloading laundry bags and plastic baskets full of dirty clothes out the trunks of their cars. Wasn't just the summer people, either. All the St. Clairs and everybody else from Ruffins Inlet washed their clothes in our living room. And the colored people from back in the woods all around the Inlet. Man, them washers and dryers were going hot and heavy most all the time. Seemed like there was always at least one humming away.

Aunt Sissy got this big old sign painted up saying LUCILLE'S LAUNDROMAT in red letters, to let people know that they could wash their clothes at our house. But Mama never put up the sign. Wasn't no need to. People just seemed to know they could wash their clothes at our house. The sign Aunt Sissy had painted is still leaning up against the side of the house, right where the guys put it when they took it off the truck.

On Sundays now, after we get home from church, me and Mama get all the money out the machines and put it in little paper roll-up things that Aunt Sissy gets from the bank in Ocean City. All the quarters get rolled up together, and all the dimes. After we get the quarters and dimes all rolled up, we count the rolls to see how much money we've took in. I always get bored with that part, but Mama never does. After we count it, she puts most of the money in an envelope and I take it over to Aunt Sissy. Mama explained to me that Aunt Sissy had paid out all the money to buy the washing machines and dryers and we have to pay her back. That's what the money I take over to Aunt Sissy is for.

From the time we first moved to Ruffins Inlet, on every Tuesday afternoon and again on Friday, Mr. Frank Jenkins would drop by our house, regular as a clock. All his visits were alike. He'd bring us some vegetables from out his garden, like snap beans or okra (ugh), or sometimes he'd bring a cake that Mrs. Jenkins had made. He'd take his hat off first and hold it in his hand. Then he'd knock on the back screen door and say, "Lucille, it's Frank." And Mama would go to the door and be surprised that it was him and tell him how nice it was for him to drop by. She'd always say for him to come in and have a glass of ice tea to cool off. Most times he'd say No, that he was in a hurry and couldn't stop, that he'd just dropped by to see if there was anything she needed. But every once in a while he'd come in and him and Mama would sit down at the kitchen table and drink ice tea and talk about olden times. About how Mr. Frank and Papa had been best friends. Him and Papa had been on the Ocean City High School football team together one year when Ocean City was the champion over all the other teams in the whole state of South Carolina. And him and Papa had been in the United States Navy together in the World's War.

Mama and Mr. Frank never talked much about Papa being sick. The only time they did was the day she got another Hospital letter. This one wasn't good. It said the medicine hadn't worked and Papa had gone back to being like he was before. Withdrawn, Mama called it. Not talking to anybody, not listening to anybody. Just sitting there scrunched up in a little ball. After Mama told Mr. Frank that, they both sat there and stared at their ice tea until time for Mr. Frank to go home.

One real hot day when Mr. Frank came by, he said Lucille, how about sitting on the back porch to catch the breeze. And Mama said Didn't she wish they could, but that the back porch wasn't screened in and the flies were so bad they'd drive you crazy if you sat out there. You know what Mr. Frank did? That very next Saturday him and that guy that works for him at the Western Auto Store came over and screened in the back porch. Took them almost all day to do it, too. Mama was real pleased. She kept thanking Mr. Frank and then thanking him again.

The back porch was so nice after it was screened in that it got to be our living room. We didn't miss the old living room after that. Mr. Frank moved the swing off the front porch and put it on the back. And Mama put some chairs out there and a table with a lamp on it, and we sat out there all the time, except when it was raining hard and blowing in. There was almost always a nice breeze out there when it was hot everywhere else.

After he screened in the back porch, it seemed like Mr. Frank stopped by to cool off with a glass of ice tea more often than before. I said to Mama that Mr. Frank liked sitting on the back porch better than sitting in the kitchen, and Mama laughed and said that was because Mr. Frank was such a gentleman. I said, "How do you mean such a gentleman?" And Mama said, "When you're out where people can see you, then they can't gossip about you." I said "What kind of gossip? Is Mrs. McKenzie making up stories?" And Mama said that Mr. Frank was making sure she couldn't.

When Mr. Frank would stop by for ice tea, he'd sit in the swing and Mama would sit in the rocking chair and they'd talk. I'd sit on the floor and play solitaire and listen to them. They'd start out a lot of their talking about Mr. Frank and Papa being together in the Navy or in High School.

One time Mr. Frank told Mama about the time when Aunt Sissy was the head cheerleader at Ocean City High School. Mr. Frank laughed and slapped his knee and said Now that was *some* time, ha ha, that Ocean City hadn't been the same since. He said Aunt Sissy really set that school on its ear.

Mama said she bet Aunt Sissy was awful pretty when she was a young girl, before she got fat. (Mama likes to talk about Aunt Sissy being fat, maybe because Mama's pretty skinny.) Mr. Frank said that, without a doubt, Aunt Sissy was the prettiest girl at Ocean City High, and that she had the prettiest shape and was the snazziest dresser. He said that Aunt Sissy always looked like a million dollars. Mama said Mercy, that the Basket Shop must have done very well to support the family, and buy Aunt Sissy fancy clothes, too. Mama said she didn't think Papa's and Aunt Sissy's Daddy had ever contributed much toward taking care of the family, because he never could hold a job for very long. Mama said she was surprised that Aunt Sissy had money to buy clothes with.

Mr. Frank laughed and said Sissy St. Clair never had a piece of trouble making money. Maybe she wasn't too sharp in school, he said, but when it came to making money, Aunt Sissy had a mind like an IBM computer. Mr. Frank said that if it hadn't been for Aunt Sissy that all them St. Clairs would have starved to death.

Mama said that Mr. Frank probably wasn't going to believe it, but up till that night when him and Mrs. Jenkins came over with the shad roe and told her different that she'd always thought that Mother St. Clair started the Basket Shop. Mr. Frank looked surprised at that and said No, it was Aunt Sissy's Basket Shop, and he wondered why Papa didn't tell her the truth. Mama said that Well, Papa didn't really lie, that what Papa said was that Mother St. Clair had a little Basket Shop and that's how she supported the family. Mr. Frank said that Yes, Mrs. St. Clair ran the Basket Shop all right, but that was because Aunt Sissy and Aunt Caroline and Uncle Benny and Papa had to go to school.

Then Mr. Frank laughed. He asked Mama who she thought paid the bills for Papa to go off to college in Virginia. Mama looked kind of surprised at Mr. Frank for asking that question. Why, Mama said, Papa told her he *worked* his way through Randolph-Macon. Mr. Frank laughed again and said he guessed Papa liked to think he did, but that wasn't the case. Mr. Frank had been swinging slowly, back and forth, in the swing up till then. He stopped the swing and looked at Mama real serious and said maybe he shouldn't be telling her all this stuff, that it was something he thought she knew. No, Mama said, that she appreciated Mr. Frank telling her what he was telling her, that Mr. Frank must have known that Papa and Aunt Sissy didn't get along too well, that Papa went to school in Virginia and settled in Richmond just to get away from her. Mr. Frank said Yeah, he knew that. Aunt Sissy was supporting the whole family, he said, and she felt like that gave her the right to tell everybody what to do. And that Papa never could stand anybody telling *him* what to do.

Up till then I'd been sitting in the doorway, half in the kitchen and half on the porch, playing cards and watching seven ants tote a dead cricket across the porch, listening to every word Mr. Frank was saying. But then Mama said, "Ches, honey, why don't you run see if you can find Bootsie and Eugene and go play somewhere." I told her that I'd rather stay right there and play cards and listen to them talk, that I was having a good time listening.

Mama looked over at Mr. Frank kind of funny and then she said, "But it'd be better for you to be out playing in the sunshine. I'll tell you everything we say later. You won't miss a thing."

Mama says that, but then Mama never gets around to telling me anything. I guess she means to, but she just doesn't do it. So I said, "But Mama, I'd rather stay here." Then Mr. Frank looked at me real stern and said, "Son, run along and do what your Mama tells you to." So I said "Yes Sir" and made my voice go way down low when I said it so they'd know I was mad. I kicked open the screen door and went outside. Mama said, "That nice screen door Mr. Frank put there isn't going to last very long with that kind of treatment." I pretended I didn't hear her. I walked real slow around to the front yard, but as soon as I got to where they couldn't see me, I ran fast as I could the rest of the way around the house to that clump of Snowball bushes at the corner of the kitchen by the back porch. I was even closer to Mama and Mr. Frank than I'd been when I was sitting on the porch with them. I couldn't see them good, but I could hear every word they said.

Mama was saying Well, she didn't know that, and Mr. Frank was saying Yes, that was exactly how it happened. It was right then that Catlin walked up behind me and stuck her fingers in my ribs and said, "Gotcha!" I hate it when she does that, but she does it anyway. I never hear her coming and then she scares the daylights out of me. I jumped back behind the corner of the house.

"C'mon," Catlin said. "Cooter jus' told me 'bout a place where you can catch a hundred crabs in no time, fast as you can pull 'em in."

"Sh-h-h-h, they'll hear you," I said, pointing around the corner to the back porch.

"I don't give a shit."

"Sh-h-h-h. I wanta hear what they're sayin'." Catlin makes me *so* mad sometimes.

"Suits me," Catlin said, talking softer. "What're they talkin' 'bout?" She sat down on the ground next to me and leaned back against the house. Booze came up from nowhere and laid down by her feet.

"They're talkin' 'bout Aunt Sissy."

"I know all 'bout Miss Sissy. Whatcha wanta know? Ask me."

"I don't know."

Catlin leaned her head toward the corner of the house next to the back porch and listened a minute. "They're talkin' 'bout the' Boardin' House," she said. "I'll tell you all 'bout th' Boardin' House. Miss Sissy started that when she was sixteen. You know that big house the Fraziers live in over on King Street? That's where th' first Boardin' House was. Cap'n Will told me. Th' house ain't got but five bedrooms and they were full all th' time, year 'round, with fishin' people."

"Sh-h-h-h," I whispered to Catlin. "I can't hear what they're sayin' when *you're* talkin'." Catlin stopped talking.

Mr. Frank was telling Mama something about Aunt Sissy and the First Federal Bank in Ocean City. They had a run-in, he said. Aunt Sissy wanted to get some money to start a boarding house and the Bank didn't want to give it to her because she wasn't but sixteen years old. Aunt Sissy told the man she was taking her business to another bank. Mr. Frank laughed and said he could see her doing it. He said Aunt Sissy got all the way to the door and was walking out when the Bank man called her back and said that they'd figure out some way to lend her the money.

Then Catlin started talking again. "Hey, you goin' crabbin' with me or ain'tcha?"

"Doggone it, Catlin," I hissed at her. "I'm tryin' to hear somethin' an' you won't let me."

Catlin got up off the ground. "Okay, asshole," she said. "Listen all you wanta. Listen to your heart's content. I don't want you goin' crabbin' with me anyway." She brushed the sand off the seat of her shorts and stuck her tongue out and gave me the finger. Then she walked off around the other side of the house.

I may as well have gone crabbing with her, though. When I leaned around the corner to listen to Mama and Mr. Frank some more, they were all through talking and Mr. Frank was saying Goodbye. Mama told him it was always nice when he dropped by. She missed having a man around, she said. I guess she misses Papa a lot.

When I think about Papa, calm and soft-talking, I miss him too. But the times I remember him mad and screaming I don't miss him at all.

XI

Making the living room into a Laundrymat sort of messed up the dining room, too. All the furniture that had been in the living room, the couch and chairs and stuff, got squeezed into the dining room, around the big old dining table. That meant there wasn't no extra room to walk around in. If you wanted to get to the other side of the table, you either had to move the furniture or crawl under the table or over top of it.

The worst thing was about Mama's piano. When the Brooks truck brought it from Richmond, Mama barely had enough to pay for it. She had only a dollar and sixty cents left after paying for it. But worse than that, there wasn't no place in the house to put it. There was plenty of room in the garage, though, because we don't have a car. So that's where the piano got put, in the garage.

And that's where Mama went once every day, out to the garage to play her piano. She could only play and sing songs that she already knew by heart. Because, even with both garage doors wide open, there ain't enough light in the garage to see the music by. You know how hard it is to see all them little bitty notes.

And there wasn't no way Mama could give music lessons out there, either. It ain't only dark in the garage, but the mosquitoes are real bad, too.

Mama tried making *me* practice for a while. But the only piece I knew all the way through by heart was named "Sonatina by Clementi" and there wasn't no way to get to know more pieces when you can't see the notes to go by. After a while I think Mama got sick of hearing "Sonatina By Clementi" because she quit bothering me about practicing.

Every day, though, Mama'd be out in the garage for more than an hour playing through all her pieces she knew by heart. Mostly Chopin. Mama knows a lot of Chopin pieces. And a lot of Debussy pieces. Sometimes when I was out somewhere, maybe sitting under Manor House or else on the dock talking to Catlin, and the wind was just right, I'd hear Mama's piano sounds coming through the air. Like that Chopin piece I like, the one Mama calls "B Minor Prelude." It'd sound real cool. Soft and nice and sad.

One time Mama got Mr. Frank to bring her a whole bunch of extension cords from the Western Auto Store and we hitched them together and put a lamp on the end out in the garage so that Mama could see the music, and learn some new pieces. But it didn't work out. The plugs were always coming loose. And then one time a possum bit through the cord and electrocuted hisself. So Mama went back to playing in the dark again. I asked Mama how come she didn't get Mr. Frank to fix her a light out there, but Mama said when somebody was as nice as Mr. Frank is, you have to be careful not to impose on him too much. She'd rather play in the dark than impose on Mr. Frank anymore.

I was glad when Mama quit making me practice. I hated it! And I never could figure out why Mama liked going out to the garage every day and practicing. When I asked her about it, Mama laughed and said that playing the piano was her escape and that's all she'd say. But I never knew exactly what she meant she was escaping from. The Laundrymat wasn't much trouble at all, except that you had to keep it clean. That meant sweeping it out a couple of times a day. And Mama would wash off the machines every once in a while. And then you had to be sure you had quarters and dimes around all the time to make change for people when they don't have nothing but dollar bills.

It took a while getting used to the machines rumbling away all the time. They rumbled away day and night because some people only like to wash clothes late at night. Don't ask me why. They'd always come over after Mama had locked the front door for the night. And they'd knock on the door and wake us up and say Please, could they get in to wash just a little bit of stuff. And Mama'd let them in and then have to wait till they got through with their washing before she could lock up the Laundrymat and go back to bed. So Mama decided to leave the front door unlocked all the time to let people get in and do their wash anytime they wanted to. She got Mr. Frank to put a good lock on the door between the Laundrymat and the dining room. We kept that locked all the time so that people wouldn't wander into our part of the house from the Laundrymat.

After I got used to the washing machines rumbling and tumbling, I got so I even liked it. Sometimes I'd wake up in the middle of the night and hear one of the machines humming away up in the front of the house, and it would just sort of hum me back to sleep, like riding in a car at night lying in the back seat with your head on your Mama's lap.

XII

Mama had a bridge party, and I'll tell you who all came. Aunt Sissy and Mrs. Lazenby and Mrs. Jenkins and Aunt Adelaide. Aunt Sissy wasn't supposed to come because she'd said No, she couldn't make it. But then she came anyway. Everybody was all dressed up and smelling sweet from perfume, sitting out on the back porch, holding plates and napkins on their laps, eating little bitty sandwiches with the crust cut off. Mama always makes me eat the crust on my sandwiches because she says it's wasteful when you don't. But then, when she makes sandwiches for her lady-friends she cuts off the crust. Mama made me put on a clean white shirt and pass glasses of ice tea on a tray.

Everybody was there except Aunt Sissy. But then nobody knew she was coming until the big black Cadillac pulled around the side of the house and there she was. It was raining a little bit, and Cooter hopped out of the car and ran around with an umbrella to hold up over Aunt Sissy so she wouldn't get wet walking the little ways to the house.

Mama said What a pleasant surprise, and held the screen door open for Aunt Sissy to come in. Aunt Sissy said that she didn't know there was a screen porch on the back of this house. Mama laughed and said There didn't used to be, and told her how Mr. Frank had screened-in the porch for her. Aunt Sissy allowed as how that was very nice of Mr. Frank and said for Mrs. Jenkins to tell him to let her know how much it cost and she'd send him a check. Mama said No, that wasn't necessary, that she was paying Mr. Frank a little bit at a time. Mrs. Jenkins said Don't be silly, that nobody was paying Mr. Frank for a thing. That Mr. Frank had screened-in the porch because he wanted to do something nice to welcome his best friend's wife to Ruffins Inlet, and she didn't want to hear another word about paying for the screen porch. Aunt Sissy said that was okay with her, that she just didn't want anybody going broke doing favors for *her* family.

While they were talking about who was going to pay for the screen porch and who wasn't, Aunt Sissy was walking around looking at the screen and knocking on the wood posts holding it up, checking it out. After she'd gone all around the porch, she came back and sat down in the swing next to Mrs. Lazenby, where Mama had been sitting. She said to Mama that the screen in the corner at the other end of the porch could use another nail or two. Mrs. Jenkins sat up quickly and said to Aunt Sissy, What's that mean? Aunt Sissy said Oh, Ethel—that's Mrs. Jenkins's first name—that she wasn't criticizing Mr. Frank's work, that everybody knows what a good job Mr. Frank always does. But, she said, he must have had something else on his mind when he did that.

Mama said Does anyone care for another sandwich, and passed the plate around with the little sandwiches. She whispered to me to please get her one of the folding chairs from the other end of the porch by the card table we'd borrowed from Aunt Adelaide. After I did that, would I please pass Aunt Sissy some ice tea.

When I passed Aunt Sissy the ice tea, she said Ain't you got something stronger? Mama laughed and said No, that she meant to buy some sherry but that she'd forgotten to at the last minute. So Aunt Sissy drank the ice tea and ate the little sandwiches.

Mrs. Jenkins said What's Benny up to these days, Adelaide? She said that somebody told her Uncle Benny was putting on rooster fights. Aunt Adelaide turned her head away and started talking to Mrs. Lazenby like she hadn't heard what Mrs. Jenkins said. But Mrs. Jenkins wanted to know about the rooster fights, so she waited till Aunt Adelaide got through saying what she was saying to Mrs. Lazenby. Then she asked Aunt Adelaide all over again What's Benny up to these days? Aunt Adelaide said that he was in a new business venture, but she wasn't sure exactly what it was. She said Uncle Benny never talked business with her because, she laughed, Uncle Benny knew what a poor head she had for that sort of thing.

Aunt Sissy made a noise like a pig snorting and said Well she wouldn't kick a dog in the behind for Uncle Benny's business head, either. She said it wasn't fighting roosters anyway, that it was fighting cocks and Jesus!, she didn't know how *anybody* figured they could make money with fighting cocks in Ruffins Inlet.

Aunt Adelaide smiled and shrugged, and said that Uncle Benny told her that everything was going along real well. She said Uncle Benny told her that there'd be *two* big Cadillacs in Ruffins Inlet before much longer. Aunt Sissy said Maybe instead of buying Cadillacs that Uncle Benny ought to think about paying back people he owed money to. Aunt Adelaide said she wished they'd talk about something else because she just wasn't good at talking business things. Aunt Sissy said That was just the point. That Uncle Benny wasn't good at business things, neither. That she wished he'd concentrate on making money at the Filling Station instead of hatching all these crazy ideas to get hisself rich in a hurry. She sounded a little bit mad.

Mama said she'd like to know who all wanted lime sherbet and she asked me to collect all the dirty plates and put them in the kitchen. Aunt Adelaide and Aunt Sissy said they'd like some sherbet and Mrs. Lazenby said she'd love some except that she was on a diet and better not. Mrs. Jenkins didn't say yes or no about the sherbet, she asked did anybody know what a cock fight was like. I wasn't thinking about what I was saying and I said "It's awful!" Then quick, before anybody could ask me how I knew that, I said "I saw pictures of one once. The chickens kill each other and get all bloody while they're doin' it."

Mrs. Jenkins said Mercy, that was sure something she could go the rest of her life without seeing, and Mrs. Lazenby said her, too. Aunt Sissy said that she'd been to a cock fight when her and Uncle Will were in Cuba one time and it didn't bother her one bit. They're just stupid old chickens, she said, and besides she'd won over two hundred dollars.

Mama brought out dishes of lime sherbet on a tray and passed them around. She'd fixed a dish for everybody and nobody turned it down. Mrs. Lazenby ate hers faster than anybody, saying she knew she shouldn't everytime she took a big mouthful. Between mouthfuls she asked Aunt Sissy how Uncle Will was, that she hadn't seen him in a long time. Aunt Sissy said Uncle Will was still just as crazy as ever. She laughed when she said "crazy" so you knew she liked him that way. She said she didn't know how she'd ever let that nut talk her into marrying him. Mrs. Jenkins said Sissy Ruffin you are something! Everybody knew, she said, how Aunt Sissy had chased Uncle Will all up and down the east coast till she caught him. Aunt Adelaide said Did you blame her? That Uncle Will was the best-looking boy she'd ever laid *her* eyes on, and he was smart, too. He never got nothing but straight A's all through high school and college. Aunt Sissy laughed and said When your name is Sissy St. Clair you don't settle for nothing but first class.

Mama said Let's get to our bridge, girls. Aunt Sissy said No, thank you, that she really couldn't stay and play bridge. She said that if they were going to play poker maybe she'd hang around, but not for bridge. Aunt Adelaide laughed and said she *figured* Aunt Sissy would be leaving before the bridge game started, that she'd never heard of Aunt Sissy playing bridge in her whole life.

Aunt Sissy said that before she left she'd like to walk around front and take a peek at the Laundrymat. She opened the screen door and leaned her head out and called to Cooter. Mama said to the others Excuse me a minute girls, that she'd walk around and show Aunt Sissy the Laundrymat and be right back. Aunt Sissy said No, that Mama shouldn't leave her guests, that maybe Chester could show her the Laundrymat. So I did.

It wasn't hardly raining at all, but Cooter held the umbrella up over Aunt Sissy till we walked up on the front porch. There were three ladies in the Laundrymat and they had all but one of the washing machines going and both of the dryers. I've got to tell you that Aunt Sissy really looked that place over like you wouldn't believe. She looked at the front of the machines and she looked at the back. She said to the three ladies How good it was to have a Laundrymat in Ruffins Inlet now, that they'd needed one for such a long time. All the ladies nodded their heads and one of them, the black lady, said That's the Lord's truth.

Aunt Sissy asked me quietly so the ladies couldn't hear her, "Y'all had any trouble with these machines?"

"No ma'am, Aunt Sissy," I told her. "We ain't had a piece of trouble."

"They run okay, huh?"

"Yes'm. They all run jus' fine." The machines were all brand new when Mr. Frank put them in, so I didn't know why Aunt Sissy'd be thinking there was anything wrong with them.

"If there's any trouble, son," she said, "you lemme know. Okay?"

"Yes'm," I said.

We walked back around the side of the house to where Cooter had parked the Cadillac. It had quit raining, but Cooter held the umbrella up over Aunt Sissy anyway. And held the car door open for her to get inside, then he ran around and got in the driver's place. They backed out the yard and drove off down the road. I think Aunt Sissy waved to me when they drove off, but I'm not sure. Anyway, I waved back. Then I went back and sat down on the doorstep between the back porch and the kitchen, and listened to Mama and them talk. They were still talking about Uncle Will. Mrs. Lazenby said she never would understand how come

Uncle Will turned down that big government job in Washington after he got out of M.I.T. to come back to Ruffins Inlet and run an old fishing boat. How can you be so smart, she said, and so dumb at the same time. Aunt Adelaide said No, no, that wasn't hard to understand at all. She said that anybody who knew Will Ruffin, knew how much he loved Ruffins Inlet and them old fishing boats. That Uncle Will would never be happy living any place else.

Mrs. Lazenby said Well, it was too much for *her* to understand. Mrs.. Jenkins said Everybody knows how people talk, but that she'd heard an entirely different story. She waited a minute until Mrs. Lazenby said What was that? and then she said she'd been told on good authority that what got Uncle Will to give up that big government job was a brand new fishing boat. Nobody ever knew where he got the money to buy it, she said. Mrs. Lazenby said Nobody ever knew, huh? and her and Mrs. Jenkins winked at each other and laughed.

Mama said she was thinking about starting a garden club in Ruffins Inlet. Mrs. Lazenby said that there was a crying need for a garden club in Ruffins Inlet.

Aunt Adelaide said she bid two spades.

It wasn't as good listening after Aunt Sissy went home. I got bored and changed my shirt and went looking for Catlin.

XIII

Catlin's dog Booze is near-about the ugliest dog I ever saw in my life. I mean, you know how some dogs got long hair and some got short hair? Old Booze has got both long hair *and* short hair. He looks like a rat's been chewing on his hide because where you think the long hair ought to be, that's where the short hair is. And the other way around. He's about the color of creek water so that don't help much, either.

But Booze is evermore smart. Smart as a whip. He does anything Catlin tells him to do. Like she'll say, "Booze git me that stick over yonder," and point at a stick. And old Booze will go fetch it. Sometimes he picks up the wrong stick and Catlin'll say, "Not *that* one," and Booze'll mess around till he gets the right stick.

Here's another thing Booze can do. Catlin will say to him, "Booze go home and fetch my red sweatshirt." And, doggone, if Booze don't go get her red sweatshirt for her. Catlin won't tell me how she taught him to do that. But she told me that the red sweatshirt is the only thing Booze'll fetch from home. She tried to teach him to get other stuff, but Booze always ended up bringing back the red sweatshirt. She keeps it hung on the doorknob where he can get it. But I think that's pretty smart anyway.

Booze gets along good with most people, but not Bootsie and Eugene. He don't like them worth a drat. That's because Bootsie and Eugene tease Catlin all the time. One of them will call out to her and say, "Catlin show me your pussy." And the other one'll say, "Catlin ain't got one," and then they'll laugh. That makes Catlin real mad. And what makes her even madder, is when they start telling her that her Mama drank whiskey and was drunk all the time. That's when she sics Booze on them. But they're smart enough to be where they can climb up a tree or else get up on top of somebody's garage or something, where Booze can't get at them to bite them. When they're up high, like up in a tree or on top of a garage, they spit down on Booze when Booze is trying to get up at them. They really aren't nice sometimes.

Eugene knows better than to go anywhere without Bootsie. He knows he might run into Catlin and she'll beat the fool out of him. She can whip Eugene easy. But Bootsie is another thing. He's almost fifteen and he's a lot bigger than any of us, and he's real strong.

I don't know why Catlin gets so mad at Bootsie and Eugene for calling her Mama a drunk. Uncle Will told her that her Mama hardly ever drank whiskey, that her Mama didn't like it. So if she didn't drink whiskey how could she be a drunk?

XIV

You know that thin bumpy line of little white sand hills you can see from Aunt Sissy's front porch, way out across the creek and marsh? It's an island named Palmetto Island.

Catlin said, "Le's go over to Palmetto Island and look for shark's teeth." We were sitting on the joggling board on Aunt Sissy's front porch.

"*Real* shark's teeth?" I asked her.

"Whatcha think, boy?" Catlin asked. "You think I'm goin' way over yonder to Palmetto Island an' waste my time lookin' for fake shark's teeth?"

I don't know why, but thinking about real shark's teeth made me feel wiggly all over. I couldn't hardly keep still. I got up and went over and sat on the front steps.

Catlin followed me and sat down on the steps beside me. "Bes' shark's tooth huntin' anywhere in th' whole world," she said. "Cooter found twenty-eight over there one time."

"Twenty-eight? Wow! What'd he do with 'em?"

"Sold 'em to Miss Caroline for th' Gift Shoppe at th' Boardin' House," Catlin said. "Miss Caroline gives you ten cents for th' big ones and a nickel for th' middle-sized ones. She don't like th' little ones. For fossil ones she gives you more."

"Wha's she do with 'em?"

"Sells 'em to th' people at th' Boardin' House. An' all them people from Ocean City an' all roun' that come over to go deep-sea fishin' with Cap'n Will." Catlin got up off the steps and started walking toward the creek. "C'mon," she said.

"What about Shirley Mae?" I asked her. "Ain't we gotta take her along with us?"

"Shirley Mae's got her period," Catlin said. "She's gonna stay home. Ramona'll look after her."

"She's got a period?"

"You know," Catlin said. "Her monthly."

"I don't know what that means," I told her.

"Ain't your Mama ever tol' you 'bout periods?"

"Sho ain't."

"Well, lemme see." Catlin came back and sat on the steps and stretched out her right leg and started drawing lines and circles in the sand with her big toe. "I don't know exactly how to tell you." She drew another circle in the sand, and then took her other foot and ran it back and forth over what she'd drawn, erasing it. "It's got to do with havin' babies."

"Oh." I was sorry I'd asked her.

"Seems like every month ladies get an egg in their bellies. That's to make babies with." She stopped a minute and looked like she was thinking. "I ain't sure I exactly understand it, either. But th' way Ramona tol' me is if th' lady don't screw an' get pregnant, then th' egg comes out an' a whole lot of blood comes with it."

"Yuk," I said. "Is that th' truth?"

"Tha's what Ramona tol' me. I wouldn't lie to you. Cross my heart an' hope to die." Catlin crossed her heart with her pointing finger and then raised her hand up in the air to show me she was telling the truth.

"Well, it sho don't sound right," I told her. I was having a hard time understanding it. "How come she don't bleed to death?"

"She don't bleed *that* much, I guess."

"How much?"

"Don't ask *me*. I ain't had a period, yet." She thought for a minute. "Can't be much, though. They put this little cotton thing down in your pants to catch th' blood. 'Bout this big." She shaped her hands to show me how big. "Ramona showed me one. They ain't big enough to catch much blood, so th' lady mus' not bleed much."

I shook my head. I was wondering how come Mama never told me about periods. But then Mama never liked to talk about anything that had to do with peeing and pooping. And she'd never told me anything about making babies. Junior Cargill, next door in Richmond, told me about that.

"When you get yo' period sometimes you don't feel so good,"

Catlin said. "All Shirley Mae wants to do is lie in bed an' watch TV."

We walked down to the dock and borrowed Cooter's rowboat. Booze sat up in the front of the boat, I sat in the middle and paddled, and Catlin stood up in the back of the boat and pushed us along with Cooter's pole that he always keeps in his boat. Catlin can pole pretty good, but not near as good as Cooter can. When Cooter gets to going good with that pole, you zip right along. You go so fast you almost think there's a motor hitched up on back of the boat.

But Catlin can't pole as good as Cooter, and I ain't the best paddler around either, so it took us a good while, going around all them bends in the creek, to get to Palmetto Island. It was hot and there wasn't hardly any breeze. But when we got over to the island and crossed the sandhills, the cool breeze off the ocean made us forget how hot it had been paddling and poling over. Booze ran ahead of us and waded out into the water and ducked his head in the surf to cool off.

The tide was coming in and the waves were breaking big and making loud booms when they broke. Catlin found a shark's tooth right off. It was just a little one, but it was a fossil, she said, and she thought maybe Miss Caroline might give her a dime for it.

I started walking down by the ocean because I like to wade and let the little waves slosh up around my ankles. "You ain't gonna find no shark's teeth down there," Catlin yelled at me. "Get your ass up here near th' sandhills. Up where th' high tide leaves 'em. This is th' best place." I wanted to stay down close to the water so I could wade a little bit and hunt a little bit. But I figured Catlin knew more about hunting shark's teeth than I did. And she did. Soon as I got up near where she was, I found one. It looked pretty tiny to me, but Catlin said it was a middle-sized one and that it was a fossil.

"How can you tell it's a fossil?" I asked her.

"It's black, dummy," she said. "That means it's a fossil. New shark's teeth are gray. It takes a million years to turn 'em black."

"A million years?"

"Yep."

I had to think about that for a little while. For a million years that little shark's tooth in my hand had been laying out there in the sand, getting washed around this way and that way by the ocean when the tide came in and went out. While I was thinking about that, I found two more shark's teeth. Then I didn't find any for a long time and Catlin didn't, either. So we got tired of hunting and sat down on the sand.

"Le's take our clothes off," Catlin said to me. She grinned when she said it, and she had a different look on her face than the one she usually has.

It surprised me, what she said. And it kind of embarrassed me, too. "S'pose somebody sees us?"

"Ain't nobody gonna see us," Catlin said. "An' who cares if they do?" She jumped up off the sand and pulled her shirt off over her head and slipped her shorts down her legs—that was all she had on—and she went running down the beach holding them up in the air so they waved in the breeze like a flag. Booze ran after her, barking and jumping up in the air, trying to grab the flapping clothes away from her.

A funny sort of giggle came up from inside me somewhere and busted out of my throat. All at once I felt like taking my clothes off, too, and never putting them on again. All I had on were old jeans, and as soon as I unbuttoned them, they fell down on the ground and I was naked. I grabbed them up and chased after Catlin, holding them high in the air and letting the wind fill up the pant legs.

I tried to sneak a look at Catlin's crotch, but we were running too fast for me to see anything. And then we got to playing, and I forgot all about me and her being naked. It felt good not having clothes on, running and letting the cool air go where it don't usually go.

Catlin ran up to the top of a big sandhill and picked some sea oat stalks and started throwing them the other way down the sandhill like she was throwing spears at some bad guys. "We'll kill them dirty pig-fuckers!" she yelled back to me. And then she ran down the other side of the sandhill to where I couldn't see her. I ran up the sandhill to catch up with her. When I got to the top, I had to hold up a minute and catch my breath.

The sun was going down. And from the top of the sandhill I

could look way off and see Ruffins Inlet across the marsh with the sky all pink and orange and purple where the sun had been. I could see the steeple of the Episcopal Church, and I could tell where Inlet Manor was because of all the cars parked out front, even though the trees covered up the house so you couldn't see it. Looking the other way, on the ocean side, the sky was getting real dark down where it touches the ocean. While I was watching, the moon jumped up over the edge of the water, cool and yellow.

All at once I felt like yelling. Don't ask me why, but I felt like yelling. So that's what I did. I yelled. Just as loud and as long as I could yell. Catlin heard me and came running back up the sandhill to see what was wrong with me. When she saw there wasn't nothing wrong but just that I felt like yelling, she commenced yelling, too. Laughing and yelling. We'd stop when we got out of breath and take some deep breaths and then we'd yell and laugh some more. Then's when I grabbed Catlin and hugged both my arms around her neck and kissed her. We lost our balances and fell down in the sand, but it didn't hurt. When we rolled over on our backs my peter was poking up. I didn't even know it was hard till I saw it.

Catlin sat up straight and looked down at my peter. "I never seen one hard before," she said. "That's pretty tricky." She leaned over to get a closer look. "Okay if I touch it?"

"Sho," I said. I didn't hardly know what I was saying and I didn't care. I felt crazy. Like I never wanted to be anywhere else but right here naked, with the ocean and the waves and Catlin and the sand and the sky and the moon.

After Catlin looked at mine, she showed me hers. It was different from what I thought it would be. I don't know exactly how it was different, but it was different. I didn't understand how it worked and what things were for. How in the world it could make babies I sure don't know.

We didn't talk much in the boat going back home. I didn't feel like there was anything to say, and if there was, I didn't feel like thinking it up and saying it. Catlin didn't say anything, either. Every now and then I'd look at her and she'd kind of smile and I'd smile back at her. But there wasn't no need to talk, so we didn't. It didn't seem like it took nearly as long getting back to the Inlet as it had took getting over to Palmetto Island. But it was all-the-way dark when we got home.

Ever since that day on Palmetto Island, I don't feel funny taking off my clothes in front of Catlin. Oh, I don't mean I pee in front of her or anything like that. I go off somewhere, behind a tree or something, to do that. But I don't feel ashamed being naked in front of Catlin. And she don't feel funny being naked in front of me, either. Now when we are crabbing or fishing and get hot, we take off our clothes and cool off in the creek. It's sort of nice being naked with somebody and not feeling funny about it.

XV

Uncle Will makes a lot over Catlin. You'd almost think she was his child the way he calls her "sugar" and "darling." The funny thing is, that he never calls her them things when Aunt Sissy's around. When Aunt Sissy's there he don't hardly pay any attention to Catlin at all. Aunt Sissy don't ever go near Uncle Will's dock though, and when me and Catlin go over there to watch the fish boats come in, that's when he does it. Gives Catlin Cokes and Dr. Peppers and candy bars and anything she wants. And hugs her and tells everybody how pretty she is and how smart she is.

I asked Catlin one time how come Uncle Will only makes over her when Aunt Sissy ain't around. Catlin said she didn't know exactly. She said Uncle Will explained it to her but she really didn't understand it very good. Something about Aunt Sissy having a falling out with Catlin's Mama. And about how pretty Catlin's Mama was.

"But your Mama's dead," I said.

"Yeah," Catlin said. "But Cap'n Will says I'm th' spittin' image of my Mama 'round th' eyes." She stopped in the middle of the road and poked her head over at me so I was looking straight in her purple eyes. "Nobody can look at me without rememberin' 'bout my Mama."

"Well I sho don't see what your Mama bein' pretty has got to do with Aunt Sissy."

"Me, neither." Catlin shrugged her shoulders and we went on walking down the road again. "Anyway, Cap'n Will says Miss Sissy gets mad every time she sees him makin' a fuss over me. He says th' bes' thing to do is to cool it when Miss Sissy's around. That way she don't get mad an' tha's easier on everybody. Cap'n Will says Miss Sissy's got a lot on her mind. A lot of people dependin' on her. An' that makes her easy to get mad."

It was six o'clock in the morning and me and Catlin were on our way over to Uncle Will's dock. Ramona had fixed us tomato sandwiches for lunch, and Uncle Will was going to take us fishing on the *Inlet Queen* for free. The *Inlet Queen* is the regular boat, the one that goes just plain deep-sea fishing. The other one is the fancy one, the *Inlet Lady*. That one goes all the way out to the Gulf Stream and it costs forty dollars to go on it.

"What's th' Gulf Stream?" I asked Catlin.

"Damn if I know," she said. "It's about Mexico an' water bein' warm an' fish liking warm water." She threw her arm out toward the ocean. "All I know's it's way th' hell out yonder. Tha's why th' *Inlet Lady* got that big mother of an engine on it. Tha's so it can get out to th' Gulf Stream in a hurry."

"You ever been out on th' *Inlet Lady*?"

"Naw. I don't much like deep-sea fishin'."

"How come? Ain't it fun?"

"Oh, it's kinda fun. But I get seasick all th' time."

And she did again. Before we'd hardly left the dock, Catlin was throwing up. And she kept it up so long she was looking green around her eyes. But even when she was throwing up, she had her fishing line out. She'd throw up for a while and fish for a while. The lady fishing next to her was real nice. She was skinny and brown and had curly yellow hair and laughed a lot. She gave Catlin some Coca-Cola and a seasick pill. It looked like that was doing the trick, but then the loud-speakers said "All lines in" and all the people pulled in their lines and the boat took off, likity-split, for another fishing place and Catlin threw up again.

"Honey, I know jus' how you feel," the lady with the yellow curls said. "Used to be I couldn't look at a boat without th'owin' up all over th' place. But I got over it. I *had* to get over it. I never got to see sweet Andy, here." She poked her elbow in the ribs of the grinning guy sitting on the other side of her. "Andy was always goin' fishin' an' leavin' me home. Either I had to quit th'owin' up or get a *di*vorce." She laughed and the guy laughed. Then she bought a ginger ale and got Catlin to drink some of that. Catlin threw that up, too.

Uncle Will's got these guys named George and Dean and Tommy that go around the boat putting bait on ladies' hooks that don't want to mess with the bait themselves. George and Tommy are colored guys, and Dean is a white guy. The bait is an octopus named squid and I don't blame nobody for not wanting to put it on his hook, because it's pretty sickening. But if you hold your breath while you're doing it and don't look anymore than you have to, it don't bother you much. I made myself do it because I didn't want Catlin thinking I was chicken. Anyway, this guy Tommy came along about the time Catlin was throwing up the ginger ale and he said "Sugar, don't you want to go lie down?"

Catlin shook her head. "Naw, Tommy. I'm okay," she said. But Tommy must've gone and told Uncle Will about it because it wasn't no time before Uncle Will was right there hugging Catlin and asking her "What's th' matter, darlin'?" While he was asking her that, he told Tommy to reel in Catlin's line because she had a bite. There were two sea bass on her line. Good big ones. That made Catlin feel better. Only she was mad that it was Tommy pulled them in and not her.

"Gimme th' line," she said to Tommy. "Ain't nobody gonna catch my fish for me." Uncle Will and Tommy and the lady laughed for some reason. But anyway, after that Catlin didn't throw up no more. When Uncle Will saw Catlin was doing okay, he left us and went off talking to all the fishing people. Up one side of the boat and down the other one. The people all acted like they loved it when he stopped and talked to them. Maybe that's because he's the captain.

Ain't no doubt he's the captain. He's got on this blue captain's hat with gold stuff on it. And he's got on one of his shirts, the kind he said Aunt Sissy gets sent down from New York, that says "Captain Will" on the side where a pocket ought to be. His brown face has got a zillion lines on it, mostly running up and down, except the ones on his forehead that go cross ways.

He likes to laugh and joke and I reckon that's what Uncle Will's main job is, keeping people laughing and having a good time. It's a cinch he don't have much work to do. He doesn't drive the boat. Walter does that. He doesn't help dock the boat or bait the hooks or sell lines. George and Tommy and Dean do that.

You know what they do? They sell a piece of string with a little metal thing on the end of it for a dollar and a half. That's for you to string your fish on. Seems like to me you got to buy one of them strings or how else you going to carry your fish home with you? So they got you. Course, Tommy gave me and Catlin one free.

All around the boat they got these red and blue plastic laundry baskets for people to put their fish in while they're catching them. Then, when you get a minute from catching fish, you take what you've done already caught to the back of the boat and put them in the cooler so they don't spoil. The cooler's a big orange chest on the tail end of the boat that's cool like a refrigerator. It stinks to high heaven, let me tell you. That's from all the fish that's been put in it before, I guess. Anyway, you got to hold your breath when you lift the lid to put your fish in, or the smell will knock you down.

I heard some ladies teasing Dean about how come he don't wash the cooler and get that stink out, but Dean laughed right back at them. It didn't bother him that they were laughing at him. He told the ladies that him and the boys wash the cooler out two times a day, and that there just ain't no way possible to get that fish smell all the way out. One of the ladies, that had red hair with a handkerchief tied around it, said 'Awww, go on, Dean, admit it. You ain't washed out that cooler in more'n a month." I'll tell you, it smelled to me like the lady was right.

Me and Catlin got tired of fishing after a while, so we followed Uncle Will around, listening to him joke and laugh with everybody. And we checked everybody's laundry baskets to see what they'd caught. Everybody was catching plenty of fish. Sea bass and red snapper, mostly. That's what Catlin said they were.

When Uncle Will got through joking with all the people, he went back upstairs to the driving room. He calls it the bridge. Me and Catlin went with him. It's really great up there. There's Walter, the guy that drives the boat for Uncle Will, and he's watching the radar machine that tells him where big schools of fish are. While we're watching him, Walter spots a big school of fish on the radar. "We 'bout fished out here, Cap'n Will," he said. "Whatcha say we move on? Looks like a pretty good mess of 'em off yonder." He pointed at the radar. Uncle Will didn't even bother to look. He said "Okay, Walter, le's move it."

Walter picked up a microphone hanging by the driving wheel and said "All lines in!" into it. He made the motor go "hud'n, hud'n" a few times, waiting for the people to pull in all the lines. Then we made a sort of little turn and took off. Catlin looked a little sick for a minute or two, but then she was okay. When Walter got us to where the fish were, he cut off the motor and said into the microphone "Okay folks, you can drop 'em in. There's plenty of fish down there."

Uncle Will gives you your money back if you don't catch any fish when you're out on the *Inlet Queen*. But you got to be a real dummy not to catch at least one fish when the boat's sitting right over top of a zillion fish.

After Walter got the boat to the new fishing place and cut the motor off, him and Uncle Will sat down in a couple of them cloth and wood folding chairs. Me and Catlin were looking out the window, watching the waves come at us like moving sandhills and feeling the boat rising to the top of a sandhill and then sliding down the other side. Catlin had to quit looking, because she was getting seasick again.

"Sugar, reach me a High Life," Uncle Will said to Catlin. Uncle Will's got this refrigerator up there in the driving room—the bridge—just to keep his beer in. Uncle Will don't drink whiskey when he's out on the boat, only beer. But he drinks a lot of that. I reckon that's why he's got a fat belly. He's skinny everywhere else except his belly.

Catlin got a can of beer out the refrigerator and popped the top off for Uncle Will. He took the beer and said "Thank you," and took his other arm and put it around Catlin's waist and pulled her over to him so that she was sort of half sitting in his lap and half standing on the floor.

"You havin' a good time, Sugar?" he asked her, taking a swallow of his beer.

"Yessuh. I'm havin' a real good time."

"How many fish you catch?"

"Not countin' them two Tommy pulled in, I caught a snapper an' a sea bass." She held up two fingers. "An' Ches caught four bass."

"Tha's good fishin'!" Uncle Will said, looking over at me and smiling. "Hold this," he said, giving Catlin his beer. He took off his captain's hat and scratched the short white and gray hair on top of his head with his little finger and the one next to it. He does that a lot, and kind of winks one eye when he does it. "Thanks," he said, putting his hat back on his head and taking the beer from Catlin. He took a big swallow of beer and then started talking real soft to Catlin so I had a hard time hearing what he was saying.

"You an' Miss Sissy gettin' 'long okay?"

"Yessuh."

"She ain't been pickin' on you?"

"No suh, Cap'n Will. Me an' Miss Sissy gettin' 'long jus' fine."

Uncle Will nodded his head and winked. "Good," he said, and gave Catlin a hug.

Then he gave me and Catlin a Coke and he drank another High Life. Me and Cat drank our Cokes and worked the radar for a little while, watching the line swing round and round the circle, until Walter made us quit.

Then we climbed back down the ladder and watched people fish some more. Uncle Will says we can go fishing again anytime we want to go. But that ain't going to be soon. It gets boring after a while, with nothing to do but fish or watch people fishing. And anyway, Catlin don't want to get seasick anymore, for a while.

XVI

There was another night Catlin came over and knocked on my bedroom window and woke me up. That night we went over behind Aunt Caroline's Boarding House and peeped in the windows. Around back of the Boarding House, you can sit on a sandhill and see a whole lot of bedrooms lit up in front of you. Like a stage or a lot of little stages. Some people pull down their window shades, but a lot of people don't. That first night I was there, there wasn't much going on. There was a man and a lady sitting on a bed playing cards and eating sandwiches and drinking beer. He had on his pajama pants and she had on her nightgown. That ain't much to look at. In another window there were two guys in their underwear hugging each other.

"What're they doin'?" I asked Catlin.

"They're faggots," Catlin whispered. "Don't talk so loud."

I whispered back to her "What're faggots? And why do we have to whisper?"

"Cause your Uncle Benny will hear us," she hissed back at me. I didn't understand what she was talking about, so I said "What?" and Catlin pointed her thumb over her right shoulder. I looked at where she was pointing to. A little ways away from us there was a big cedar tree with two little round lights coming out of it. It took me a minute to figure out that it was the reflected lights from the Boarding House shining on the big end of some binoculars. And there was a man behind the binoculars watching the Boarding House.

"S'your Uncle Benny," Catlin whispered. I squinched my eyes and pushed my glasses up my nose to see better in the dark. The binoculars were covering up the guy's face, but he did look kind of like Uncle Benny. At least he looked like the guy Catlin said was Uncle Benny the night we sneaked a look at the chicken fights.

"What's he doin' here?" I whispered.

"Peepin', same as us."

"I mean, how come he ain't at th' chicken fights?"

"They don't have chicken fights 'cept on Saturday nights now," Catlin said. "A lot of people quit comin' on week nights," Catlin snickered. "Besides, your Uncle Benny likes to peep. He spends a lot of time out here, sittin' on that same damn limb, there, with th' binoculars stuck to his eyes jus' watchin' and watchin'."

"I'll be doggone" was all I could think of to say. I looked back at the Boarding House windows. "Don't look like much to peek at."

"Sometimes you don't see much," Catlin said. "And then again, sometimes you see a lot. You know, people naked and stuff like that. Twice I saw some people doin' it."

"You swear?" I asked her. I couldn't believe it.

"Swear to God," Catlin said, crossing her heart and raising up her hand. "Mos' times you jus' see people gettin' naked an' puttin' on their pajamas. But two times I saw people doin' it." She raised her hand up again.

"How do you know when they're doin' it?"

"You can tell. Th' guy was layin' on top of th' lady an' humpin' away, jus' like dogs do. You can tell."

I looked back at the Boarding House windows again. Didn't look like anybody was doing it tonight. Everybody had clothes on or else pajamas or something. Except the two guys hugging in their underwear.

"What're faggots?" I whispered.

"They're guys that like to do it with guys."

"How d'ya mean, do it with guys?"

"Jus' watch."

But one of the guys got up and pulled down the window shade right then, and we couldn't watch.

"Oh, shit," Catlin said. "Why couldn't they leave th' fuckin' shade up? Then I wouldn't have to s'plain what they do."

"Well, what *do* they do?"

"Listen," Catlin said. "If I tell you what they do, you ain't gonna believe me. So le's come back another night an' maybe they won't pull th' shade down. Then you can watch an' see for yourself what they do. If I tell you, you ain't gonna believe me."

I didn't understand why Catlin couldn't come right out and tell me about faggots, but I was getting real sleepy and I wanted to go home and go to bed. So I said "Okay."

We went home after that. We left Uncle Benny sitting up in the cedar tree. The light from the Boarding House shining in his binoculars made him look like a big old hoot owl.

XVII

Bootsie and Eugene know more dirty words than anybody I know. More than Catlin, even. Well, maybe not *more* than Catlin, but it's different the way Catlin says dirty words and the way Bootsie and Eugene say them. When Catlin says them they're just cuss words, but when Bootsie and Eugene say them they turn into the things they're saying. Catlin says "shit" and it don't mean anything. But when Bootsie and Eugene say it, it makes you think of what the word means.

Bootsie and Eugene live down the road a ways from me and, like I told you, they got this apple basket hung up on a pole in their backyard where we play basketball. That's pretty much the only time I play with them. When they're playing basketball, they play good and we have fun. But other times they don't want to do anything but watch TV. There are plenty of other cousins in Ruffins Inlet to play with. But I like playing with Catlin the best. The things she likes to do are more fun than what the others like to do. She likes going in the creek and catching crabs and shrimp and all them things you catch in the creek. And I do, too. But we're the only ones that do. Bootsie and Eugene don't care a thing about crabbing or fishing or shrimping or anything like that. If they ain't playing basketball, they're watching TV or else just fooling around.

One time when we got tired of playing basketball and their Mama wasn't home, they showed me how to play strip poker. Catlin wouldn't play and she wouldn't let Shirley Mae play, either. She said it was a dumb game and she took Shirley Mae home.

The way you play strip poker is this. You put all the cards out on the table with the numbers and faces down. And then everybody picks a card. The one that picks the card with the lowest number has to take off some clothes, like a shoe or a sock. Only it's summertime and we ain't got on sox or shoes. All we got on is shirts and pants. So it didn't take much card-picking before we were all naked. Me looking at them, and them looking at me. When you ain't seen somebody naked before, you kind of pretend you ain't looking at them but you are.

Bootsie's and Eugene's peters look different from mine. They got more skin on theirs. And Bootsie's got hair growing over top of his. I reckon when I get to be almost fifteen I'll get hair there, too.

After you play strip poker and take your clothes off and see what everybody looks like with his pants off, there ain't much else to do. Bootsie said "Le's jerk off." I didn't know what that meant, and I didn't want them to know I didn't know. So I said I had to go to the store for my Mama. And I put on my pants and shirt and went home.

XVIII

Ever since that time when Mama started to tell me about plat-eyes and then didn't, I've been wanting to know what they are.

"Catlin, you know 'bout plat-eyes?" I asked her. It was rainy and yukky outside, so her and me were sitting under Inlet Manor in her secret chimney room with our knees up under our chins drinking Coca-Cola. What made me think about plat-eyes was the spooky shadows the candlelight was making on the walls. The east wind blowing under the house was making the candle fire bounce all around.

"Course I know 'bout plat-eyes," Catlin said. She moved one knee from in front of her mouth so she could take a sip of Coca-Cola. "Everybody knows 'bout plat-eyes."

I said "I don't," and waited a minute to see if she was going to tell me what they were, but she didn't. So I asked her "Well, what *is* a plat-eye?"

"Shh-h-h-h," she said. She cocked her head to one side and pointed her right ear up to the black hole over our heads that goes up the chimney to the kitchen. Ramona and Christine and Blossom were laughing and talking. Catlin giggled. I listened a minute but they were talking Gullah and I didn't understand a word they were saying.

"They're jokin' 'bout Mr. Benny," Catlin whispered. She turned her ear back up toward the kitchen to hear some more.

I didn't care who Ramona and them were talking about. I wanted to know about plat-eyes. "Catlin, what's a plat-eye?" I asked her again. She was listening hard to the kitchen talk and shook her hand at me to be quiet. That makes me real mad, somebody shushing me like that so I said "What's a plat-eye?" louder, almost loud enough for them to hear me upstairs.

"It's a ha'nt," Catlin hissed at me and turned her ear back to listening to Ramona and Christine and Blossom. Their talking and laughing sounded like it was coming from the other end of a rain pipe. But it's a waste of time for me to try and understand Gullah-talk.

"Is a ha'nt like a ghost?" I asked Catlin.

"What?" Catlin asked, straightening up, then leaning her head over to hear me better.

"A ha'nt," I whispered, "is that like a ghost?"

"Yeah," Catlin said. I could tell by the way she said it, that her thinking wasn't about plat-eyes. But I wanted to know more and Catlin was the easiest one to ask.

She straightened her head again and leaned over to whisper "Mr. Benny's upstairs seein' Miss Sissy." She put her hand over her mouth and giggled.

"Wha's so funny 'bout that?" I asked her.

"Only time Mr. Benny goes upstairs to see Miss Sissy is when he's needin' money."

"Ain't he makin' money at th' Texaco Station?" I asked. "An' how 'bout them chicken fights?"

"Shh-h-h-h. Wait a minute," Catlin said. Blossom had just laughed a big whooping laugh and Catlin cut her head up sideways to listen. Christine said something that ended with "true" and Ramona and Blossom laughed.

"What'd she say?" I whispered.

"I dunno. Something 'bout cock fights. She said, 'it's for true'."

"I *know* that," I said. It was the only word I'd understood.

Then the kitchen was quiet for a little while, so I said to Catlin "A plat-eye's a ghost, right?"

"Naw," she said. "A plat-eye's a ha'nt."

"An' you said a ha'nt's a ghost, so a plat-eye's a ghost."

"Wrong." Catlin shook her head. Then she stopped and scratched behind her right ear. "Well, a plat-eye *can* be a ghost if it wants to be. Or it can be a dog. Or a pig. Anything a plat-eye wants to be it can be."

"Yeah?" I lifted my teacup and took a swallow of Coke. We'd brought down some ice cubes when we came, so the Coke wasn't warm like usual. But the bubbles were all gone.

"Christine's Daddy can talk to plat-eyes," Catlin said.

"For true?"

"He rings th' bell over at th' church an' he says a plat-eye shape like a owl flies up to th' steeple an' talks to him all th' time."

"I don't belive *that*."

Catlin gets mad when you don't believe what she says. She stuck her chin up and turned the corners of her mouth down and said "I'm jus' tellin' you what was tol' to me. I don't give a shit whether you believe it or not."

I didn't want her to get mad because I wanted her to tell me more about plat-eyes. "Okay," I said. "I believe you. Tell me what plat-eyes do to you."

But Catlin wasn't listening to me. Ramona and them were talking again. I waited a minute while Catlin listened, and then I asked her what they were talking about now.

"I be dogged," Catlin said. "Mr. Benny had to close up the cockfights."

"How come?"

Catlin shook her head. "Didn't nobody but six people show up las' Saturday night. An' one of 'em was Mr. Lazenby an' he ain't got no money to bet."

"An' he closed up th' chicken fights?"

Catlin nodded her head. "But all them rooster guys want their money."

"What money?"

"Chester"—she looked at me kind of disgusted—"them guys don't bring their roosters there an' get 'em kilt for nothin'." She talked like she was explaining it to a dumb person. "Mr. Benny promised them a bunch of money."

Booze was scratching on the shutter, so I opened it for him to get in and for me to get out. Ain't nobody going to talk to me like I'm dumb. I slammed the shutter back shut and hoped the racket went right up to the kitchen. Catlin said something nasty back to me, but I didn't hear what it was and I didn't want to hear. I stayed there a little while on my knees in the sand looking around and wondering what I wanted to do. It was still raining and that old east wind was blowing, so there wasn't any place to go. Bootsie and Eugene were at their house and I could go there without getting too wet. But they were probably playing strip poker or something stupid like that. There wasn't *anything* to do.

I got up and humped my back and hobbled over to the hole in the floor under the family table. It was only afternoon and not time for anybody to be eating dinner, but I just went over to check anyhow. When there's nothing to do, you do things like that just to be doing something.

Naturally nobody was there, just like I knew they wouldn't be. I could see Cooter's and Sweetpea's bare feet hustling around this way and that way, putting clean tablecloths and silver on the tables and lighting the candles in the fishnet glasses. I could hear what they were saying when they got close to the family table. But then they'd head off in another direction and I couldn't hear so good. It was like listening to the radio and turning it up loud and then down soft and then loud and then soft, loud, soft. They were talking and laughing just like Ramona and them in the kitchen were doing. Only they weren't talking about Uncle Benny. They were talking about a lot of other things. About Grandpa's Funeral Day and Sweetpea said he had got hold of something good and he was saving it for Grandpa's Funeral. They were talking kind of quiet then, so I don't know exactly what it was they were talking about. It sounded like Sweetpea said Coke, but that's dumb because Catlin told me that Aunt Sissy always takes plenty of Cokes up for Grandpa's Funeral. Anyway Cooter said Man, he thought that wasn't very smart, and Sweetpea said Nobody would know a thing. Then their voices quieted down to a mumble. I don't know what they were talking about because they were setting tables over next the creek side. The only thing I heard real clear was when Cooter said for Sweetpea to be careful with them candles else he'd set the place on fire.

When they came back closer, they were talking about almost getting caught doing something. Shirley Mae was the one that almost caught them. Sweetpea laughed and said he'd never seen nobody jump up any faster than Cooter did when Shirley Mae opened the door. And Cooter said Shit man, that he didn't want nobody seeing him naked like that. Sweetpea laughed and said Too late, that he was sure Shirley Mae saw him. And then he said something about Hell, if he had a tool like that he'd want everybody to see it. Then Cooter must have hit him because Sweetpea said Owwwww, and then I could hear one of them running off into the little dining room with the other one chasing after him. They ran from the little dining room into the big one and then back out on the dining porch. It was Cooter chasing Sweetpea, and he caught up with him and wrastled him down to the floor and grabbed him in the crotch. They were real near the family table then and I pulled my head back through the hole so they wouldn't see me. They were both giggling and having a good time. Then I heard Ramona yell out from the kitchen for them to Cut out the horsing around and get them tables ready, the crowd would be here soon. And she yelled to Sweetpea that his Daddy was looking for him.

Almost as soon as Ramona said it, Uncle Benny came out on the dining porch and said to Sweetpea, Son I want to talk to you, and Sweetpea said Yessuh and the two of them sat down at the family table right over top of my head and started talking. I laughed to myself about how Catlin was sitting in the chimney room listening to the kitchen girls talk about Uncle Benny, second-hand, and me getting it straight from Uncle Benny, first-hand.

Uncle Benny said to Sweetpea that he needed to borrow a little money from Sister—that's what he calls Aunt Sissy—but that she was in a bad mood and wasn't going to lend him none. Sweetpea asked his Daddy how much money it was that he needed. Uncle Benny said Only five hundred lousy dollars, and that he didn't know why Sister was being so damn stingy. I heard the screen door slam shut and Aunt Adelaide talking to some people she was bringing in to eat dinner.

Then I felt Catlin pulling on my leg. I didn't even have to look to know that it was her. I stooped down just a little bit so that my head was part way under the house and said to Catlin "Whadda you want?"

"Who's up there?"

"None of yo' business," I told her. And I started to stand up straight so I could hear better what Sweetpea and Uncle Benny were talking about.

Uncle Benny was asking Sweetpea Would he go upstairs and try and soften up Sister with a little sweet talk. And Sweetpea said that he didn't know whether it'd do any good or not. He said Aunt Sissy had told him that she'd already let Uncle Benny have too much money. That all Uncle Benny did was throw it away. All she was doing was throwing good money after bad, and it was time for her to quit.

Catlin put her head up close to the hole in the floor so I could hear her talking. "C'mon Ches," she said. "Tell me who it is." I didn't pay her any attention.

Uncle Benny was telling Sweetpea that Sister was putty in

Sweetpea's hands and would do anything Sweetpea asked her to do. Uncle Benny said Please, would Sweetpea go upstairs and talk Sister into letting him have five hundred dollars? Five hundred lousy dollars?

Catlin was pulling on my leg. "Ches, if you tell me who it is up there, I'll tell you 'bout plat-eyes." I waited a minute but then she said "You better tell me or I'll kick yo' damn ass. You hear?"

I ducked my head down out of the hole in the floor. "It's Uncle Benny an' Sweetpea," I hissed at her. "I was gonna tell you anyhow. Now hol' your damn horses." I stuck my head back up through the hole. But now only Uncle Benny was sitting there. Sweetpea was gone. Uncle Benny yelled for somebody to please, bring him a drink of bourbon. When he did, Aunt Adelaide came hustling over to the table saying to him Honey, please don't make so much racket, that he was disturbing the other diners.

Uncle Benny said to her that Sister wouldn't let him have the lousy five hundred bucks. Aunt Adelaide said that she didn't think that Honey understood what Sister was saying, because Sister was such a generous sweet lady. Uncle Benny said Thank you to somebody that gave him his bourbon drink and said to Aunt Adelaide Maybe she'd like to go upstairs and tackle Sister. Aunt Adelaide allowed as how it was busy time right now and she had so much to do she couldn't run upstairs and see Sister, but that Uncle Benny should remember that Sister had always been very generous with them.

Catlin wanted to know "What're they talkin' 'bout?" I told her "I'll tell you when they get through talkin'." She said "You'd better be straight with me, Chester St. Clair, or you gonna be Goddamn sorry."

Sweetpea came back to the family table then. He asked his Daddy what he did to make Aunt Sissy so mad, and Uncle Benny said Well, she made him pretty mad too. So mad he'd took out a contract on her. What's that mean, Sweetpea wanted to know. Uncle Benny said Aw hell, that it was only movie talk, that it meant knocking off the guys that didn't do what you wanted them to, ha ha. Sweetpea said he hoped his Daddy wouldn't be mad at him, but that Aunt Sissy had said she wasn't going to give Sweetpea any money to give his Daddy.

The dining porch was pretty full up now. I could see the waitress girls' white shoes hustling by on all sides.

When Sweetpea told his Daddy that Aunt Sissy said No, that she wasn't giving him any more money, Uncle Benny said God-damn. Then he said it over and over again, each time it got louder. Then Sweetpea told his Daddy not to get all upset like that because he'd just been joking with him, that Aunt Sissy had give him the five hundred dollars. Uncle Benny said Damnit, Sweet-pea shouldn't do stuff like that to his old Daddy. Sweetpea must have give him the money because right after that he got up and left.

I told Catlin what all Uncle Benny and Sweetpea had been saying to each other. About Uncle Benny getting Sweetpea to ask Aunt Sissy for five hundred dollars, and Sweetpea getting the money for him.

Catlin smiled when I told her Sweetpea got the money. "That Sweetpea's something, ain't he? Miss Sissy jus' can't say no to that boy. Tha's a cinch."

Booze was scratching a flea and every time he lifted his back leg to scratch, he threw sand on me. I pushed his behind around so the sand went another way.

"Now tell me 'bout plat-eyes," I said.

"Tha's all Mr. Benny an' Sweetpea said? You swear?"

"Cross my heart an' spit." I crossed my heart and spit in the sand to show I was telling the truth.

"Okay," Catlin said. "C'mon. I got some more Co'Cola. Le's go drink it an' I'll tell you 'bout plat-eyes." She ape-walked back over to her secret room with me behind her. We eased back the shutter and slipped into the cool dark of the chimney. Catlin struck a match and lit the candle on the stool-table and said "Whatcha wanta know?"

I'd got so interested in Uncle Benny getting his five hundred dollars that I had to stop and think what it was I wanted to know about plat-eyes. "Oh"—I remembered—"What do they do to you?" Catlin thought a minute and then shrugged her shoulders. "Nothin'" she said. "Oh, they can scare th' shit outa you. But tha's about all. I never heard of 'em hurtin' anybody." She pulled a can of Coca-Cola from under the stool-table and popped the top off of it.

"How you know when it's a plat-eye scarin' you?" I asked her. "I mean, if it makes itself into a horse or somethin', how you know it ain't a real horse?"

Catlin put the Coca-Cola down on the stool-table and made her eyes get real big. She was play-acting, I could tell. "Oh, you know it ain't no horse." She nodded her head up and down real slow.

"How you know?"

She leaned across the table so her face was almost touching mine and pointed to one of her eyes. It was open so wide there was white all around the seeing part. "By his eye," she said, making her voice sound spooky. "He's got an eye that looks jus' like th' devil's. Shiny, like there's a flashlight behind it. An' reeee-al eeeee-vil lookin'. Th' dark part can get skinny like a cat's eye."

The candle fire waved back and forth from the wind blowing through the shutters, and made our shadows jump around on the brick walls. It was *real* spooky. I said "Le's go. It's gettin' scary in here." I started to push open the shutter, but Catlin grabbed hold of my arm. "Don't goooooo," she said, making the words long and ghost-sounding. "I ain't tol' you 'bout th' Gray Man, yet."

I giggled. It was one of those funny giggles that kind of bubbles up from your stomach like a burp. I felt like getting up and running out of the chimney room, getting back to the daylight outside. But I wanted to know about the Gray Man, too.

"Who's th' Gray Man?" I asked Catlin.

She laughed and quit talking spooky. "He's a good guy." She poured Coke into the cups for her and me.

"He's a guy?" I asked. I picked up my cup and took a sip. We'd used up all our ice, so the Coke was warm but I kind of like it warm.

"Naw, th' Gray Man ain't a guy. He's a ghost."

"A ghost can be a good guy?"

"Sho he can. All ghosts ain't bad, you know," Catlin said, like I ought to know that. "Th' Gray Man is good."

"How you mean *good*?"

"He keeps people from gettin' kilt by hurricanes."

I waited for her to tell me some more.

"Everytime there's gonna be a bad hurricane, th' Gray Man walks up and down the beach an' tells everybody that there's a big storm comin' an' for them to get off th' beach 'fore they get washed away."

"You ever see him?"

"Naw." Catlin shook her head. "But Ramona's seen him. And Tommy has, too. Cap'n Will says his Grandmama saw th' Gray Man jus' before th' storm of 93."

"Wha's a storm of 93?"

"Not *a* storm of 93, *the* storm of 93," Catlin said. "It means 1893, but everybody says storm of 93 when they talk about it, so I do, too. Tha's when th' big tidal wave hit Palmetto Island and drownded everybody there."

"But there's nothin' *on* Palmetto Island," I said. "There ain't nobody there. How could a tidal wave drown everybody when there ain't nobody there?"

"There ain't nobody there *now*, but that don't mean there ain't never been nobody there. Cap'n Will says that one time lots of people lived on Palmetto Island in th' summertime. More'n all th' people in Ruffins Inlet, even. With lots of houses an' stores, an' even a railroad train that come up from Charleston to take people back an' forth."

"F'true?"

"Tha's what Cap'n Will says."

"I'll be dogged."

"But then th' tidal wave came an' washed everybody away 'cept Cap'n Will's Grandmama 'cause she got off th' island when th' Gray Man tol' her to."

"Th' Gray Man didn't tell nobody else?"

"Yeah, but they didn't pay him no mind. So th' tidal wave washed them away." Catlin stopped sipping her Coke and looked at me. "You know what a tidal wave is?"

"Naw." I felt kind of dumb, her knowing all this stuff that I didn't know.

"A tidal wave's 'bout th' biggest wave there can be. She held her hand up over her head. "Bigger'n a house." She put both hands over her head. "Bigger'n a damn mountain."

"Wow."

"In th' storm of 93, this big fuckin' tidal wave came up out th' ocean, with th' wind blowin' like a son-of-a-bitch an' *whoosh*" —

Catlin swept her hand in front of her across the stool-table almost knocking over our cups—"washed everything away. All th' people an' all th' houses an' everything."

I didn't say anything. I was trying to think up in my mind what a wave that big looked like, and whether you could run faster than it could and keep from getting drownded or not.

Catlin picked the Coca-Cola can up off the floor and divided what was left between our cups, a little bit for me then a little bit for her, back and forth, till it was all gone. She set the empty can back down on the floor and took a sip of her Coke. "Tha's when th' Moonlight Rider started ridin' up an' down Palmetto Island," she said, starting to talk spooky again.

"We didn't see no Moonlight Rider when we were there."

"It wasn't night time, dummy."

"Not all th' way night time, maybe. But th' moon was up."

"Well, it's gotta be all th' way night before th' Moonlight Rider comes out."

I gave in. "Okay. So it's gotta be night time. Wha's he do when he comes out?"

"He rides up an' down th' beach on a horse."

"How come he does *that*?"

"Cap'n Will said his Grandmama tol' him about it. His Grandmama even knew th' guy's name an' everything. Mr. Lenirieux was his name. Anyway, he'd been off somewhere up-country on business—to Columbia or someplace like that—an' he was on his way back home th' night th' big tidal wave hit. Hurryin' to get home in time for supper. An' jus' when he gallops his horse up this big sandhill where he can see his house, this big fuckin' tidal wave rolls in, an' lifts his house up an' floats it right back out into th' ocean. Before his very eyes. It was supper time an' all th' lamps were lit in th' dining room. He could see in th' window an' see all his family sittin' down at th' table, his wife an' eight children, an' th' servants, *everybody!*, floatin' off in th' ocean." Catlin pretended her hands were the house and moved them slowly in the air like they were getting washed away by a big wave.

"You're makin' that up," I said.

"No damn such a thing," Catlin said. "It's th' truth, swear to God." She crossed her heart and held her hand up to prove she was telling the truth. Then she pointed her finger at me. "But *that* ain't th' scary part."

"I don't wanta hear th' scary part."

Catlin kept on telling me anyway. "Here's th' scary part: Sometimes on stormy nights you can see th' house floatin'—way out yonder on th' Ocean. You can see through th' windows an' see Mrs. Lenirieux an' her children eatin' supper." She stopped a minute like I was supposed to ask her "Then what happens?" but I didn't. She went on anyway. "An' then you hear this gallopin' comin' down th' beach, an' it's th' Moonlight Rider ridin' by on his horse, dressed up in ol' timey clothes like they wore back then. He's gallopin' an' callin' to his wife 'Gwennn-do-lynnnnnn, Gwenn-do-lynnnnnn'." Catlin called out the name soft and ghosty, like the wind blowing through pine trees. "But his wife can't hear him callin' 'cause she's way out yonder in th' damn ocean. An' th' fuckin' wind's blowin' a hunnerd miles an hour. An th' damn waves are makin' so much racket. But he keeps on callin' anyway, 'Gwennn-do-lynn, Gwennn-do-lynnnnnn'."

I reached over and pushed back the shutter to get myself out of there. But Catlin grabbed my arm again. "I wanta tell you some more 'bout th' Gray Man," she said. She was grinning, but I wasn't having fun at all.

"I don't wanta know no more right now," I said.

"I'll tell you 'bout Leland th' witch."

"Catlin, you're scarin' me," I said. "Lemme go."

She giggled and turned loose my arm. I jumped down out of the chimney room so fast I almost stepped on Booze. All I wanted to do was get out from under the house, back in the daylight again. Even the raining daylight.

XIX

Sometimes in the afternoon when there ain't nothing to do, I go over and sit on Aunt Sissy's dock and watch the people driving up to eat dinner at Inlet Manor. Sometimes with Catlin and Shirley Mae, but most of the time all by myself. I don't sit in the Lookout House on the end of the dock like other people do. The roof of the Lookout is scary. One of the poles holding it up got rotten and broke off and fell in the creek, so the roof is just hanging there on three poles waiting for a breeze to blow it down on top of you. When I go there, I stay on the walkway because that's in better shape. Some of the boards in the walk are rotten, but you know which ones are good ones and which ain't and you're careful to only step on the good ones.

There's a board nailed across the handrails blocking the walk-way to the dock. Aunt Sissy got Cooter to paint KEEP OFF on it. Cooter didn't leave enough room in between the words so it looks like KEEPOFF, but everybody knows what it means. It's supposed to keep the people that come to Inlet Manor for dinner from walking out on the dock and falling in the creek and breaking their necks or legs or something. Because then the people could sue Aunt Sissy for letting them fall in the creek and it'd cost her a lot of money.

When I'm out on the walkway by myself, I like to lie down on my stomach and look down in the creek flowing along underneath me. You can see all kinds of things there, especially when the tide is out. Low tide uncovers all kinds of goings-on that you don't know about. Everything's trying to eat everything else, the fish eat the shrimp, the crabs eat the fish, and the birds eat crabs and fish. I guess they've got to do that or die.

On one side, when the tide's out, there's a zillion fiddlercrabs crawling all over, looking like dirty peanuts with crawly legs stuck on each end. They got their little holes dug in the black mud and they're walking around picking in the mud with their little claws, looking for stuff to eat. When I wave my arms, they all run down into their holes. But then if I lay real still and quiet, in a little while they sneak back out and start picking in the mud again. Some of them got one little claw and one big white one that's as big as their bodies. The big-claw ones are the boys. The girl ones got two little claws. Catlin told me that, and I have to take her word for it on account of when you catch fiddlercrabs and turn them over and look at where the boy and girl parts ought to be, you can't tell the difference. The way the lines go on the bottom part of their shells is different and that's supposed to tell you which ones are boys and which ones are girls. Catlin says that's how they do it and make babies—with their shells. I said "You 'spect me to believe *that*?" And she said she don't give a shit whether I believe it or not, that Cap'n Will told her it was so and Cap'n Will don't lie. So I reckon it's so, only I'll be doggone if I can see how fiddlers do it. I'm glad the boy ones got a big claw and the girl ones don't. That makes it easy to tell them apart.

I've laid down on the dock and watched fiddlercrabs messing around a lot. To see if what Catlin says about them is true. But I've never seen them doing it. Most of the time all they do is pick around in the mud, picking up stuff that's so little you can't see it, and shoving it into their little sliding-door mouths.

Every now and then one of the boy fiddlers will raise hisself high up on his legs and move his big claw up and down in the air. Catlin says that's when they're playing their fiddles. It always looks more to me like they're praying.

Down at the end of the walkway underneath the Lookout House is the place to watch oysters. A long time ago somebody throwed some old bed springs in the creek and that's what the oysters have hitched themselves onto. Oysters don't do much but squirt water up in the air a little ways. But you can watch the blue crabs slipping along the edge of the oyster bed in the water trying to catch a shrimp or a minnow. And the little brown woodcrabs crawling around in the oysters at low tide when the oysters are out of the water. Did you know that oysters got little pink crabs inside them? Well, they do. I saw them one time when I was helping Cooter and Sweetpea shuck oysters for the Manor. Every now and then we'd find a crab inside. A little fat pink crab. And Cooter and Sweetpea would eat them. Just pick them out of the oyster and stick them in their mouths and chew them up. Alive!

Cooter said the crabs were sweet like candy and he tried to get me to taste one. But I could't make myself put that wiggly thing in my mouth.

One time I was lying on the dock watching a wood-crab crawl up a stalk of marsh grass. All of a sudden a marsh hen came out of the marsh grass and gobbled up the little crab. Then right behind the marsh hen came two little baby marsh hens. I kept extra still so as not to scare them away. They messed around in the shallow water for a while catching minnows. The baby marsh hens couldn't catch good so the Mama one gave them some of the minnows she caught. Afterwards they slipped back between the blades of the thick marsh grass and were gone, almost like magic. Marsh hen mamas are a dirty grey-brown color and ain't very pretty. But the baby ones are almost black and the cutest things you ever saw.

The pretty birds you see in the creek, the big white ones, are cranes. Catlin says they ain't cranes, they're egrets. But cranes suits them better then egrets, so I call them cranes. Most of the time when you see them they're a long ways off, tip-toeing around in the water on their long legs, catching fish. Or sometimes they'll be sitting on the end of a dock or on top of a post quietly looking around or sleeping. Every now and then they'll come around the bend of the creek and be so busy looking for minnows they don't see me. If I keep real still, I can watch them catch their dinner.

They got real long necks and they hold their heads back over their bodies, like a rattlesnake getting ready to strike. Then they sneak around on their long stick legs searching out minnows in the shallow water. When they see one, they hold real still for a second and then that head shoots out on that long neck like a snake striking. And the head comes back out the water gobbling up a fish. They go so fast they hardly ever miss. You wouldn't believe how fast they can zip out that head. Like a bullet.

When I'm all by myself, that's what I do. Watch the crawly things and critters that live in the creek. I don't pay no attention to the dinner-people's kids that want to come out on the dock. They call to me and say "Can'tcha read? Th' sign says keep off." But I don't bother even looking up at them, except every now and then when they slip under the KEEP OFF sign and start to come out on the dock. Then I tell them to get off the dock or else they'll get put in jail. They always want to know how come I can go on the dock and they can't, and I tell them it's because I own it. Then they say "You're lyin'. You're too little to own anything." And I tell them "Step on out here if you wanta go to jail." That usually shuts them up and they go back up on the front porch and wait for Aunt Adelaide to call them in for dinner.

The times when Shirley Mae and Catlin are with me, we spend more time watching the dinner people than watching cranes and things. The dinner people come from all over. Virginia and Ohio and Illinois. Ontario, even. (That's in Canada.) We look at the color of the license plates and try to guess which state they come from. Some states got the same color license as another state, and then you look at the color of the numbers and letters to figure out which state it is. More cars come from North Carolina than any other place. Don't ask me why.

Me and Catlin and Shirley Mae saw the Governor of South Carolina one time. He had a whole bunch of people along with him. Three big Cadillac cars full of people. Aunt Sissy told us he was coming. Somebody had called her up from Columbia and wanted to save three tables for the Governor. Aunt Sissy told them that Inlet Manor don't save tables for nobody. Not even the Governor. She told them that everybody is equal at Inlet Manor and that she'd love to have the Governor and his party come down, but that they'd have to wait for a table like everybody else. She told them they could probably get a table if they came early.

When the Governor came, Aunt Sissy didn't even come downstairs to see him. Hell, she didn't vote for him, she said, and she wasn't going to make a fuss over him. I caught her peeking out the window, though, when them Cadillac cars drove up in the front yard and all them people got out. Seven guys and five ladies. They didn't go directly up to the Manor when they got out of the cars. Instead they all walked down to the edge of the creek. One of the guys was wearing a white suit and the lady holding onto his arm had on a long dress that reached all the way down to the ground. It had big yellow flowers all over it with green leaves. I figured the guy in the white suit must be the Governor, and I was right, because when Catlin called "Hidy Mr. Governor," the one in the white suit said "Hello there" back. Shirley Mae called out to the lady "Tha's a mighty pretty yellow dress you got on," and the lady called back "Thank you."

Catlin looked at me and said "I talked to the Governor." And stuck her nose up in the air.

Shirley Mae said "Me, too," even though it wasn't the Governor she talked to, it was the lady.

So I had to call out something, too. I said "Eat good, Mr. Governor," and the Governor said he would and everybody laughed. It wasn't what I meant to say. I meant to say "Have a nice dinner," or something like that, but it came out "Eat good Mr. Governor," and sounded dumb. But anyway I'd talked to the Governor, too.

Maybe Aunt Sissy wouldn't come downstairs for the Governor, but there's this Senator fellow that she comes downstairs for everytime he shows up. I don't know what his name is, but he shows up at the Manor once every week or so. Most times he comes by hisself, but sometimes with his wife. They got four children and every now and then they come along, too.

The Senator never has to wait in line for *his* table. And Aunt Sissy always comes downstairs to say "Hey". Then she takes him into the dining room and gets him a table. Even when there's thirty people waiting outside, the Senator gets a table. Sometimes Aunt Sissy even eats dinner with him. She says he's an old Bow, whatever that means. I thought he was a Senator like the Congress kind in Washington D.C. But Catlin said No he ain't, that he's just a State Senator and she explained to me how they got Senators up in Columbia, too. It ain't a big deal like in Washington D.C., she said. But that don't keep the Senator from acting big shot. The way he walks around and tells people what to do, you'd think he owns the world.

XX

On Grandpa St. Clair's Funeral Day it wasn't Monday, but the Inlet Manor closed up anyway. And just about everything else in Ruffins Inlet was closed up. Cap'n Will's Deep-Sea Fishing and the Texaco Filling Station. Everything except the Piggly-Wiggly. Just about everybody was going to the picnic.

Chico drove me and Mama up to Greenleigh Hall in his station wagon. Him and Bernadette in the front seat with the baby, named Choo-choo, sitting in the middle in one of them chair-things that hang on the back of car seats. Me and Mama sat in the back seat with stuff piled all around us. Chico's station wagon is the small kind that ain't no bigger than a regular car. And with picnic baskets, and a suitcase full of diapers, and a baby-pen for Choo-choo, there wasn't much room left for Mama and me. Choo-choo cried a lot and pooped in his pants and stunk up everything.

Mama was car sick all the way but she didn't want anybody to know it, so she kept herself from throwing up. She came close to it a couple of times, I could tell. But she held it back and that ain't easy. She had got up extra early that morning, at 5:00 A.M., and fried a whole mess of chicken. Counting wings and necks, there were 107 pieces of chicken. Mama said that ought to be enough for fifty people. Aunt Sissy had told her to bring gingerbread and lemon sauce for dessert. But Mama had been saving extra quarters and dimes from the Laundrymat every week and she decided to spend it all on chicken, and surprise everybody. In Richmond, people were always telling Mama how she could fry chicken better than anybody. And I reckon Mama wanted to let everybody in Ruffins Inlet taste how good she could fry chicken.

Going out to Greenleigh Hall in Chico's little station wagon, I had to scrunch my feet to one side to make room on the floor for one roasting pan of chicken. Mama had to hold the other one in her lap, because the baby-pen and all the stuff for Choo-choo was taking up so much room. We hadn't gone very far down the road when Mama whispered "Ches, honey, hold this chicken in your lap for a little while. Th' smell is getting to me." That's when I knew she was sick in the stomach. When Mama's tired or not feeling good, any kind of smell gets her stomach upset. Holding the roasting pan didn't bother me none. The chicken smelled good.

Bernadette and Chico were talking Spanish at each other and sounded like they were fighting. But you never can tell about them. Lots of times when they sound like they're fighting, they ain't. I don't think Mama could tell, either, because she said "I declare, Bernadette, you can really speak Spanish beautifully," and it sounded like she was trying to break up a fight. Bernadette smiled at Mama and said "That's what two years with th' Peace Corps in Chile will do for you." But then she went back to talking to Chico in Spanish. Chico don't talk English very good. He knows all the Filling Station words and he can count money, and that's about it. Not that he ain't nice. But talking English ain't his strong suit.

The reason that Bernadette went back to talking to Chico was because she was telling him that she'd forgotten and left Choo-choo's baby food back in Ruffins Inlet and that we had to go back and get it. So her and Chico *were* kind of fighting, because Chico didn't want to go back.

After Bernadette got Chico to turn the car around, she explained to Mama and me what they'd been talking in Spanish about. "We're gonna be late and Aunt Sissy'll be mad, but we've got to go back," she said. "Choo-choo's got a special formula, and if he drinks anything else he gets gassy and that means he is up all night screaming bloody murder."

We drove back to Ruffins Inlet and got the baby food and that made us the last ones to get to Greenleigh Hall.

Seeing Greenleigh Hall in the daylight is a lot different from seeing it at night. Them big old oak trees that go along the sides of the road aren't spooky at all in the daytime. The big branches come together overhead and make a long tunnel all the way to the house. Looking down the tunnel, the house looks real fancy, way at the end. But when you get down to it and get a good look at it in the daylight you see it's just an old wood house. Like Catlin said, the front steps are the fanciest part of all. But it's been so long since anything got a coat of paint, that even the steps don't look so great. And boy! do they need fixing. Looks like when a board wears out all they do is lay another board of top of it. Don't nail it down or anything. Just lay the new board on top of the old one. Some steps got two or three boards on them, and the boards are warped. So when you walk up the steps to the front porch, you rock back and forth and get a little dizzy. It's fun. I went up and down a bunch of times till Mama made me stop.

Where the picnic is is down in the graveyard where we came to see Laura that night. It's way off to one side of the house down a little hill under some more big old mossy oak trees. In the daylight everything looked different. There ain't many tombstones in the graveyard—twenty maybe, or thirty—and they're real old and got this gray cruddy stuff growing on them, like mold on a piece of bread. The only tombstone that ain't gray and cruddy is the biggest one in the whole graveyard. (Mama says I should call it *cemetery*.) It's the one with the angel we sat beside the night we came to see Laura, and it belongs to Grandpa and Grandma St. Clair. It's two tombstones hitched together, one for Grandma and one for Grandpa. On top of the tombstones, there's this big, rock angel standing there looking down at everybody. Like I said, it's the biggest tombstone in the cemetery and it's white and kind of new looking, and don't seem to match none of the other tombstones. It's like it's in the wrong cemetery, or something. Most of the dead people are named Ruffin, except Grandpa and Grandma are named St. Clair.

Running down between all the tombstones, the gray ones, they got this real long table, covered with red and white checkerboard tablecloths brought from Inlet Manor. On top of the table, there's all this stuff to eat. Ham and roast beef, and potato salad, and hopping-john, and pork chops, and collard greens, and lots of other stuff. At the end of the table nearest the house, in front of Grandpa and Grandma's big white tombstone, are three white chairs, the kind made out of that twisted stuff like they make baskets out of. Aunt Sissy's sitting in one, Uncle Will's sitting in one, and the old colored lady that lives at Greenleigh Hall is sitting in the third one. They're the only ones that get to sit down.

Everybody else is standing around down at the end of the table where the whiskey and ice are, or else sitting on a tombstone, talking and drinking and eating boiled peanuts. Aunt Adelaide and Uncle Benny and Cousin Teresa and Aunt Carolina and Uncle Luke and a whole lot of people I don't know.

"We must say 'Hello' to everyone," Mama whispered to me. She pushed on my shoulder and steered me down the table, all the way to where Aunt Sissy and Uncle Will and the old lady were sitting. Uncle Will's got on his white "Captain Will" shirt and his captain's hat and he's smoking a cigar, same as usual. But Aunt Sissy and the wrinkled lady are dressed up very special. Aunt Sissy's got on a long yellow dress and she's got yellow flowers in her hair. The wrinkled lady's got on a dress like old ladies wear to church—dark blue with little white things all over it—except that it's long, all the way to the ground.

I said "Hello Aunt Sissy." Aunt Sissy smiled at me and went right on talking to Aunt Adelaide. She said Adelaide when a man's got fingernail polish on, you'd better watch out. Aunt Adelaide said Didn't she know it! and the guy had a big diamond pinky ring on to boot.

Mama said to me "Now you're going to meet a very special person. Chester-Junior this is M'um Janey." We were standing in front of the wrinkled lady. "M'um Janey was your Uncle Will's nurse from the day he was born." When Mama said Uncle Will's name, the old lady got a big smile on her face and a lot more wrinkles. "I helped birth Baby-boy," she said, leaning over and giving Uncle Will's arm a pat. Uncle Will smiled back at her and patted her hand. I didn't want to shake M'um Janey's hand because I thought it would feel cold and dead, but it was warm like anybody else's hand, only wrinkled. She said I should read the Bible and grow up good like Baby-boy.

Aunt Adelaide said the Pinky-diamond-guy told her he was restaurant critic for *Holiday* magazine. Cousin Teresa said You don't mean it! Aunt Sissy said she wished she had a nickel for every jerk who'd tried to get a table at Inlet Manor with *that* crappola.

M'um Janey asked me did I read my Bible and I said "Yes'm" because I knew if I told her the truth she'd give me a lot of talk.

Mama was busy listening to Aunt Adelaide and didn't hear me.

Aunt Adelaide said the Pinky-diamond-guy kept shoving a ten-dollar bill in her hand. The aunt named Bessie said You swear? Aunt Sissy made a snort then turned it into a laugh and said The guy must be from New York, because New York people think ten dollars will buy them into anyplace. Uncle Benny said he'd have took the ten and asked for ten more. Aunt Sissy said That goes without saying, that everybody knew how Uncle Benny's hands stuck to money. That made Uncle Benny mad and he said he was getting damn sick and tired of Aunt Sissy always putting him down.

I said "Hello Aunt Adelaide," and she said "Ches-Junior you're growing like a weed. First thing you know you'll be big as Sweet-pea." Then she said to everybody else that even if she'd wanted to take the ten dollars she couldn't, because there wasn't a table to be had right then. Uncle Will said Aunt Adelaide, as usual, had done the right thing.

Aunt Sissy said that if Uncle Benny didn't like it, he knew what he could do. Uncle Benny said You damn betcha he knew. And that he was going to do it! He turned around to go the other way, but he tripped over a footstone and fell down on the ground. Mama said "Oh," and Aunt Adelaide said "Mercy!" and hustled over to help Uncle Benny up. Aunt Sissy busted out laughing and some of the others laughed, too. Uncle Will got up out of his chair, not laughing, and said That's quite enough, Sissy, and he went over to help Uncle Benny, too. They got him up and dusted the grass off him and Uncle Benny went up the hill toward the big house, marching like a soldier. He was really mad.

Aunt Sissy held her empty glass up in the air and yelled for Christine to give her a refill. Cousin Teresa and Aunt Bessie almost knocked each other down trying to get to Aunt Sissy's glass first. Cousin Teresa was closer, but Aunt Bessie was faster.

Mama whispered to me, "Ches honey, let's go get the chicken." We went up the hill and got the big pans off the back seat of Bernadette and Chico's wagon and were back down pushing some things aside to make a place for them on the long picnic table, when Aunt Sissy called to Mama "Whatcha got in th' pans, Lucille?" Mama put two pieces of chicken on a blue paper plate and me and her walked back down to where Aunt Sissy and them were, so Mama could show everybody her special fried chicken. Mama was smiling big when she held out the plate to Aunt Sissy.

"Jesus Christ—fried chicken." Aunt Sissy shook her head. "We got enough fried chicken to put Colonel Sanders outa business."

"It's fried in butter," Mama said. "Everybody up in Richmond used to compliment me on my special butter-fried chicken. So I fried some for this special day."

Aunt Sissy groaned and shrugged her shoulders. "Okay," she said. "Put it over there with the rest of the chicken. I don't want none now." She straightened the skirt on her dress and poked her two little feet out from under the bottom. Her shoes were yellow like her dress, and had big yellow daisies on the toes. It was already hot even though it was still morning, and Aunt Sissy was fanning herself with a fancy black lace fan she must have brung with her from the Manor. There was an electric fan sitting in the grass behind her, blowing air just on her, not on Uncle Will or M'um Janey. The electric cord ran off through the grass like a snake. I don't know what it was plugged into. We were a pretty good ways from the house, and besides, there's no electricity there anyhow. But the fan was humming away, blowing air on Aunt Sissy.

"Just leave the gingerbread in the car till we get ready for dessert," Aunt Sissy said to Mama. She held her glass up in the air over her head. It was empty again. "Teresa, Addie—somebody get me a drink, wouldya please?" This time Aunt Adelaide got there first and snatched the glass out of Aunt Sissy's hand and went off toward where the whiskey bottles and ice were, on the end of the picnic table.

Aunt Sissy stuck her feet out from underneath her dress again and made little circles in the air with her toes. "Ain't anybody gonna tell me how they like my new shoes?" she asked. The minute she said that, Aunt Bessie and Cousin Teresa and just about everybody all said at once that they thought Aunt Sissy's new yellow shoes were near-about the prettiest they'd ever seen.

Mama said, "Sissy, I brought my special fried chicken *instead* of gingerbread." She smiled a little smile and the edge of her mouth twitched. "Everybody's gonna eat so much chicken they won't feel like having dessert."

Aunt Sissy took the fresh glass of whiskey that Aunt Adelaide was holding out for her and looked up at Mama. "Lucille, can't you do anything I ask you to? Just one little teeny thing?" Mama said something, but I couldn't make out what it was because Aunt Sissy was talking on top of her. "We have *always* had gingerbread and lemon sauce at Grandpa St. Clair's Funeral," she said. "It was Grandpa's favorite." She took a swallow from her glass. "Here I am, counting on Lucille St. Clair to bring the most important thing to Grandpa's Funeral and she goes off and fries some God-damned chicken." Aunt Sissy drank all the rest of her whiskey without stopping, and held the empty glass up in the air again. "Get me another one, please Addie," she said to Aunt Adelaide.

Mama turned away, and me and her walked up the hill to where the cars were parked in front of the house. She was sniffling a little bit and she didn't want anybody to see her crying. I took hold of her hand. "I'm gonna eat lots of your fried chicken," I told her. "So don't pay no 'tention to that ol' bitch." Mama hugged me to her when I said I was going to eat lots of her chicken. But when I called Aunt Sissy an old bitch she stopped hugging and pushed me back to where she could look at my face.

"Chester St. Clair! Wherever did you learn such language?" she wanted to know.

"Catlin says it all the time."

"Well, I don't think I want you playing with children that talk like that."

"Ain't jus' Catlin," I told her. "Eugene and Bootsie talk thataway too. And so do Chico and Uncle Benny. And yesterday I heard Bernadette say 'Shit'."

"Well, children should not talk like that!" Mama said, very stern. "And soon as we get home you're going to get your mouth washed out, young man." Then she gave me a little hug, so I'd know she didn't mean it. "Now, run along and play with the other children."

The other children weren't hard to find because they were making so much racket. They were down on the riverbank. Bootsie had killed a snake he said was a cottonmouth. Him and Eugene were picking it up on a stick and throwing it at the others. Everybody was running to get out of the way and laughing and yelling a lot. Eugene was teasing Shirley Mae the most on account of Shirley Mae was screaming the loudest. "Okay, leave her alone," Catlin told Eugene. But Eugene wouldn't quit. So then Catlin grabbed the snake off the stick with her bare hand and threw it in the river. That made Eugene real mad and he was going to hit Catlin, and Bootsie was going to help him. But Catlin picked up a big piece of driftwood that was laying there on the bank and held it up over her head. "Git yo' damn ass 'way from me," she said, "else I'll knock yo' fuckin' head off." Eugene knew she meant it, so he backed down. And him and Bootsie went off up the hill saying they were hungry and going to get something to eat.

Me and Catlin and Shirley Mae and Jo-Jo and two cousins named Hester and Matt went exploring along the river's edge. We found a turtle and a dead fish and then we found a swing somebody had made with a car tire tied on the end of a rope they'd hung up in a tree. We took turns swinging each other. You'd swing way out over the river and you kept hoping the rope wasn't rotten, and wouldn't break and dump you in the river. That was fun, but then Catlin noticed Shirley Mae wasn't with us anymore. She'd slipped off when we weren't looking.

"Damnit," Catlin said and spit in the grass. "Seems like I spen' half my life lookin' for Shirley Mae. I don't know why that girl can't stay put. How come she's gotta go slippin' off all the time?"

"Ain't that her up yonder?" Jo-Jo asked. He pointed up the hill at the house. "Comin' out the back door with Chico?"

"That's her all right," Catlin said. She sounded glad about it. She took off up the hill and we all raced after her. "Shirley Mae, damn you," she yelled, panting from running so fast. "We been lookin' all over for you."

"I been right here with Chico," Shirley Mae said. She looked at Chico and giggled. Chico giggled too, and said "Jes." That's the way he says "Yes". Chico says words different from how you're supposed to.

Catlin took Shirley Mae's hand, and we all walked across the yard and down to the cemetery to get something to eat. Mama filled up a paper plate for me, and the other kids' mamas fixed them a plate or else they got it themselves, and we went back up the hill and sat on the wobbly front steps to eat. All the grown-ups were back down in the cemetery picking over the table, stuffing themselves. I don't know where Bootsie and Eugene went off to. But me and Catlin and Shirley Mae and Jo-Jo and Hester and Matt were sitting on the steps with plates full of potato salad and all kinds of junk I don't like. I ate two pieces of Mama's fried chicken—but not the skin. I hate the skin.

Then's when Aunt Sissy almost got run over by the pickup truck. Jo-Jo saw it first. He said "Looka that fool pickup drivin' off by itself." That's exactly what it looked like it was doing—driving down the hill to the cemetery all by itself. Wasn't nobody behind the wheel. All us children got to laughing and put our plates down and ran after the truck, but the old thing was going so fast we couldn't catch up with it.

We yelled "Hey, look out!" but nobody looked out. They all went right on talking and drinking and eating. And that's how Aunt Sissy almost got run over. Because nobody listened when we called "Look out!" to them. Aunt Sissy just sat there talking to Uncle Will and Cousin Teresa.

Then I don't know exactly what happened. But all at once Aunt Sissy's legs went flying up in the air and she screamed like a wounded eagle and turned a backwards somersault in her yellow dress. One of her new daisy shoes went sailing right by my ear. The pickup truck missed Aunt Sissy, but it ran over her chair and went crashing into Grandpa and Grandma St. Clair's tombstone.

They laid Aunt Sissy on top of a red-checkered tablecloth they'd spread out on the grass. Mama and Bernadette were washing her face with ice water. Aunt Sissy was breathing hard, like she'd been running a race, and saying over and over "They tried to kill me, they tried to kill me." Mama kept saying "There, there" like she does to me when I'm mad. And she kept telling Aunt Sissy that nobody would ever want to kill her.

Aunt Sissy saw me standing there watching and she said "Git me a double, boy," like she could hardly get the words out. I got her a double, and that seemed to make her feel better. I didn't really *get* the double. Aunt Adelaide already had one fixed and she handed it to me and I handed it to Aunt Sissy.

The pickup truck missed Aunt Sissy, but it sure knocked Grandma and Grandpa St. Clair's tombstone crazy. Knocked the big angel down on the ground. And bent the tombstone over so it wasn't straight up and down anymore. The angel was lying with her face in the grass and the end of one wing broke off. Uncle Benny and Sweetpea and Cooter and all the men tried to set it back on top the tombstone again. But they weren't strong enough to lift it that high. They tried and tried. And then they got tired. So they just pushed on it till it was standing straight up. And they left it there beside the crooked tombstone aimed at Grandma and Grandpa's graves. Me and Catlin thought it looked dumb. But all the grownups said it looked just fine.

Then Aunt Sissy allowed as how she'd had enough excitement for one day, so Ramona and Christine and the ladies packed up what was left of the food. And folded all the tablecloths and put the tables—the long table was really three short tables put together—under the house. "Ready for next year," Ramona said. Then Shirley Mae got lost again and it took a while to find her. She was up at the house all the time and didn't hear everybody calling her. She was with that cousin, the guy with the big teeth that poke out in front. I forget his name.

XXI

There was this day when somebody saw us. We'd gone to a new place Catlin found near Palmetto Causeway where you can catch all the crabs you want. Drop your line in and you got a crab on it, sometimes two. In the middle of crabbing, we took our clothes off and went swimming to cool off. Then went back to crabbing, not bothering to put our clothes back on. That's when this person—I don't know who it was—saw us. It wasn't Cooter and it wasn't Sweetpea, I don't think. Neither one of them would have snitched on us, least of all snitched to Aunt Sissy.

That's what the person that saw us did. He—maybe it was a she—went and told Aunt Sissy.

When me and Catlin paddled Cooter's boat back up to the dock, there was Cooter, sitting on the end of the dock with his skinny feet hanging in the water, waiting for us. He didn't ask us how many crabs we caught like he usually does. He right away told us that Aunt Sissy wanted us.

"Y'all in bad trouble," he said.

"What kinda trouble?" we asked him. We weren't paying him much mind on account of we thought he was kidding around. Then we saw that he wasn't smiling when he talked. He really wasn't kidding. Aunt Sissy wanted us.

"Miss Sissy's got a mad on like I ain't seen in a long time. I don't know wha's wrong, but you better get up to th' house in a hurry." That was all he'd tell us.

And boy! Cooter was right. Aunt Sissy was mad as could be.

"Git in here!" she yelled when Catlin knocked on her door and told her it was us. That deep-down voice of hers sounded like a big dog growling. "Well, Goddamn," she said when we slipped into her room, "if it ain't Adam an' Eve fresh back from th' Garden of Eden."

I didn't understand what she was talking about. But Catlin had it figured out right away. "It's real hot out there today, Miss Sissy," she said. "You're real smart to stay up here with that big ol' air conditioner turned up high."

Aunt Sissy looked at Catlin for a minute—like she hadn't heard a word Catlin said. Then she said, "Well, what're you gonna name th' baby?"

That stumped me again. I couldn't figure why Aunt Sissy was asking us about naming somebody's baby. I tried to think about who had a new baby, or what lady was poking out in front. But I couldn't think of a soul. So I asked her, "Somebody got a new baby, Aunt Sissy?"

Catlin whispered to me sideways out the corner of her mouth, "She's talkin' 'bout you an' me."

Aunt Sissy heard her. "You damn right I am," she said.

I still didn't understand. It was too much for me to figure out. I just looked at Catlin. Catlin whispered, real soft this time to be sure Aunt Sissy couldn't hear "She thinks you an' me been doin' it."

"Doin' it?" I was so surprised I didn't know what to say. Why would Aunt Sissy think a thing like that?

"Tha's a right bad thing to think, Miss Sissy," Catlin said.

"Well what am I s'pose to think, Miss Smarty?" Aunt Sissy was talking real sweet now—too sweet. "What am I s'pose to think when you two been out there in broad daylight, naked as th' day you were born. What am I s'pose to think? Tell me that, if you would please."

"You ain't s'pose to think *that*," I said. It made me mad for Aunt Sissy to think me and Catlin would do anything like that.

But Catlin never got mad at all. "Wasn't nothing dirty, Miss Sissy. We jus' got hot an' took off our clothes an' went swimmin'. Ain't nothing wrong with that."

"Nothin' *wrong* with it?" Aunt Sissy spit the words out, real nasty. "I'll tell you wha's wrong with that. You're a girl an' he's a boy. Tha's wha's wrong with that. Boys an' girls ain't s'pose to run 'round naked together." She stopped a minute to catch her breath and then she started up again. "An' don't han' me that crappola 'bout it bein' so hot outside. Looka what you got on. A T-shirt an' shorts. Betcha ain't even got on underwear—"

"Yes'm I have," Catlin said and pulled up the corner of her shorts so Aunt Sissy could see her underwear. But Aunt Sissy wasn't looking or listening.

"—You don't have to take nothin' off to get cool. You're close to naked already. So don't han' me that crappola." Aunt Sissy was talking louder and louder all the time so that when she finished she was near-about screaming. And red in the face and panting for breath. She looked so mean it scared me, so I didn't say nothing.

Catlin wasn't scared one teeny bit. She straightened up her back and stared Aunt Sissy right in the eye. And that funny little piece of smile sneaked backed on her face. That smile she'd smiled that other time when Aunt Sissy was yelling at her.

I don't know whether Aunt Sissy saw it or not. She never let on if she did. But all at once she quit yelling and went back to talking natural again. "Ches-Junior, here, don't know better," she said. "He's jus' a baby."

Even when I'm scared I don't like nobody calling me a baby and I said "Ain't no baby, neither" tough as I could make it sound.

Aunt Sissy went right on talking like I hadn't said a word. "Ches don't know better. But *you* do. You're twelve years ol', almost in high school. *You* oughta know better."

Catlin stood there with her back straight and her neck stretched out and didn't answer back.

"Now you listen to me, chile. I don't want you teachin' this boy anymore of yo' cracker ways. You hear me? No more. Maybe you think it's okay to go runnin' 'round naked with boys—God only knows what goes on in crackers' heads. But I'm tellin' you now it *ain't* okay. This boy's name is St. Clair. An' St. Clairs don't run 'round naked. So you jus' remember that."

Me and Catlin just stood there looking at Aunt Sissy. For a minute nobody said anything. Then Aunt Sissy said for us to get the hell out on account of she had a headache. When she said that, I ran out in the hall, to get out of that room as fast as I could. Then I had to wait for Catlin. It took *her* forever to turn around and walk out of that room. She closed the door slow and easy, like nothing had happened. As soon as the door was closed, she winked at me and we ran downstairs and out of the house.

XXII

In the morning after everybody's eaten their breakfast, Ramona has her loafing time. Sometimes she goes home to loaf. But a lot of mornings she loafs right there at Inlet Manor. She'll say "Le's have a game," and she'll pull her white-painted chair with the curving arms up to the big wood table in the middle of the kitchen and get out her sunshine face deck of cards with the rubber band around them, ones Sweetpea got off an airplane when he was coming home from college one time. So we all get around the kitchen table and spend Ramona's loafing time playing cards. The reason Ramona has loafing time is because she works all day and till late at night.

Ramona's the boss of everybody at Inlet Manor, except Aunt Sissy and Uncle Will. One time I even heard her bossing Aunt Sissy. Her and Aunt Sissy have been friends ever since they were little girls. They lived next door to each other and they used to play together all the time. Ramona has two sisters named Juanita and Doreen. Juanita lives in Baltimore and LeRoy belongs to her. LeRoy's staying with Ramona this summer. Doreen lives in New York and she ain't married. Ramona is the oldest one and she lives by herself because her Mama and Daddy died and she never got married to anybody.

Shirley Mae wanted to know why Ramona didn't live at Inlet Manor. "Lordy honey, I spen' enough time 'round this place," Ramona said. "I don't have to sleep here too, do I?" She shifted her big behind and pulled her chair up closer to the long wood table. She was sitting on one side, Shirley Mae and me at the end, and LeRoy and Catlin on the bench on the other side. "Sleepy time comes I gotta be in my own little bed in my own little house." She picked up her playing cards and fanned them out in front of her face, checking out the corner of her eye to be sure nobody was peeking in her hand.

"Does Aunt Sissy own yo' house like she does ours?" I asked Ramona. "It's yo' turn LeRoy," I said to LeRoy.

"No Siree," Ramona said. "Nobody owns Ramona's house but Ramona." She pulled on the piece of purple cloth with the little bumble bees all over it that was wrapped around her head and tied in a knot at the back. She wears a different one every day. And when you see her at the Manor, she's always got a long white apron on over her skirt. Christine and them other girls wear dresses that just go down to their knees. But Ramona's dresses hang way down, almost to the floor. Ramona don't dress in style, but what she wears looks like good style for her.

"Aunt Mona, gimme all your sixes," Leroy said. We were playing "Go Fish" because LeRoy don't know how to play anything else. When he ain't there, we play "Gin Rummy" or "Black Jack," with matches for money.

"Go fish," Ramona said to LeRoy. LeRoy picked a card off the top of the pile in the middle of the table. When he looked at it, he made a face and stuck it in with the other cards in his hand.

"LeRoy, gimme all yo' sixes," Catlin grinned and held out her hand to LeRoy. "Dawgone you," LeRoy said and gave Catlin his six. Catlin collected the two sixes and laid them down on the table in front of herself.

Shirley Mae asked Ramona, "Ramona, was Cooter's Daddy as pretty as Cooter is?"

Catlin giggled. "Boys ain't pretty, Shirley Mae. That's what girls are. Boys are good-lookin'."

"You can call it good-lookin' if you wanta," Shirley Mae said. "Cooter's pretty to me."

"He looks pretty to me too, baby," Ramona said and smiled. She put her hand up to Shirley Mae's cheek and patted it.

"Was his Daddy pretty, too?"

"I never knew Cooter's Daddy," Ramona said. "But his Mama was pretty. Real pretty."

"Ches gimme all yo' aces," Catlin said to me. I don't know how she knew I had an ace, but she did. I threw it across the kitchen table to her, but it flipped off to the side and fell onto the floor. Catlin picked it up and giggled.

"Tell me 'bout her," Shirley Mae said.

"Cooter's Mama? Honey, I tol' you all about her."

"Tell me again. Pleeeeeease?"

"Ain't much to tell." Ramona put her cards face down on the table and fixed the catch on the little gold earring on her right ear. "She wasn't hardly nothin' but a baby herself. Not old as you, even."

"Tell 'bout her birthin' Cooter an' then dyin'," Shirley Mae said. "Tha's real sad."

"Tha's what happened?" I asked Ramona.

"Honey-baby, le's talk 'bout somethin' else," Ramona said. "Tha's too sad for Ramona to talk about."

Shirley Mae said to me "Tha's what happened. Cooter's Mama done th' birthin' all by herself. Out in th' woods. An' when Tommy, off th' fish boat, found her she was mos' dead. Ain't that right, Ramona?"

Ramona nodded her head and said "An' Cooter been here ever since. Cap'n Will an' Miss Sissy th' only folks tha' boy ever had."

"Tha's sad," I said.

"Cat, it's still yo' turn," Ramona reminded Catlin. You could tell she didn't want to talk about Cooter's Mama.

"Shirley Mae, gimme all yo' jacks."

"Fish."

"Ramona, you been workin' for Aunt Sissy a long time, ain't-cha?" I asked Ramona.

"Ever since I can remember," Ramona said. "I started helpin' Miss Sissy an' her Mama at th' Basket Shop when we was in th' eighth grade. Tha's a *long* time ago." She stuck her hand into the neck of her dress and pulled at something near her left shoulder. "After her Mama got sick, I run th' Basket Shop by myself."

"An' you worked at the Boardin' House, right?" Catlin asked her.

"I never worked in that little Boardin' House, th' one Miss Sissy made out th' ol' Frazier place on Willow Street," Ramona said. "That wasn't nothin'. Only six rooms. But when Miss Sissy built th' big Boardin' House—that same one there on Manor Road—*everybody* had to work, we was so busy. Miss Caroline, Miss Teresa, me. Even Mr. Benny."

"Not Aunt Adelaide?" I asked.

"Miss Adelaide an' Mr. Benny wasn't married then," Ramona explained. "They wasn't even courtin'."

"Oh."

"Whose *go* is it?"

"It's yours Ramona."

"Okay. Gimme all yo' jacks, Cat."

Catlin handed over her jack to Ramona. Ramona studied the three cards left in her hand a minute, and looked around the table at each one of us. "Honey-baby," she said to Shirley Mae, "gimme yo' threes."

"Oh phooey, Ramona," Shirley Mae said. "You looked in my hand." She threw the card at Ramona.

"No such a thing," Ramona said. "I never looked in yo' hand." She reached over and pushed Shirley Mae's hand so that her cards were closer to her face. "But you oughta hol' yo' hand up so nobody *could* look."

Shirley Mae lifted up one side of her behind and let out a little squeeky poot, like the noise from a Hallowe'en horn. I couldn't hold back a giggle.

"It ain't funny," Ramona said to me. She shook her head and looked stern at Shirley Mae. "Honey-baby, don'tcha do that no more. Why, if yo' Mama heard you do that she'd be *real* upset."

"Catlin does it all the time," Shirley Mae said.

"Do *not*."

"Y'do too."

"Don't."

"Do."

Ramona slapped her hand down on the table. "Well, ain't nobody gonna do it no more. Y'hear?"

"Yes Ramona."

"Catlin. Y'hear me?"

"Ramona I ain't been fartin' like that. Shirley Mae made that up," Catlin said.

"You heard what I said, Catlin?" Ramona said. "No more."

"Yes Ramona."

The rest of that game was very quiet. Nobody had much to say. Ramona asked for my seven, and LeRoy's ten and the game was over.

"One mo' game," Ramona said. "Then I gotta get to fixin' some lunch for everybody." She started dealing out the cards.

"Le's teach LeRoy how to play somethin' else," Catlin said. "I'm sick of 'Go Fish.' "

"Ain't got time now," Ramona said. "Maybe tomorrow."

Then's when we heard shuffling coming up the back steps and Cooter and Sweetpea came in the back door toting a basketfull of crabs they'd caught. "Git right outa here," Ramona said, "an' wash them crab off. An' wash them dirty feet too, Mr. Allison St. Clair. Don't go drippin' that ol' creek mud over my kitchen."

Sweetpea grinned at her. "Don't git yo' bowels in a uproar, Ramona."

"I'll uproar you, boy, for messin' up my kitchen," Ramona told him. "Now gitcha self outa here."

Sweetpea scooped up the basket of crabs and started out the door. Over his shoulder he told Cooter "I'll wash off th' crabs. Yo' feet ain't muddy. You stay here an' put th' water on to boil."

Ramona finished dealing and stacked the rest of the deck in the middle of the table. We all picked up our cards and fanned them out and straightened them in our hands. I had two nines and two jacks. That's pretty lucky from just dealing. While I was waiting for the others to get their cards straight, I said "Cooter, Shirley Mae thinks you're pretty," and giggled.

Cooter lifted the big black pot he'd been filling with water up out of the sink and set it down on the stove, and turned the burner up high. "Shows she got good taste," he said. He didn't look at me or at Shirley Mae when he said it. Just kept his eyes looking at the pot.

Catlin leaned across the table and cupped one hand on the side of her mouth. "Don't tease Shirley Mae," she whispered to me.

"Why?"

"Jus' don't."

I shrugged. "I don't see why not."

Shirley Mae got her cards straight and said "Cat, gimme yo' aces."

Catlin flipped an ace over to her.

"Thank you." Shirley Mae smiled and put the aces down on the table in front of her. "An' Ches gimme yo' tens."

"Fish."

She picked up a card from the fishing pile and said "Ha, ha. I got it" real loud. She held up the ten so that everybody could see she wasn't cheating, and then booked it with her other ten. "Ramona gimme yo' queens."

"You gotta fish for that one, honey," Ramona said.

Sweetpea's bare feet came flopping up the sandy back steps. "Cooter, you got that water ready?" he called in through the screen where the steps pass one of the back kitchen windows.

"Almos'," Cooter called back to him.

I said "Eights, Cat?"

"Fish."

I fished and got a queen. LeRoy held his hand in front of me so I could see his cards. "What should I oughta ask for, Ches?" he wanted to know.

"Dummy," Catlin said. "Don't let him see yo' cards."

"He'll know what to ask for next turn, LeRoy," Ramona explained to him.

LeRoy grinned a silly looking grin and said "Oh. Tha's right, ain't it." He had an ace in his hand, so I whispered "Ask Shirley Mae for her aces," to him.

"Okay Chester, damn you. Tha's cheatin'," Shirley Mae said. "I ain't playin' no more." She threw down her cards on the table.

"Me neither," Catlin said. She threw her cards down, too. And then everybody else did the same. Ramona scraped her hands across the table, sliding all the cards together and picking them up. Then she tapped the sides on the table to even up the edges and slipped the rubber band around them.

"I didn't wanta play anymore, anyhow," I said. "I'm gonna watch Sweetpea an' Cooter."

Sweetpea and Cooter were standing by the stove dumping crabs out of the bushel basket into the big pot of boiling water. Two big crabs slipped out the side of the basket and scooted across the stove top and down onto the floor. I think Sweetpea let them loose on purpose on account of when Shirley Mae and LeRoy yelled and stood up on their chairs, Sweetpea and Cooter laughed like it was a big joke. Catlin snatched a wooden spoon out of Sweetpea's hand and chased one crab till she had it pinned under the spoon. Then she picked it up by the back flippers where he can't bite you and walked over and dropped it in the pot. Cooter had caught the other crab and was doing the same thing. When the crabs hit the boiling water, their back legs quivered for a second or two before they slipped down into the water. I don't like watching them die like that, so I looked the other way.

"Hey man, did you see *that*?" LeRoy asked, looking around at everybody and grinning. LeRoy starts all his talking with "Hey man." "Hey man, tha's cool. Throw in another one," he said. I reckon he'd never seen crabs get boiled to death before. He stayed there and watched Cooter and Sweetpea dump the rest of the crabs in the water.

"Who's gonna help pick?" Sweetpea asked.

"Not me," I said quick.

"I don't know how," LeRoy said.

"I'll help, Sweetpea," Catlin said.

Sweetpea gave her a hug. "I knew I could count on my bes' girl," he said.

"I'll help too," Shirley Mae said, "if Cooter's gonna pick."

"You gonna have to pick at th' other table," Ramona said, pointing to the square table in the corner of the room. "I gotta have this one to work on."

I left everybody there picking crab. I hate picking crab. Shirley Mae was sitting next to Cooter and trying to do everything the same way he did. She likes Cooter a lot.

I said "Goodbye pretty Cooter," and raced out the back door to keep from getting hit by the wooden spoon Shirley Mae threw at me.

XXIII

Three days after Aunt Sissy yelled at me and Catlin for taking our clothes off, we went over to Palmetto Island and stayed the whole afternoon. Shirley Mae didn't go with us. She wanted to stay at the Manor and help Ramona and Christine and Cooter get ready for the dinner crowd. Usually Ramona don't want her around that time of day, but this time she said "Okay." And Cooter said he'd help keep an eye on her. Catlin said she wasn't worried no-how, because Shirley Mae won't sneak off when Cooter's around.

As soon as we got on the beach, we took our clothes off and went swimming. Catlin is teaching me to ride waves. I'm getting pretty good at it, but not good like her. She can catch any wave that comes along and ride it all the way to shore, till her stomach is dragging on the sand.

After we went swimming, we looked for shells. I found a pretty wing shell. Yellow and pink. And Catlin found a sea biscuit. We looked for shark's teeth, too, but only found one. A little one that I think was really a piece of oyster shell.

While we were in the ocean swimming, I didn't feel naked at all. But it's funny. After we got out of the water, I kept feeling like I ought to cover up my peter with my hands to keep Catlin from seeing it.

Catlin must have felt the same way because after a while she said "Le's put our clothes on."

And that's what we did.

XXIV

Aunt Sissy thinks Uncle Benny was the one that tried to kill her with the pickup truck on Grandpa St. Clair's Funeral Day. That's what Mama told me. Aunt Sissy said Uncle Benny took the brake off and aimed the pickup at her and give it a little push to get it going down the hill.

"You reckon he really did?" I asked Mama.

"Oh child, I don't think so," Mama said. "Ben wouldn't do a thing like that."

"How come Aunt Sissy thinks Uncle Benny wants to kill her?"

Mama put down her sewing and looked across the dining room table at me. Then she turned her head around to the side next the Laundrymat and listened a minute to see if anybody might be there to hear what we were talking about. Then she said "Chester, now you mustn't ever tell a soul. This is family talk and what I'm gonna tell you you mustn't ever tell anybody. Not Eugene or Bootsie. Not Catlin. Not anybody, you hear?"

"Yes'm."

"Your Aunt Sissy says that Uncle Benny owes her a considerable amount of money and he's trying to get out of paying her back."

"How much money?"

"I don't know how much. I couldn't ask Sissy *that*."

"A hundred dollars?"

"More than that."

"A thousand? A million?"

"Ches honey, I told you I don't have any idea of the amount. Your Aunt Sissy just said it was a lot of money."

"How come he owes her a lotta money?"

"I'm not sure exactly." Mama made wrinkles in between her eyebrows. "But I think she loaned him money to open up a Picture Show one time. And another time he started a miniature golf place. And then the Topless—." Mama stopped talking and looked down at her sewing. Her face got real red.

"Mama I know what a 'Topless' is," I said.

Mama looked at me and her eyebrows went up high. "You do?"

"Yes'm. I seen Bootsie's *Playboy* magazines. He's got a whole stack of 'em. Topless is when ladies don't wear nothing on top an' show their boobs. Ain't that right?"

Mama had picked up her sewing, but she dropped it again. "Chester St. Clair!" she said.

"Well, ain't it?"

"Well, yes. I guess you could say it that way. But there *are nicer* ways to say it. D'you hear?"

"Yes'm."

"You could have said 'bosoms' or something like that even."

"Yes'm."

"Now I don't want to ever hear you talking like that again. Y'hear?"

"Yes'm." Lordy, I thought, what'd she say if she knew that the *Playboy* ladies don't wear no bottoms either.

Then Mama got quiet and picked up her sewing and started stitching again.

"Mama?"

"Yes?" She didn't look up from her sewing.

"What about Uncle Benny an' th'—you know—th' bosoms place?"

"We won't talk about it anymore," Mama said. I knew by the way she said it not to ask her any more about Uncle Benny. Now I'll never know about the topless place or how come Uncle Benny tried to run Aunt Sissy over with the pickup truck. Mama always quits talking when it gets real interesting. She tells everybody that I'm her "little man" and how much she depends on me now that Papa's not here. And how grownup I am. Only she never talks grownup with me. And I never find out anything.

XXV

I think it was August that was the time when Mama had to have a bad operation. Aunt Adelaide was going to drive her to Charleston to the Hospital, but then Aunt Adelaide wasn't feeling good, so Cooter took Mama in the pickup. I didn't go with them on account of Mama said it'd be better if I stayed home. That it wasn't fun being at a Hospital, it wasn't no place for children to be.

"I'll only be gone a little while," she told me. She'd made me some oatmeal cookies. And she'd put two clean pairs of shorts and four shirts and some jeans and underwear and my toothbrush and comb in a Piggly Wiggly shopping bag for me to take to Aunt Sissy's with me. That's where I was going to stay while Mama was gone.

"How long?" I asked her.

"Not long. A week, maybe."

"Tha's *long*."

"I'll be back before you know it," Mama said. She held out the Piggly Wiggly shopping bag and the little suitcase that she was taking to the Hospital with her. "Put these on the porch so we'll be ready when Aunt Adelaide gets here. We don't want to keep her waiting." Mama's hand was shaking a little bit.

I took the shopping bag and the suitcase out on the porch and set them down at the top of the steps and sat myself down beside them. Mama was sweeping out the dining room again. She'd swept it twice already. She messed around in the house a little bit longer and then she came out on the porch with me.

"Now help Aunt Sissy as much as you can, y'hear?" she said. She had her pocketbook hung on her arm and was carrying an alarm clock in her hand. She leaned over and stuck the clock in my Piggly Wiggly bag. "You know how to set it, don't you?" I nodded my head. "I won't be here to get you up in the morning, so you'll have to let the ol' alarm clock do it." She smiled a little smile. "Try and get over here nice and early every morning so you can give the Laundromat a good sweeping before anybody gets here. Keep it nice and clean like you do when I'm here. Aunt Adelaide'll take care of everything else. She knows what to do." Mama was walking up and down the front porch putting on her white gloves. "Now let me see. Have I thought of everything?"

But thinking time was over because right then Cooter drove up in the pickup and said Aunt Adelaide was sick and couldn't come, and that he was going to drive Mama to Charleston.

I could see that Mama didn't think much of going to the

Hospital in a pickup truck, but there wasn't much else she could do. I cried a little bit when she said "bye" and gave me a kiss and a hug. And after they'd drove off, I sat on the steps a little while longer, so I'd be sure I didn't have to cry anymore. Then I walked down the road to the Manor.

I couldn't find Sweetpea when I got there, so I went upstairs and put my Piggly Wiggly bag in his room anyway. Sweetpea's got this great room. Really cool. Like he's got all these things nailed up on the wall. There's a big fish that he caught one time when Uncle Will took him out on the Gulf Stream Boat. And there's a deer's head that he found in the attic at Greenleigh Hall that the rats had chewed the ears off of. And a big board with all the shark's teeth he ever found glued on it. And a big road sign that says SLIPPERY WHEN WET. Plenty of things to look at.

On one side of the room there's a great big wood bed with a headboard that goes up almost to the ceiling. Sweetpea's got pictures of naked girls stuck all over that with Scotch tape. Really naked girls without their hands over their crotches. Then, there's a dresser with a big round mirror over top of it. And a rocking chair that's got long necked ducks for arms, carved in wood.

That's all the furniture, except for the cot that had been set up for me at the foot of the big bed. That ain't a whole lot of furniture for such a big room. But the walls are something else. Almost every piece of wall has got something stuck on it or nailed to it. There's a lot of pictures of Sweetpea on the beach with his surfboard, with other guys and their surfboards. And hanging down from the ceiling there's a model of an old-timey airplane, the ones that had two wings. And there's a plastic submarine that's got one side made out of glass so you can look inside and see what's going on, engines and men working and stuff like that. The submarine's hung up high and you have to stand on a chair to see it good.

I looked at everything, and then I looked some more. Then I got to thinking about spending the nights sleeping in Sweetpea's room and not being home with my Mama. And thinking about Mama being operated on and all, I started feeling like crying some more. So instead I ate an oatmeal cookie and went downstairs and looked for Sweetpea.

This time there wasn't no trouble finding him. He was in the kitchen rolling forks and knives and spoons up in paper napkins, getting ready for the dinner crowd.

"Here's my roommate," Sweetpea said when I walked into the kitchen. "Sit right down here next to me." He pulled a stool out from under the table to make room for me. "I'm gonna put you to work. Tonight you're gonna be my assistant. How you like that?"

"Okay," I told him. I don't mind helping Sweetpea because he tells jokes and fools around and makes it fun. He showed me how to hold the spoons and forks and knives and roll the paper napkins around them. After we'd finished that, I helped put clean table-cloths on the tables. And put ice in glasses for ice tea. And spread out baskets so they'd be ready for hush-puppies when Ramona got through frying them. Ramona and Christine said I did real good. Ramona said I did better than Sweetpea on *his* first day. But she laughed when she said it, and Sweetpea laughed and made like he was punching her, so I think she was just funning me.

Me and Sweetpea ate supper first so we'd be ready to work when the crowd started coming in. We sat at the family table and Mary Ellen waited on us. While Sweetpea and me were sitting there eating, I thought about the hole in the floor and I stuck my head down under the table to see what it looked like from the top side. The piece of iron wasn't as big as I figured it'd be.

"Whatcha doin' down there?" Sweetpea wanted to know. He leaned way back in his chair and held up the edge of the checkered tablecloth so he could see me. "I dropped my napkin," I told him.

We barely finished our supper before cars started winding into the driveway, scatter-parking around the front yard. All jammed with people ready for dinner. Just a few cars at first, but before we knew it they really began piling in one right after another. After that nobody had any time to talk to me. Ramona put a stool off in one corner of the kitchen for me and said Sit! And I sat there and watched everybody else work. Spreading out plates. Filling them up with shrimp or fish or crab or some of everything. Pouring ice tea, and Coca-Cola, and coffee, and sometimes milk. Dishing up vanilla and chocolate ice cream for dessert. As fast as Ramona and Christine and Blossom could fill up the plates, one of the wait-resses would snatch them up and run out into the dining room with them, sometimes holding four and five plates at the same time. Sweetpea and Cooter kept rushing in with red plastic tubs full of dirty dishes. Back and forth, back and forth. For a while Cooter washed dishes and Sweetpea cleared tables, then they switched off and Sweetpea washed dishes and Cooter cleared tables. Catlin came in one time to get supper for her and Shirley Mae, but I didn't see her anymore after that. Ramona got me to pouring ice tea and I forgot about everything except pouring tea till a lot later when the crowd was gone and just a few people were there waiting to get fed. Then I helped Cooter and Sweetpea wash up all the dishes that were left and that took a lot of time. I helped dry.

After that I was really tired, but Sweetpea said us workers needed to take a ride to cool off. So we got in the jeep and drove down some dirt roads and then across the causeway and a little wood bridge over to Palmetto Island. We spent the next hour speeding up and down sandhills. Sweetpea and Mary Ellen were in front and me and Cooter were up in the kitchen chairs in back. I had to hang on real tight to keep from getting bounced out. The way Sweetpea went sailing over them sandhills! Sometimes the jeep would go up in the air off the ground, and then come back down, bam, and bump your behind. One time my hand slipped and I almost went sailing through the air except that Cooter grabbed ahold of me just in time. Everybody was laughing and having a good time. Even getting your behind bumped was fun.

Then we drove to Ocean City and rode the Ferris wheel and the Hurricane. The Hurricane is what they call the roller-coaster. Sweetpea knows the guy that runs the Ferris wheel, and the guy let us ride free for a whole half an hour. While the Ferris wheel was turning over and over, Sweetpea and Cooter climbed around all over the wheel-part. Every now and then they'd stand still long enough to let the wheel turn over and get them almost upside down. They were showing off for Mary Ellen and she was squealing and carrying on worse than anything.

I decided I didn't want to ride on the Hurricane. It looked scary. You could hear people screaming like they were dying while they were riding on it. That didn't bother Sweetpea and Cooter and Mary Ellen none. I stood at the fence near the first hill—you know the *real* steep one—and watched them flying down, and Mary Ellen looked like she wished she'd stayed with me. That's what she said when she got off "Ches, I wish I'd stayed with you!"

Then Sweetpea drove back to Inlet Manor and left me and Cooter there, and him and Mary Ellen took off somewhere. When I got upstairs I didn't do any of the things Mama told me to do. Not brush my teeth, not wash my face and hands, not wash my feet, not put on my pajamas or anything. I laid down on the bed and went to sleep. With all my clothes on.

XXVI

The next morning, me and Shirley Mae were in the kitchen eating breakfast with Ramona and Christine. And Catlin came in with her BB gun. She'd got up early like she always does and gone off snooping around the Inlet. She tells us that Mrs. Lazenby's got a alligator in her lily pool and he's eating up all her goldfish. Mrs. Lazenby'll give a dollar to whoever gets rid of the alligator for her, she says.

"A real live alligator?" I asked her.

"You better believe he's live," Catlin said. "Chew yo' fuckin' arm off."

"Catlin!" Ramona roared like a lion from over by the stove where she was fixing Aunt Sissy's breakfast tray. "Watch yo' mouth!"

"I'm sorry, Ramona," Catlin said. "It slipped out."

"Better not be no more slippin'. Y'hear?" Ramona frowned and held up her pointing finger. "Else th' word goes straight upstairs. Ya' got me?"

"Yes, Ramona."

Then Ramona changed her frown to a smile. "That little BB gun ain't gonna bother no alligator," she said. "He ain't even gonna feel it."

"It oughta sting him a little bit, don'tcha think?" Catlin held the BB gun out in front of her and looked at it.

"Naw. Y'need somethin' bigger'n *that*."

"I got my sling shot," I said.

Ramona laughed. "Y'need Sweetpea's twenty-two rifle. Tha's what you need."

"Y'reckon he'll loan it to us?" I asked her.

"I don't hardly think so," Ramona said. "Maybe if he goes 'long wid you he will."

"I'll go ask him," I said and I ran out of the kitchen and up the stairs.

Ramona called after me "Ches, don't you go bustin' into Sweetpea's room now. Y'better knock first!"

But I figured Sweetpea's room was my room too being as I was sleeping there and all. So I walked right in. Ramona was right, I should have knocked. Sweetpea got real mad like I'd never seen him get before. He said No, I couldn't borrow his twenty-two rifle. And he told me that I should always knock on the door and wait till he said Come in, and then it was all right for me to come in. He said it two times. Even Aunt Sissy knocks before she comes into his room, he said.

I swore I wouldn't do it no more, that I'd always knock first. But it didn't help. Sweetpea was still mad. And I'll tell you, I don't know how come he got so mad. I mean, I'd slept right there in the room the night before. And I'd hardly been out of the room more than half an hour, just long enough to go downstairs and get breakfast. Wasn't nobody but him and Cooter in the room. Sweetpea's lying there on his bed naked, but it ain't like I ain't seen him naked before. He sleeps naked all the time.

I tried to sleep naked like Sweetpea one time. But I didn't like it much. I kept feeling like somebody was looking and I kept covering up my crotch with my hands. And it's not easy to go to sleep feeling that way. So I got up and put on my underwear pants and slept that way. That's sort of halfway in between sleeping naked and sleeping in pajamas. That's what I sleep in most of the time—pajamas. Mama likes me to sleep in pajamas.

Anyway, Sweetpea was lying there in his bed naked. And Cooter was changing his clothes or something because all he had on was a T-shirt. He was standing with his front turned the other way so I couldn't tell if what Ramona and Christine and Blossom were kidding about was true or not. You know—his big thing. Anyway Sweetpea got so mad he wouldn't even talk about letting us use his twenty-two rifle.

So we had to go over to Mrs. Lazenby's with only a BB gun and a sling shot. We sat by Mrs. Lazenby's pool real still and waited and waited, until finally the alligator poked his head up out of the water. Not his whole head. Just his eyes and nose. Catlin had to point him out to me, because the way his head was poking up it looked just like an old stick floating on top of the water.

Ramona was right about the BB gun, too. BB's didn't bother that alligator one little bit. We shot a zillion at him and he didn't even feel them. He just kept sort of gliding around the pond slow and easy. Every now and then he'd move quick and we'd think we'd hit him but he'd just be gobbling up another one of Mrs. Lazenby's goldfish. The sling shot wasn't no better. I hit him twice on the snoot with a rock and it could just as easy have been a fly lighting on his nose for all he cared. Then I hit him with a bigger rock, one almost as big as a matchbox. He felt that one okay, because he went down under the water and stayed there for a while.

Bootsie and Eugene came over not long after that. They had a twenty-two rifle along with them that belongs to their Daddy. But Catlin never let them get a shot at the alligator. She set Booze on them, and Booze chased them away. That made Bootsie and Eugene mad and they said they'd come back after we left and get the alligator. They said nobody could kill a alligator with a BB gun, that they'd come back and knock him off with their Daddy's twenty-two rifle and get the dollar from Mrs. Lazenby.

Mrs. Lazenby came out on her back porch to see what all the racket was about, and we told her it was some of the summer people from the Boarding House. And they'd been teasing Booze. Mrs. Lazenby stood there on the top step with her hands on her hips looking at Catlin like she didn't believe a word of it. But we all just smiled at her till directly she turned around and went back in the house.

We took turns shooting at the alligator, me and Catlin and Shirley Mae. Catlin's a dead-eye shot, but she never could hit the alligator in the eye. That's where we were trying to hit him because Catlin said that was the only place to shoot alligators to kill them. Hit him anyplace else and you're wasting shot, she said. Seemed like to me we hit that critter in the eye a whole bunch of times. But that old guy didn't act like he noticed a thing, let alone got kilt by it. He just kept on easing hisself around the pool, gobbling up goldfish.

Then it got to be two o'clock and time to eat dinner, so that's what we did. Went back to Inlet Manor and ate. When we got through eating and started back for Mrs. Lazenby's, Catlin said for me and Shirley Mae to go on ahead, that she'd catch up with us. We got all the way to Mrs. Lazenby's house before she ever caught up with us. She was toting Sweetpea's twenty-two rifle.

Me and Shirley Mae were real surprised to see her with the rifle after Sweetpea had told me No, we couldn't use it.

"How'd you get *that*?" Shirley Mae asked her.

"You filched it!" I said.

"Did *not*," Catlin said.

"How'd you get it, then?"

Catlin looked a little bit shy. "Sweetpea don't say no to me," she said.

"Tha's th' truth," Shirley Mae nodded her head. "Catlin's Sweetpea's girlfriend. He'll do mos' anything she wants him to."

"That ain't so," I said. "Mary Ellen's his girlfriend."

"Only till I grow up," Catlin said. "Sweetpea's waitin' on me to grow up."

"I don't believe it."

Catlin held up the twenty-two rifle. "I got th' gun don't I?" She wasn't looking shy anymore. She was looking big-shot again.

"Yeah," I said. I still didn't believe it, but there wasn't no sense arguing. And she *did* have the gun.

Booze was sniffing, and running around, and peeing on everything, like dogs do. And he ran into Mrs. Lazenby's backyard ahead of us. Wasn't more than a minute after Booze ran down one side of the house before Bootsie and Eugene came running out from around the other side, with Booze right behind them biting at their jeans. Bootsie was swatting at Booze with his Daddy's rifle and Eugene was hitting at him with a stick. But neither one of them could touch Booze. Old Booze dodged back out the way every time they'd make a swing at him. Then he'd jump in and nip at them some more before they could swing again. Only thing was that they were making so much racket we were scared Mrs. Lazenby might chase us off. So Catlin called Booze over and held onto him till Bootsie and Eugene could get away.

Catlin had a box of bullets in her pocket that she'd gotten from Sweetpea when she got his gun, but the box only had eight bullets in it. So me and Shirley Mae said it was okay for Catlin to go first because she's the best shot. Doggone if Catlin didn't hit that old alligator in the eye first shot. The alligator made a big splash and flipped his tail up in the air, and then he didn't move no more.

It took a lot longer to get him out of the lily pool than it did to shoot him. We got a pitchfork and a rake and dragged them along the bottom of the pool till we got the alligator in a place where we could pull him up over the side. Three times we thought we had him and he slipped back in. When we finally got him out on the grass I was surprised. He was just a little fellow. He wasn't no longer than half a rake handle, maybe a little bit more.

"He's so little," I said.

"Big enough to chew *yo'* ass off," Catlin said.

We dragged him by the tail across Mrs. Lazenby's backyard and up on her back porch. And we called to her through the screen door to come see the alligator and give us our dollar.

I think Mrs. Lazenby must have been taking a nap, because we had to call her a bunch of times before she answered us. And then when she came out on the back porch she wasn't very nice. She said she didn't think that little alligator Catlin was holding up by the tail was the same alligator that had been in her lily pool eating her goldfish. She said we must've got it from somewhere else and brung it over and put it in her lily pool. She said she sure wasn't going to give us no dollar for showing her the wrong alligator.

So we called her a lying, stingy, old fart-face, and left her there on the porch and went and throwed the dead alligator back in her lily pool.

"That 'gator's gonna smell real bad in a couple of days," Catlin said, when we were walking back to Inlet Manor. We made up jokes about Mrs. Lazenby's stinking backyard and how nobody would ever go see her again because her yard stunk so bad. And we laughed and laughed.

But that wasn't the end of it. Mrs. Lazenby called Aunt Sissy on the phone. And me and Shirley Mae and Catlin had to go back to Mrs. Lazenby's house and tell her we were sorry for calling her all them bad names. We explained to Aunt Sissy how Mrs Lazenby was a cheapskate and how she'd promised to give us a dollar to kill the alligator and then wouldn't give it to us. But Aunt Sissy made us go anyhow.

We left the dead alligator in her pool, though.

XXVII

Me and Catlin had a argument the other day. We were going to the Piggly Wiggly Store to get Ramona some black-eyed peas and fatback. Me and Catlin and Shirley Mae and Booze. On the side of the road there was a bunch of them little white flowers growing—the ones with the white petals and the teeny yellow middles, like little daisies. I wasn't really thinking about flowers, but then Catlin says "Don't pick none of them flowers, yonder," and I say "How come?" and she says "Them's pee-beds. If you pick 'em you'll piss in yo' bed tonight." Shirley Mae giggled and said "Tha's right."

Well, I don't know what you call them little white flowers

alongside the road, but they ain't pee-beds. I know what pee-beds look like and that ain't them. Pee-beds are solid yellow. Yellow petals and yellow centers, no white at all. So I tell Catlin and Shirley Mae "No them white flowers ain't pee-beds," and I tell them what real pee-beds look like. That made Catlin mad and she started calling me "Yankee" again, and telling me I didn't know my ass from a pee-bed. Then she dared me to pick one.

So I picked a bunch of them. As many as I could pick, a whole armful. Because I wasn't going to take a dare from her.

I knew I was right about them flowers not being pee-beds, but you know what? Catlin was so sure they were that it made me wonder. I woke up three times in the night that night, and thought about pee-beds, and felt down to see if I'd wet the bed. I hadn't. Even if I had I wouldn't have told Catlin.

XXVIII

Every year in April Aunt Sissy goes away for two weeks. That's what Mama told me. Mama said Aunt Sissy goes to a place named Lasvagus where people play cards and bet money. Aunt Sissy likes to play cards and bet money. She takes Ramona with her and the hotel where Aunt Sissy stays sets up a cot in the room so that Ramona can stay right there in the room and take care of Aunt Sissy. Aunt Sissy goes to Lasvagus in April and she goes to New York in December. That's to do her Christmas shopping. These are the two times every year when Aunt Sissy goes away. Other times she stays right here in Ruffins Inlet and don't hardly go out the house. In fact, Aunt Sissy don't hardly ever go out of her and Uncle Will's bedroom. She stays up there writing in her ledger books and playing with Flossie and Myrtle and watching television and talking to people that come to visit her.

Except this morning.

This morning her and Aunt Adelaide took Shirley Mae off to the doctor. I figured that would make Catlin glad on account of she didn't have to spend all day looking after Shirley Mae. And me and her could play and have some fun. We could go clamming or something like that, stuff we never can do when Shirley Mae's along with us. Shirley Mae's no fun to have along when you go in the creek. First place, she don't like it much. She'd rather be home watching the TV. And second place, all she does when she's with us is fuss the whole time, and say "I ain't havin' no fun" and "When are we goin' home?" And that ain't good because you can't keep your mind on fishing or crabbing when Shirley Mae's fussing so much.

So this day, when Aunt Sissy and Aunt Adelaide have took Shirley Mae off to the doctor, me and Catlin go clamming. Way back across the creek, beyond Herkum's Crossing, over to our new secret place. And the clamming was good. We were bringing them up by the handfuls. Only Catlin can't keep her mind on clams. She kept talking about Shirley Mae and the doctor.

"Tha's th' 'bortion doctor they goin' to," Catlin said. We were standing in the creek and it was low tide so the water only came up to the top of my bathing suit. I was holding the bucket and floating it in the warm gray water. We were wiggling and pushing our toes around on the squshy bottom feeling for clams. Along your legs you could feel baby shrimp pecking their sticker heads at you, tickling your legs with their gentle pokes. Every now and then you'd hit an oyster shell with your toe, and man!, they can cut bad if you ain't careful. You've got to feel your toes around in the mud extra easy to keep from slicing them on the sharp oyster shells.

"Wha's a 'bortion doctor?" I asked Catlin. But Catlin was thinking and not listening.

"Shirley Mae's gone an' got pregnant again."

"How can she get pregnant?"

"Beats me."

"You been watchin' her good."

"Yeah." Catlin dove down under the cloudy water. In a minute she came back up with a clam and dropped it in the bucket.

"Ain't Shirley Mae got to do it with somebody before she can get pregnant?" I asked her.

"Yeah."

"But she ain't done it with nobody, 'cause you been watchin' her, right?" Then my toes felt a clam. More than one clam, maybe four. "There's a whole family down under my big toe," I told Catlin and pointed down at my left foot. She dove down under the water and I felt her fingers touch my knee and then slide down my leg to my big toe. I moved my foot out of the way so she could get at the clams. When she came up out the water she only had two clams.

"Hey, there's more'n two down there," I told her.

"Tha's all I could find."

"I bet there's at least six more."

"Get 'em yourself, then, smarty," Catlin said, and she took the bucket from me so I could dive down. I took a deep breath and dived down under the water, but when I felt around on the bottom I couldn't find the right place anymore. I wasn't about to go back up without anything, so I felt around some more till I found a clam before I went up. I almost gave out of air before I found the clam. It was a big one, thank goodness.

I held it up for Catlin to see, and then I dropped it into the bucket. The bucket was getting pretty full. It don't take long to get a mess of clams, if you know the right places like me and Catlin do. We got a few more just for fun, and then headed back home.

When we got back to the Manor, Aunt Sissy and Aunt Adelaide were still gone. And they stayed gone pretty near all day. Me and Catlin sat on the dock and waited for them. It seemed like they weren't never coming home. We got Ramona to give us some bread, and were dropping hunks of it into the creek and watching the little minnows snatch it to pieces. After the bread gave out, we watched the people coming into the Manor for dinner, parking their cars, and walking across the big yard up to the porch. The grownups walk around the big tree roots that spread around the bottom of all the oak trees, like spider legs. Or else they step over them. But the children do like me and Catlin do all the time. They walk along the tops of the roots and balance like it's a tightrope. When you get to the end of one root, you try to jump to the next root without stepping on the ground.

Me and Catlin watched a heap of people coming and going before Aunt Sissy and them finally drove up in the yard. We said "Hey" and "How you feelin', Shirley Mae?", but didn't nobody answer. Aunt Sissy was on one side of Shirley Mae and Aunt Adelaide was on the other side. They looked like they were holding her up in between them. Shirley Mae didn't look like she felt so good.

We walked alongside of them up to the Manor and up on the front porch. Catlin ducked around everybody to hold the front door open for them. Aunt Sissy usually says "Thank you" when anybody does that for her. But this time she said "Catlin, get me a double. Fast! And tell Ramona to fix a bowl of chowder for Shirley Mae."

I fixed the double and took it upstairs to Aunt Sissy quick as I could. Catlin was just going into Shirley Mae's room with the bowl of chowder when I got back out in the hall.

"I don't want it," Shirley Mae told her. "Ol' fish piss." She'd put her nightgown on and was lying back on her bed with the air conditioner on full blast.

"Miss Sissy says you need it," Catlin said, holding the chowder out to Shirley Mae.

"Well, I ain't gonna eat it."

"Eat it an' I'll getcha a Coke."

Shirley Mae looked at Catlin. "You swear?" she asked. Catlin nodded her head and Shirley Mae put the bowl of clam chowder up to her mouth and drank it without taking it down, like it was a glass of water. When she got through she said, "Do I hafta eat th' pieces?" Catlin nodded again.

It took her longer to eat the pieces. And while she was doing that, I went downstairs and got her a Coke from Ramona. When I got back upstairs with the Coke, Shirley Mae was telling Catlin about the 'bortion doctor.

"I hate Dr. Ellison," she said. "He's mean and hateful."

"Tha's what you said," Catlin said.

"He hurt me."

"Bad?"

"Real bad. Worse than th' other time. He put them straps on my legs jus' like before. Mama an' Aunt Adelaide hel' my arms. I screamed as loud as I could. He stuck that damn ol' thing up me an' it hurt sooo baaaaad." She started crying. Catlin patted her on the arm, but I didn't know what to do so I didn't do nothing.

"I hate him," Shirley Mae said.

"Me too," Catlin said.

I said "I reckon I do too." I don't even know who Dr. Ellison is. But I guess if he makes Shirley Mae hurt, I hate him. Doctors are supposed to make people feel better.

Catlin leaned back in her chair, locked her fingers together across her stomach, and hooked her feet around the front legs of the chair. "Shirley Mae, I gotta tell you this," she said. "If you don't want to go back to Dr. Ellison no more, you gotta quit doin' it with all these guys. Else you're gonna have to go back an' get hurt some more."

"I didn't do it with nobody, Cat. *Honest!*"

"Shirley Mae," Catlin said with a disgusted sound to her voice, "now I tol' you before. Th' only way you can get a baby in yo' stomach is for some guy to do it to you."

"I didn't do it with nobody," Shirley Mae said. "Honest I didn't, Catlin. You said for me not to do it, and I didn't."

Catlin unloosed her feet from around the chair legs and straightened up and leaned over to get closer to Shirley Mae. "Shirley Mae you gotta tell me th' truth. You know you an' me don't lie to each other, do we? We always tell each other th' truth."

"Maybe she's tellin' th' truth, Catlin," I said. Shirley Mae sounded like she was telling the truth to me.

"Chester, there ain't no way in th' world that Shirley Mae could get a baby started all by herself." Catlin shook her head at me. "A guy's gotta do it to her. I know tha's th' truth 'cause Ramona told me so. So Shirley Mae's been fuckin' with somebody." She closed her eyes and shook her head again. "Lord knows when they done it. I thought I'd been watchin' her real good."

Shirley Mae looked like she was going to say something, then she stopped for a minute, and then she said, "But he tol' me we wouldn't make a baby. He *promised* me."

"An' you let him do it?" Catlin's eyes opened wide.

Shirley Mae grinned like she was embarrassed. "It felt so *good*."

"Who did it?"

"I promised not to tell."

"Who?"

"You won't tell nobody?"

"No." Catlin shook her head. "I won't tell a soul."

"It was Henry."

Catlin looked funny for a minute. "Henry who?"

"Cousin Henry. Th' one from Mt. Pleasant."

"Th' one with th' teeth?" Catlin poked her top teeth out through her lips. "At Grandpa St. Clair's Funeral?"

Shirley Mae nodded.

"That son of a bitch."

XXIX

Ramona brought Shirley Mae's supper upstairs and said she was going to stay with Honeybaby while she ate. That's what Ramona calls Shirley Mae sometimes, Honeybaby. She sat down beside the bed and started feeding Shirley Mae like she was really a baby. Even used a spoon instead of a fork.

We watched two mouthfuls go in, and then Catlin punched me with her elbow and said "C'mon."

"Where we goin'?" I asked her. But Catlin didn't say nothing back, just headed out the door. So I followed her. She went downstairs and out the back door. Then she ducked under the house and walked hunchback over to the hole in the floor underneath the family table. I waited while she slid the piece of iron out of the way. She stuck her head through the hole, and just as quick pulled it back out again.

"She's there," she whispered.

"Who?" I whispered back.

"Miss Adelaide. All by herself."

"Ain't she s'pose to be greetin' an' sittin' people down?"

"Not tonight. She'll let Bernadette or somebody else do that. She's gonna be too busy tellin' everybody what happened today."

Catlin moved out of the way so I could stick my head through the hole and take a look. You could tell without even seeing her face that it was Aunt Adelaide sitting there. With her red and white sandals and her blue and white dress. Then she started talking to these feet that walked up to the table and sat down next to her. It was Uncle Benny. Aunt Adelaide wants to know how come he's late. Uncle Benny kind of groans and says that he's had a heavy day. And he wants to know if Aunt Adelaide and them saw the doctor. Aunt Adelaide tells him Yeah, that they saw the doctor and Shirley Mae was pregnant again, all right.

Uncle Benny gave a big sigh and asked Aunt Adelaide wasn't that Flanigan brat supposed to watch out for Shirley Mae so this crap wouldn't happen. Somebody should take a stick to that Flanigan brat, he said.

Catlin commenced pulling on my arm and hissing "Lemme look. Lemme look. It's my turn." I wasn't having much fun listening to Aunt Adelaide and Uncle Benny, but I didn't want Catlin to hear Uncle Benny calling her that Flanigan brat and saying she needed a beating. So I pushed her hand off my arm and hissed back at her, "Wait a minute."

Aunt Adelaide was telling Uncle Benny how he wasn't going to believe who the Daddy was. Uncle Benny said that the only thing he was sure of was that it wasn't him. He said it might be Chico, though. Aunt Adelaide said that was awful to talk that way about his own son-in-law. Uncle Benny said you'd have to be blind not to notice how much Chico would like to get into Shirley Mae's pants.

And Aunt Adelaide said if Uncle Benny was going to continue talking vulgar like that she was leaving, and she shuffled her feet like she meant it.

Catlin pulled on my arm and said "C'mon Chester", but I was having a good time listening to Uncle Benny talk dirty.

Uncle Benny said Okay, okay, that he was only kidding about Chico and for Christ's sake to please tell him who it was. Aunt Adelaide told him he wasn't going to believe it, again, and then she told him it was Cooter. She said that Shirley Mae had confessed on the way home from the doctor that it was Cooter. I bent my knees a little bit so my head was halfway underneath the house, but still halfway in the dining porch and said to Catlin "Didn't Shirley Mae tell us it was that cousin with all the teeth that done it to her?"

Catlin nodded her head. "Henry, th' son-of-a-bitch."

"Then how come she tol' Aunt Sissy and Aunt Adelaide that it was Cooter that done it?"

Catlin's eyes got big. "She tol' 'em it was Cooter?" Her mouth stayed open after she'd finished talking.

I straightened my knees so I was back up in the dining porch again. Aunt Adelaide was calling Cooter a worthless nigger. After all Aunt Sissy had done for him, she said, *this* was how he paid her back. She told Uncle Benny that Aunt Sissy had Cooter upstairs in her room now, giving him hell. Course Cooter was lying, she said, and crying and claiming he'd never done nothing like that.

Catlin was pulling on my pants now, saying "Damnit Chester! Lemme look or I'm gonna pull yo' pants off." And she started pulling my pants down, so I gave up and let her have a turn looking. She didn't hardly give me time to get my head out of the hole before she poked her own head through. I sat down on the sand beside her feet and waited. Catlin stood there looking headless, with her head through the hole for a minute or two, then she ducked down to tell me what they were saying. "Goddamn! Shirley Mae tol' 'em it was Cooter." I said, "Catlin, I tol' *you* that," but she didn't hear me because her head was stuck back upstairs, listening some more. I sat there thinking by myself about why Shirley Mae would ever tell a big lie like that to her Mama. Or maybe, was it me and Catlin she'd lied to?

Catlin ducked her head down underneath the house again. "Them dum' turds believe Cooter really done it. Miss Sissy's got him upstairs right now, workin' him over." She said "Poor Cooter," and something else I didn't understand because her head was back up through the hole before she'd finished saying it. She'd quit whispering and was talking almost natural loud. It was a wonder the people on the dining porch didn't hear her.

Almost as quick as her head had gone upstairs, Catlin ducked her head back down again and said "I gotta talk to Shirley Mae." She ran, hunched over like you got to to walk under the Manor, to the edge of the house and went up the back steps out of sight. I hobbled after her fast as I could, up the back steps, into the house, through the hall and up the stairs, stepping two steps at a time. When I got to the top of the stairsteps, Catlin was already going into Shirley Mae's room.

"Shirley Mae," Catlin said before the door was all-the-way open. She was panting from running up the stairs. "Damn yo' time! You *storied* to me." You could tell from outside the door that Shirley Mae was watching a cowboy show on TV. Horse's hoofs were going ninety miles an hour, turned up as loud as it would go. I followed Catlin into the room. Shirley Mae said "What?" without taking her eyes off the TV. She was lying on her bed with her little biddy nightgown not covering her behind, and a whole bunch of bed pillows stuck under her back so she was half sitting up and half lying down.

Catlin said "You tol' me a lie. You tol' me Cousin Henry was th' one you done it with." Shirley Mae was too busy watching the cowboys chase each other to hear what Catlin was saying. She just laid there on her pillows watching the TV and sucking on a grape sucker. Catlin walked over and cut off the TV. Shirley Mae sat up straight and yelled "Don't do that!" at Catlin, stuck her sucker in her mouth, and crawled on her hands and knees down to the foot of the bed to reach the television set and cut it back on. But Catlin got in between Shirley Mae and the TV and wouldn't let Shirley Mae cut it on again.

With the TV cut off, you could hear Aunt Sissy's loud talking coming from next door. She was yelling and cussing and saying "Goddamn" a lot. You couldn't hear all the words because the wall got in the way. Cooter was crying something awful. I never heard nobody cry like that before. Sobbing so, the words could hardly come out. Saying the same thing over and over. "Miss Sissy, I never done that...Swear to God!...I never done that...I never...." Aunt Sissy's words sounded nasty and mean. "Don't lie to me, Cooter...Goddamnit, don't lie...I can't stand liars...."

"Don't be hateful Catlin." Shirley Mae sat up on her knees and made a face at Catlin and stuck out her tongue.

Didn't you tell me Cousin Henry was th' one you done it with?" Catlin asked her. She stood in front of the TV with her feet apart and her hands on her hips.

"Yeah," Shirley Mae said. "Please Cat, *now* can I cut the TV back on?"

"Then how come you went an' tol' your Mama and Miss Adelaide it was Cooter?" Catlin asked her. She walked around and flopped down on the edge of Shirley Mae's bed with her shoulders slumped over. I sat down beside her and we both looked at Shirley Mae.

You could hear Aunt Sissy's voice next door, going up and down, loud and soft. Soft, you couldn't hear the words, only the mean sound. But when her voice went up, loud words came through the wall without no trouble. "... Nothin' lef' to do ... Gotta get you altered ... fixed, Goddamnit ... Can't trust you no more...." Cooter was mostly quiet now. Except for a sob every now and then. I asked Catlin what *altered* meant. But she wasn't paying any attention to me. She was talking to Shirley Mae.

I didn't hear what Catlin said to her, but Shirley Mae got shy all at once. She looked down at the bed and ran her sucker stick around the edge of a flower printed on her bedspread. She said "I love Cooter," so softly you could hardly hear her. "An' I'm gonna marry him."

"You gonna what?" Catlin asked. She leaned over closer to Shirley Mae so she could hear better.

Shirley Mae looked up at Catlin and me and a smile was all over her face. "I'm gonna marry Cooter," she said out loud.

"Shirley Mae," Catlin said disgusted-like," you can't marry Cooter."

"Why not?" Shirley Mae wanted to know. "Cooter's pretty an' he's nice an' I'm gonna marry him."

"You can't."

"Why not?"

"You jus' can't, tha's why."

"Well I'm gonna," Shirley Mae said, and nodded her head up and down like she meant what she said. "Cooter made a baby in me an' that means me an' him got to marry. Right?"

"Cooter didn't make no baby in you," Catlin said. She put her face right in front of Shirley Mae's so she could look straight in Shirley Mae's eyes.

"Yes he did," Shirley Mae said. She turned her head and started running her sucker stick around the flowers on her bedspread again.

"Then how come you tol' me it was Henry?" Catlin asked, shaking her head like she didn't know what to think.

"Maybe it was *both* of 'em" I said.

"No," Shirley Mae said. "Jus' Cooter."

"Shirley Mae," Catlin said, "how come you storied to me? You *know* you an' me don't ever story to each other."

Shirley Mae didn't say anything.

Catlin kept on talking. "I tol' you a long time ago I wasn't ever gonna story to you. An' you said you wasn't ever gonna story to me neither."

Shirley Mae nodded her head.

"An' you jus' storied to me."

Shirley Mae pulled the grape sucker out of her mouth and looked at the tiny purple ball, almost all sucked away, on the end of the stick. "But if I tell you th' truth, then Cooter won't marry me."

"Cooter ain't gonna marry you no-how, Shirley Mae," Catlin said. "You jus' get rid of that idea right now." Catlin shook her finger at Shirley Mae, not mean, but like a teacher does sometimes when she's telling somebody the *real* truth.

"He's gotta. He made a baby in me, so he's gotta."

"Yeah, but Dr. Ellison fixed you so you ain't gonna *have* a baby now," Catlin said. "Cooter ain't gotta marry you."

"He don't?"

"No he don't. All you done by tellin' that story is make your Mama yell at Cooter. Hear all that noise in there?"

Catlin pointed her thumb at the wall in between Shirley Mae's and her Mama's rooms. "Boy! What a yellin'. I'm glad that ain't *me* she's yellin' at."

Everything was quiet for a minute except Aunt Sissy's voice coming through the wall. "Goddamn low-life . . . ." Then Shirley Mae asked Catlin, "Cat, Cooter *really* don't have to marry me?"

Catlin shook her head. "He really don't."

"Then I'm gonna tell you th' truth. 'Cause I always tell you th' truth. Right?" Shirley Mae put her empty sucker stick down on the window sill by her bed and used her arms to walk herself closer to Catlin, sliding her behind along like her legs wouldn't work. "I wanted it to be Cooter," she said. Her eyes were wide open and you could tell she was telling the truth. "I wanted it to be him, but it wasn't." Shirley Mae looked real sad.

"She tol' us th' *truth* before!" I said to Catlin. I was surprised that she'd told me and Catlin the truth and told her Mama a story.

Nobody said anything for a minute. Next door Aunt Sissy yelled "Now get th' hell outa here. . . . I can't stand th' sight of ya. . . ." Then everything was quiet. She'd gotten through yelling at Cooter.

Shirley Mae said "I'm sorry I storied to you, Cat. Really I am. I jus' wanta marry Cooter. I love him a whole lot."

"I know you do," Catlin said. She kind of hugged Shirley Mae and gave her a pat on the arm like a Mama does when her little girl cries.

"But you know what, Shirley Mae?" Catlin said. "You're almos' like married to Cooter right now. Cooter lives here in the same house you do. An' you eat breakfast with him 'most every day. That's kind of like bein' married, ain't it?"

"Yeah. But I want to do it with him." Shirley Mae smiled like she was saying something she oughtn't to say.

"Shirley Mae that jus' *ain't* a good idea," Catlin said. "You can help Ramona fix Cooter's breakfast for him every mornin'. That'd be real nice to do. Ramona'll let you help. An' you can make his bed for him an' stuff like that. You better not let on to Cooter that you're playin' like you're married 'cause he might not like that.

But *you* can pretend. An' Ches an' me'll pretend along with you."

Shirley Mae looked like she was thinking for a minute. Then she smiled and nodded her head. "Now can I cut the TV back on Cat?"

Catlin said "Sho," and got up to cut the TV on herself. She reached for the turn-on knob and then changed her mind, and turned around. "Shirley Mae," she said, "you gotta tell your Mama you storied to her 'bout Cooter. Okay?"

"I really gotta?"

"Sho you do. You don't want her bein' mad at Cooter no more, do you?"

"No. I sho don't want her bein' mad at Cooter," Shirley Mae said. "I guess I gotta tell her. But in a little while, okay? Not right now. I promise I'll do it in a little while." After Shirley Mae said that, Catlin cut the TV on.

Then me and her went downstairs. Catlin went in the kitchen to get Shirley Mae a Coke. And I went outside for a little while. It was getting dark. Everything was soft and purple and quiet and lightening bugs were turning on and off all around. I went down the back steps and headed over by home to take a look. I do that almost every evening. I pretend that Mama is going to be there waiting for me, back from the Hospital feeling good. I get to thinking so hard about it that I almost believe it. And I start running down the road to get there faster. The lights are on at our house so it looks like maybe this time she'll really be there, and I run as fast as I can. But it's only the lights in the Laundrymat and only people washing clothes. Mama's not there.

It's been more than two weeks since she left. I know, because I keep count of every day she's gone. Every day I make a little mark on the floor by my cot with Sweetpea's fingernail clippers that he keeps on his dresser. There are fifteen marks now. That's more than two weeks, ain't it?

Aunt Adelaide and Mrs. Lazenby went to Charleston to see Mama last week, and Aunt Adelaide says that Mama's doing just fine. She said that Mama lookes so pretty in the nightgown and bed jacket that Aunt Sissy sent her. I don't know exactly what a bed jacket is, but Aunt Adelaide said it was the most expensive one Henriette had in her Fashion Shoppe. Aunt Adelaide told me that Mr. Frank and Mrs. Jenkins had been down to see Mama a whole bunch of times and were going again soon. I asked her if maybe I could go along with them next time they went, and Aunt Adelaide said No, that it really wasn't a good idea. And anyway, she said, Mama would be home soon. But when I asked her when, she said Soon as the Doctor says it's okay.

I'll sure be glad when Mama comes home.

XXX

Cooter took some coat hangers and twisted them around his neck and choked himself dead. In the closet up in Sweetpea's room. His good eye was open wide, almost popping out of his head, and his glass eye had fallen out and was lying on the floor. His tongue was the worst looking thing, hanging way out and looking as big as his head almost. Bigger than I thought tongues could be.

When I saw him, my throat and my stomach squeezed up and I started screaming. I tried to run, but I couldn't move. My feet were stuck to the floor. Cooter looked awful bad hanging there. I didn't even know it was Cooter at first, because he didn't look like hisself at all. His head was bent way over on one side and his face was twisted strange and sad and ugly. But he had on that T-shirt Sweetpea gave him for his birthday. The one with Groucho Marx on the front of it. That's how I knew it was Cooter.

I must have sounded like a girl, screaming like that. But I couldn't stop. The screams just came out. Like I couldn't even hardly stop to breathe. I'd get a little breath and then my chest would squeeze and push screams out again. I have a hard time, now, remembering exactly how things happened. When I try to remember, all I can see is Cooter's face looking down at me, twisted and sad, almost as real as when it was happening.

Aunt Sissy got there first, I remember that. She sucked in her breath and said "Oh my God." I can still hear her say it, deep in my ears somewhere "Oh my God. Oh my God."

And Sweetpea was there. And Ramona. I remember Sweetpea sitting on the bed, crying and saying things I couldn't understand. I remember somebody was pulling on my arm, Aunt Sissy maybe. But I couldn't make my legs move. They were like poles nailed to the floor and my body was sitting on top of them, not able to move them or feel anything in them.

Then my legs started to move and I jerked my arm away from Aunt Sissy, or whoever it was pulling on it, and ran as fast as I could. It felt like there were a zillion little bugs eating away inside my legs, and I had to get away from that place where Cooter was hanging and where all them people were making noises that scratched at the insides of my brain. Then I fell down the stairs, and that stopped me from screaming because I knocked my head and scraped my knee. I sat down on the bottom step, breathed some fast breaths, and I threw up all over the floor in the front hall. I couldn't help it. The stuff just busted out of me.

After it happened, I felt better. And I remember what happened after that a little bit better.

Aunt Sissy and Sweetpea came down the stairs behind me. I thought they were coming to get me, but they weren't. They were yelling things at each other. Sweetpea was yelling at Aunt Sissy and calling her a murderer. Aunt Sissy screamed back at him "What was I s'pose to do? Pay him? For doin' *that* to my daughter?"

"Cooter didn't do nothin' to Shirley Mae!"

They passed right by me without seeing me and stood in front of the front door spitting words at each other.

"Tha's not what *she* said, Mister!"

"She's a lyin' bitch." Sweetpea was crying hard and the words were hard to understand.

"Don't you talk that way 'bout my daughter," Aunt Sissy said. "Shirley Mae don't lie. Not to me, she don't."

"Okay," Sweetpea said. "If Shirley Mae don't lie to you, tell me when."

"When what?"

"When it happened. When Cooter an' her did it."

"At Grandpa St. Clair's Funeral. Tha's when."

Sweetpea laughed and cried at the same time. "Couldn't be," he yelled. "No way. Cooter was with *me*. All day long. He was with me!"

"I don't believe you."

"I don't give a Goddamn what you believe, you ol' bag of shit." When he said that, Sweetpea pushed open the screen door and ran across the porch and down the front steps. Aunt Sissy was right behind him, but she stopped at the top of the steps and watched, with her hands on her hips, while Sweetpea ran across the yard and got into his jeep.

"Where d'ya think you're goin'?" Aunt Sissy yelled at him, but he didn't answer her. I heard the jeep motor start up. Then I heard a big crash. I got hold of the bannister and pulled myself up off the step and dragged myself over to the front door to see what was going on.

"You idiot!" Aunt Sissy was screaming at Sweetpea. "You God-damn idiot!" Then there was another crash.

Sweetpea had run his jeep smack into Aunt Sissy's big black Cadillac car. I watched through the screen door while Sweetpea backed up the jeep a little ways off, and then came back fast and crashed into the Cadillac car again. He tried to back the jeep up and do it again, but the jeep and the Cadillac were crumpled together so that Sweetpea couldn't get loose. He raced the motor a few times and tried again, but the jeep was locked to the Cadillac. When he couldn't get the jeep loose, Sweetpea got out and started walking down the road, away from Inlet Manor. Me and Aunt Sissy stood there watching. Sweetpea never looked back, just kept on walking. Then he went around the bend in the road, and we couldn't see him no more.

Aunt Sissy stood there, watching the empty road for a minute and then she came back into the house. She didn't look at me, but when she passed by she said "Chester honey, go lie down some-where." Then she headed upstairs, hanging onto the bannister like she was real tired and it was pulling her upstairs. I followed her up the stairs, but she didn't know I was there. When she got to the top of the stairs, she didn't go into her room like I thought she would. Instead she went into Shirley Mae's room, and closed the door behind her.

I sat down on the stairsteps again. I was too tired to go anywhere. I knew I ought to clean up the vomit mess I'd made down in the hall, but I couldn't move. And I couldn't think. I couldn't do anything. Just sit. Directly, Ramona came. She picked me up and carried me back downstairs and into the kitchen. She felt warm and fat and comfortable. And everything was all right again and I cried on her shoulder.

"I'm puttin' you in Cooter's bed," Ramona told me. "There ain't no place else to put you right now. An' poor Cooter don't need his bed no more." She sniffled her nose and I could tell she'd been crying too.

"Don't leave me, Ramona," I begged her. "I don't want to be by myself."

"I'll be right back honey," she promised me. And a long time later, when I woke up, Ramona was there, sitting on the bed watching me.

XXXI

The next day I didn't feel so good. I didn't feel really bad, either. It was like I didn't have much feeling in my body. Like, I felt if somebody touched me I wouldn't feel it. In my head I *knew* I'd feel it, but I'm talking about feelings and not knowings. I stayed in bed all day and slept a little bit and watched TV a lot. When you watch TV, you don't think much. I didn't want to think, because everytime I thought, I remembered Cooter hanging in

Sweetpea's closet. It would make all the feeling go out of my body again, like all my blood had run out through my toes. I'd lie there with no feeling till Ramona or Shirley Mae or Catlin would come in the room and I'd make them touch me someplace to see if I could feel it. Everytime they did it, I'd feel it. It was just that I felt like I wasn't going to.

I stayed in bed all that day watching TV and trying not to think. Then next day was Cooter's Funeral. Aunt Sissy said I couldn't go, that I had to stay in bed. But I begged her and begged her and told her I felt real good and Cooter was my friend, and finally she said I could go.

The Funeral was at Ramona's Church. That's the little church down the Charleston Highway halfway to the turn-off to Greenleigh Hall. The one that's made out of concrete blocks with a wood steeple, all painted white. Aunt Sissy made me wear a white shirt, and she bought me some white shoes because I only had sneakers. Shirley Mae wore a white dress that had a blue collar and a blue belt. Even Catlin wore a dress. A dark green one with a white shirt like me. I'd never seen ner with a dress on before. Ramona was dressed up too. She had on a black dress and a black straw hat with some daisies on it.

Catlin and Shirley Mae and me were all dressed up and had eaten our breakfast. But Aunt Sissy and Uncle Will were still messing around upstairs getting dressed and eating their breakfast off a tray Ramona had carried up to them. Aunt Sissy kept calling downstairs to Ramona and asking her Was the car here yet? I was wondering what car she was talking about. Couldn't be her Cadillac car, because Sweetpea had bent that up so bad they had to take it to Ocean City to get it fixed.

Me and Catlin and Shirley Mae went out on the porch to wait. Ramona called to us when we were going out the door and said Don't sit on the steps and get dirty. So we sat on the Joggling board. We all had red eyes. From crying, I guess. You can't hardly help crying every now and then when your friend is dead and you know he won't ever be there to play with you anymore.

It was almost ten o'clock when a big black Cadillac car, like Aunt Sissy's only bigger, came around the corner of the house. The guy driving it had on a special suit and a cap like Uncle Will's. Ramona called upstairs to Aunt Sissy and Uncle Will and told them that the car was here. In a few minutes we heard them coming down the creaking stairsteps, then across the front hall, then the screen door swung open and out they came. Aunt Sissy looked real different. Instead of a yellow, or pink, or orange, or red dress like she usually wears, she had on a dark red dress with a hat almost the same color. I'd never seen her in a dark dress before. Uncle Will was dressed up in a brown suit and had on a tie, and he wasn't wearing his captain's hat.

Aunt Sissy had on her sunglasses, and soon as Shirley Mae saw that she had to go upstairs and get her sunglasses too. That took a few minutes because she couldn't find them and Ramona had to go search them out for her. But directly they came downstairs and we all got in the car. Catlin and Christine sat up in the front seat by the driver. Ramona and Aunt Sissy and Uncle Will sat in the back seat and me and Shirley Mae sat on the little seats that unfold in between. Catlin and me got the little seats first, but Shirley Mae started fussing and saying she wanted to sit there and right away Catlin said Okay, for Shirley Mae to take her seat. I told Catlin she could have my seat on the way back.

Nobody said anything on the way to the Church, except Uncle Will said he was glad it had cooled off a bit. Nothing worse, he said, than going to a Funeral on a sweltering hot day. Aunt Sissy nodded her head, but she didn't say anything. It was cool in the car because the driver had cut the air conditioner on.

Part-way there two motorcycles passed us. Two guys were on one and a girl and a guy were on the other one. One of the guys on the first motorcycle looked exactly like Sweetpea. I said "Sweetpea!" and pointed at the motorcycles going by. Everybody sat up straight and looked. Almost as soon as she sat up Aunt Sissy leaned back in her seat again.

"That ain't him," she said.

"But Aunt Sissy," I said, "it sho looked like him. That shirt he's got on is jus' like one Sweetpea's got."

"I tol' you that ain't him," Aunt Sissy said with a mean sound in her voice. "He's a million miles from here by now."

"But Aunt Sissy...." Ramona took hold of my arm and shook

her head at me for me to hush up. I shrugged and sat back in my seat and didn't say nothing else till we got to the Church.

The preacher was waiting on the front steps of the Church along with Christine's Daddy, that rings the bell. Aunt Sissy and Uncle Will shook hands with them. The preacher said that they were honored to have Cap'n Will and Aunt Sissy at their Church. Aunt Sissy said Reverend, it wasn't the first time she'd been in his Church, that she'd been a bunch of times when Ramona and her were growing up. Uncle Will asked Christine's Daddy how he was, and he said Thanks to the Lord he was managing okay. He held the door open, and the Reverend led the way into the Church. It was hotter inside the Church, and dark, because the pointed-top windows on each side of the Church are small and got colored glass in them so they don't let in much light. But down in front, the Church was all lit up with electric lights, lighting up the Choir all wearing white robes. And in front of them there's a zillion flowers and in the middle of the flowers there's Cooter's coffin. The Church is full of people, mostly colored people but a few white ones. We must have been the last ones there, because there weren't any back seats left and the Reverend led us up front to the very first row. There were exactly enough seats for us there. In front of us were the flowers and Cooter's coffin with a spotlight on it. It was a big coffin made out of wood with gold handles around the sides. Half the top was covered with more flowers and the other half was opened up and there was Cooter lying there, dressed up in a blue suit with a tie on. His tongue was put back in his head and his eyes were closed like he was sleeping, only he didn't look like hisself. He looked like a big brown plastic doll, sleeping.

As soon as we sat down on the bench, the Choir started singing a song about climbing up on Jesus's knee. It wasn't like the singing at our Church at all. At Ramona's Church the Choir all clapped their hands while they were singing and sort of shuffled and rocked around on their feet. It makes you want to do the same thing. First the Choir sings a part of a song, and then one of them sings a part all by hisself. Then the whole bunch sings again, and then another one sings by hisself. One time the one singing by hisself was a boy that wasn't no older than me. He sang good.

They sang loud though, and I didn't notice until the singing was over that Shirley Mae was crying again. She was looking at Cooter lying there in front of us and she was crying loud with lots of tears running down her face. Aunt Sissy leaned over and whispered something to Ramona, and Ramona whispered something to Catlin, and Catlin took hold of Shirley Mae's hand, and they both got up and started stepping over me and Christine to get out. Catlin looked like she was about ready to cry too.

"Where're they goin'?" I whispered to Ramona.

"Outside," she whispered back.

"Can I go too?"

Ramona nodded her head. So I got up and climbed over Christine and followed Catlin and Shirley Mae up the aisle and out of the Church. Everybody was looking at us. Shirley Mae was still crying when we got out the front door. We all sat down on the front steps. Catlin was careful to brush off a place for her and Shirley Mae so their dresses wouldn't get dirty. I just plain sat down. My pants are dark brown and you can't see dirt on them anyhow.

The Hearse was parked on one side of the Church with four black Cadillac cars behind it. All the drivers were leaning or sitting on the fenders or standing beside the Hearse talking and smoking cigarettes. Behind us, in the Church, they were singing a slow song about crossing over something that sounded like Jordan. This time they weren't clapping and shuffling, just singing. It was pretty and sad at the same time.

"I never saw a dead person before," Shirley Mae said, blowing her nose into the handkerchief Catlin had given her.

"I saw ol' lady Murphy when she was laid out," Catlin said. "But I never saw nobody that I knew *good* before." She tucked a corner of her shirt-tail in that had slipped out. "Ol' Cooter looked so still, lyin' there." She started crying too. Not crying hard, just sniffling.

"Yeah," I said. You feel funny when you think about that being Cooter in the coffin, and him being dead. When you think about it, all the feeling leaves your body. And you don't hardly feel like talking or crying or anything. You think of dumb things to say like "Tha's a pretty box they got him in," which is the dumb thing I said then.

"Is Cooter in heaven, Cat?" Shirley Mae asked.

"Sho he is," Catlin said.

Shirley Mae pushed her sunglasses up on her forehead so she could wipe her eyes better with her handkerchief. "I bet he's there right now, talking to God and Jesus. Don't you think?"

Catlin nodded her head.

"An' I betcha God'll fix his eye for him. Maybe give him a new one. Don'tcha think so Catlin?"

Catlin smiled and wiped her nose with the back of her hand because Shirley Mae was using her handkerchief. "Yeah," she said. "That'd be *good*. Now ol' Cooter can see out both his eyes."

We sat there not talking, just watching the cars and trucks zip by on the Highway. Listening to the Cadillac drivers talking and joking without really hearing what they were saying. And listening to the birds singing and the bugs buzzing. The Choir was singing a song about meeting Jesus on the way up to Heaven and about how happy you are when you don't hurt no more, and they were clapping and shuffling again. I like the clapping songs better. The slow ones make you feel like crying.

Catlin asked me "Was that really Sweetpea on that motorcycle?"

"Sho looked like him."

"Well, Mama said it *wasn't*," Shirley Mae said. "An' Mama knows Sweetpea better than you."

"I still think it was him," I said and I was wondering how to keep from getting into an argument with Shirley Mae when the Church doors opened and one of the Funeral guys came out and said "Okay," to the drivers. One of the drivers got in the black Hearse and drove it up in front of the steps right in front of us. About that time, the Choir finished singing about not hurting no more in Heaven and the Funeral guy opened the doors of the Church back wide. Then people started coming out of the Church. First the guys carrying Cooter's coffin, all closed up now. Behind them came Uncle Will and Aunt Sissy. And Ramona and Christine. Then the Reverend and Christine's Daddy. Ramona made signs for us to get up off the steps and stand beside them. So we did. We all stood and waited while the guys slid Cooter into the Hearse. Then the black Hearse pulled off a little ways and stopped and waited for the first Cadillac car to pull up to the steps and load up. Aunt Sissy and Uncle Will and the rest of us got into that one. Then we pulled off a little ways and waited for the other Cadillacs to load up.

While we were waiting, Aunt Sissy said she didn't care for all the crappola the Reverend said about Cooter. If Cooter wasn't lying right there in front of you, she said, you wouldn't know who the hell the Reverend was talking about. The man obviously didn't know Cooter at all. Ramona said Well, to tell the truth the Reverend *didn't* know Cooter very good, because Cooter didn't hardly ever go to Church. Uncle Will said he thought it was sort of impersonal, but it was very nice. He said that each of us have our own memories of Cooter, and we couldn't expect the Reverend to know Cooter like we all did. Aunt Sissy said she guessed so, but she still wished she'd written out what the Reverend should say and made him read it.

By then all four of the big black cars were loaded up with Aunt Adelaide and Uncle Benny and I don't know who else, and the parade started off down the Charleston Highway, going real slow. There were two State Police cars there stopping all the other cars and trucks on the Highway until all the parade got on the Highway. Out the back window I watched all the cars getting into line behind us, one by one, with their headlights on.

It seemed like it took forever to get to Greenleigh Hall. Nobody talked much the whole way, and the driver drove so *slow*. I was trying not to think about Cooter because I was scared I'd start crying in front of everybody. But you couldn't hardly think about anything else. There was the black Hearse right in front of us with Cooter in it, taking him to Greenleigh Hall to bury him in the ground. If I was at Inlet Manor I could turn on the TV and make myself think about something else, or nothing. But now all I could think about was Cooter. All at once there's this real clear picture right in front of me. I see Cooter hanging there in Sweetpea's closet with his tongue sticking out and his good eye bulging out. I was really looking out of a car window at trees and bushes and things. But I couldn't see the real things. All I could see was Cooter. I could see Cooter hanging right in front of me and it was *that day* all over again. I felt cold all over and all at once I had to scream. Like the real day when I found Cooter in Sweetpea's closet. My stomach squeezed up and shot a scream up my throat and out my mouth. A loud ugly scream. Then another one and another one. I couldn't stop them. (I don't remember this part, but Catlin told me later that I scared the driver so bad he almost drove off the road.)

I screamed and screamed. Ramona pulled me over on her lap and said things over and over to me till finally that awful picture went away and I could stop screaming. Then I cried. And there wasn't nothing I could do to stop until I got all cried out. Afterwards I felt real weak and tired. Aunt Sissy was wiping my eyes with her lace handkerchief and saying Hell, she *knew* she shouldn't have let me come to the Goddamn Funeral. It was too much for me. She was just a damn fool, she said, for letting herself get talked into it.

I was ashamed of myself for screaming and crying and carrying on in front of everybody. I felt like crawling under the seat of the car and hiding. Everybody was looking at me funny, like there was something wrong with me. I slipped off Ramona's lap and back onto my little seat in front of her. I didn't know whether I should say I was sorry to everybody or not, so I didn't. I just sat there and looked out the window at the passing woods and farms and things until we got to Greenleigh Hall.

Cooter was buried a little ways off from Grandpa and Grandma St. Clair's graves. Sort of by hisself, like Laura's grave was off by itself in the other direction. The Funeral people had put up a green and white striped tent. And underneath it there was a hole in the ground with Cooter's coffin hanging over it. M'um Janey was sitting there, waiting for us. And there were chairs there for all of us to sit on. But me and Catlin and Shirley Mae didn't sit down because Aunt Sissy said we could go walking by the River or someplace else if we wanted to, instead of watching Cooter get buried. And we wanted to.

We walked down by the river for a little ways, watching the little river waves flop around and listening to them roll up on the logs and branches and junk on the little sandy beach.

Then all at once Catlin said "Wait here," and took off back up the hill, like she had to go to the bathroom bad, or something. Me and Shirley Mae waited on her, and we waited on her, and finally we got tired of waiting and we walked back up the hill looking for her. My new white shoes had got all dirty walking along the River and so had Shirley Mae's. We pulled moss off one of the trees along the way up the hill and gave our shoes a good wiping. A lot of the mud wiped off but not all of it, and I knew I'd catch the dickens from Aunt Sissy when she saw them. Shirley Mae didn't seem to care.

We spotted Catlin up by the big house. Through the bushes and trees it looked like she was talking to somebody, but when we got up to her she was all by herself, sitting on the back steps of Greenleigh Hall. When we got up close enough I said, "Hey, how come you didn't come back? You said you would."

All Catlin said was "I didn't feel like walking by the river no more." I fussed at her for not keeping her word, and all she said was "Sorry." We sat down on the steps with her for a while. We got bored with that in a few minutes and went and looked at the billy goats. They were in a pen on the other side of the house along with two gray mules and a cow. We looked at them as long as we could, but that gets boring fast. They don't do much but stand around and chew grass and stuff. So we walked around to the front of the house and sat on the steps and counted all the cars parked out in the front yard. There were eighteen, counting the four Cadillac cars and the black Hearse.

Then Cooter's funeral was over, and people started walking up the hill and getting into their cars and driving off. Catlin and Shirley Mae and me walked down to the Cemetery looking for Aunt Sissy and them. They were all over by Cooter's grave, talking to the Reverend. The grave was beautiful, all covered with bunches and bunches of flowers. Shirley Mae took hold of her Mama's hand and stood there beside her listening to all the talk. Catlin and me stood there and waited, and we'd all still be standing there waiting if Uncle Will hadn't took hold of Aunt Sissy's elbow and started easing her up the hill. When he did that, everybody else followed along and we all walked slowly up the hill to where the Cadillacs were waiting with the driver guys holding the doors open.

Before I got into the car, something made me look back. Something turned my head and made me look down the hill at Cooter's grave. It was a pretty long ways off and there were some trees in the way, but I could swear there was somebody standing there by Cooter's grave. I didn't say nothing about it though. I didn't want to make Aunt Sissy mad telling her I'd seen Sweetpea again.

XXXII

Mama came home from the hospital last Tuesday. But she still ain't well from the operation yet. They cut off both her bosoms because cancer was in them and she's still weak and tired and can't stay up for very long. Most of the time she just lies in bed and sleeps, or else looks out the window and doesn't talk and looks like she's ready to cry. She got real skinny in the hospital, and with no bosoms she really looks extra skinny. She's got these fake bosoms she can strap on to make her look like she's got real ones. But she don't wear them. She says that as long as she's spending most of her time in bed and staying in her nightgown all day, there's no sense in putting her bosoms on. But when Mr. Frank and Mrs. Jenkins or somebody like that comes over to see her, I keep them waiting on the screen porch a while to give Mama time to put on her bosoms so she'll look like other ladies.

Anyway I have to stay in Sweetpea's room at the Manor a while longer. Sweetpea hasn't been back since he wrecked Aunt Sissy's car and left. That's more than two weeks, I think. Nobody knows where he went. I don't even think his Mama knows. I haven't heard Aunt Adelaide talk about him since he left. And Aunt Sissy won't even let you call his name around her. Catlin says she sort of knows where he is but not exactly, and anyway she can't tell me because Sweetpea said Don't tell *nobody*. But she told me this much—he's not a million miles away like Aunt Sissy thinks he is. The thing I wonder about is how come Catlin knows about Sweetpea when nobody else knows?

I miss Sweetpea a lot. He was always making jokes and saying funny things. But I like staying in his room all by myself. And sleeping in his big bed instead of that little cot. I can use his things now and I don't have to ask him if it's okay. I've been lifting his weights and my biceps are getting bigger already, I think.

But I'd still rather be home with my Mama. Aunt Sissy says Mama is too weak to put up with having me around. I told her I'd be real quiet and wouldn't be no trouble at all. But that didn't change Aunt Sissy's mind. I'm allowed to go see Mama two times every day. Aunt Sissy says that if I went anymore than that, it would wear Mama out. And then it would take her longer to get well. I go over in the morning after I've had breakfast and take Mama some hominy grits and ham or something else that Ramona's fixed for her to eat. And in the afternoon Ramona fixes a seafood platter for me to take over.

Mama doesn't eat much. Only two or three mouthfuls and that's about all. Ramona says I ought to try and make Mama eat more, that it would help her get her strength back sooner. So I sit by Mama's bed and say "The shrimp is real good tonight, Mama," or "Try an' eat one more hushpuppy, Mama," and things like that. But it doesn't do much good. After Mama decides she's through eating, there ain't hardly nothing I can do to make her take another bite.

But Mama says she's feeling a little bit stronger every day and it won't be long before I can go back home.

XXXIII

It liked to scared me to death that afternoon when two Police cars speeded in the driveway at Inlet Manor. Most times cars sort of creep in the driveway and into the front yard, because there are so many twisting roots sticking out the ground from all the oak trees and everybody's worried about busting their tires. But not them Police cars. They speeded in like race cars, like they didn't give a damn about busting tires or nothing.

Me and Catlin and Shirley Mae were lying lazy on our backs out on the dock making rabbits and ducks and things out of clouds in the sky. All at once them green and white cars came racing in with their sirens screaming and the racket made us sit straight up, all three of us at once.

Sheriff Poole and one Policeman got out the first car and two more Policemen got out the other one. They got on the same clothes they usually wear—white shirts with short sleeves and policemen hats, except the Sheriff's got on that dumb green fishing hat he always wears. Only thing different is they got guns on their belts, and they're holding on to them when they're hustling across the yard and up the front steps and into the Manor like they're ready to pull them out and shoot somebody. Me and Catlin and Shirley Mae ran up to the house right behind them to see what was going on, but we decided to wait by the steps instead of going in the house. Bunches of people were running out from the dining porch like when school's let out. And the ones on the inside were putting their faces up to the plastic-covered screen, trying to look out and see what was going on.

There was a lot of heavy talking coming through the screen door from the front hall. Then you hear Sheriff Poole telling everybody to Stand back! and the screen door flips open and two of the Policemen walk out holding Uncle Benny in between them. Uncle Benny has his head turned back over his shoulder and he's trying to talk to the Sheriff who's coming out the door right behind him. Uncle Benny is saying Ray, how can you believe this? to him. The Sheriff looks real stern and says that This ain't to his liking, but the law is the law. The Policeman with the little mustache is behind the Sheriff.

Then Aunt Adelaide comes pushing her way through the pile of people standing in front of the door to the dining porch, and when she sees the Policemen holding Uncle Benny she screams bloody murder and looks like she's going a little crazy. Benny what are they doing? she wants to know. She tries to get over to Uncle Benny but the Policeman with the little mustache won't let her get any closer. She starts crying real loud and asking the Sheriff what he's doing to her Benny?

It was quite a racket. You can't hardly follow what people are saying because everybody's talking loud and all at the same time. Aunt Adelaide is sobbing and asking Sheriff Poole to Please tell her what Uncle Benny has done. One Policeman wants to know which police car he should put Uncle Benny in. More people are coming out on the porch and asking whoever is nearest them What's going on? The Policeman with the airplane pilot's sunglasses on says they got to take Uncle Benny to Ocean City. Sheriff Poole is saying that Them things may be okay in them Spic countries but not in the United States of America. Uncle Benny is saying But it's a mistake! That he don't own any gambling business. That he don't own *any* business right now. The Policeman with the mustache says for Uncle Benny to Be quiet! Aunt Adelaide is screaming Can't anybody tell her what Uncle Benny did?

The whole group stumbled sideways down the front steps like a big crab with more legs than it needed. The Policeman with the mustache tripped and almost fell down, but did a fast shuffle and stayed standing up. Me and Catlin and Shirley Mae followed them across the yard to the police cars. Aunt Adelaide is sounding mad now, not scared like before. She's telling Sheriff Poole he ought to be ashamed of hisself putting innocent men in jail. The Sheriff is telling the Policeman with the sunglasses on that No, damnit, he didn't say put Mr. St. Clair in *his* car, he said put Mr. St. Clair in the *other* car! Uncle Benny is telling everybody on the front porch watching that Mark his words, he'll *get* Ray Poole for this. He had to yell it out because we were a pretty good ways from the porch.

Then the Policeman with the sunglasses on opens the back door of the other police car and tries to shove Uncle Benny in the back seat. But Uncle Benny shakes hisself loose from the Policeman and jumps right back out again. He tells the Policeman that Nobody manhandles Benjamin St. Clair. Sheriff Poole tells Uncle Benny again that he's real sorry to have to do this, but the law is the law. Uncle Benny says There must not be no law against screwing little nigger girls then, or else Sheriff Poole would have to put hisself in jail twice a week. That tickled the Policeman with the little mustache and he busted out laughing. Sheriff Poole told the mustache Policeman to Shut up! and he told Uncle Benny to Watch his mouth! or else he'd get hisself in *big* trouble. Uncle Benny says You don't scare *me*, Ray Poole, that he knows who, when, and where. That there ain't much goes on around here that he don't know about, he says. That the Sheriff better watch out next election, maybe he won't win so easy. After he said that part about the election, he turned around and got into the police car. Sheriff Poole put one hand on the top of the car and the other one on his hip and leaned his head way over close to Uncle Benny's head, and said that Uncle Benny better talk it over with his sister before he did anything dumb like that. Then he stood up straight and kicked the car door shut like he was real mad.

When the Sheriff said that about Uncle Benny's sister, it made me think about Aunt Sissy and I cut my eye up at her bedroom window. There she was, with the curtain pulled back just enough for her to look out. But as soon as she saw me looking up at her, she dropped the curtain and I couldn't see her. When I looked back around, the Policemen and Sheriff Poole had got in the police cars and they went speeding off out the driveway. We all stood there for a minute looking at the driveway where the police cars had just been. Aunt Adelaide was crying again.

"C'mon Miss Adelaide," Catlin said. "Le's go inside." Her and Shirley Mae got on each side of Aunt Adelaide and took hold of an arm and we all walked back to the house. Everybody on the porch stood back and made a path for us to the front door. We guided Aunt Adelaide back to the kitchen and sat her down at the big kitchen table between all the plates ready to get served, and Ramona fixed her a cup of coffee.

"You want somethin' stronger, you know where it is Miss Addie," she said and hurried back to filling plates with seafood. The kitchen wasn't no place to calm yourself down in. Ramona and Christine and Blossom were busy doing all the things they got to do at dinner time, and LeRoy's all they got to help them. He's trying to learn Cooter's job and Sweetpea's too, and not doing so good at either one. He wants to know what he's supposed to do with the glasses now, Aunt Mona? SueAnne's there fixing a drink of whiskey for Uncle Will. She said Aunt Adelaide ought to put a little bourbon in her coffee. It'd help a lot, she said. Ramona told LeRoy to put ice in the glasses. That red-headed waitress named Rita called out One broiled, one fried, and two little flounders! (Little flounders means little ones for kids.) That freckled-faced one wanted to know What happened to her four chowders?

Uncle Will came in then and asked Aunt Adelaide if what he'd heard out on the porch was true? That started Aunt Adelaide crying again. LeRoy said All the glasses got ice in them, and wanted to know what he was supposed to do next. Ramona said Cat, honey, would she do the old lady a favor and help LeRoy with the hushpuppies. Uncle Will said Goddamn! that Ray Poole must have lost his marbles. That he was going right over to Ocean City and see what this was all about. SueAnne said that Uncle Will had better have another bourbon before he went, and asked Blossom Were her shrimp cocktails ready yet.

Aunt Adelaide said she just hated Ray Poole. She said You think somebody's your friend and then you find out he's not. LeRoy wanted to know what to do with the baskets of hushpuppies when they were full. Catlin told him she'd show him, and he didn't have to ask no more questions. Christine said Thank the Lord, that she'd had more questions than she could handle. Rose, the other waitress, was in and out saying Christine I got two crabs and a platter, right? Ramona said Ches honey, go out and play someplace, that the kitchen was just too full of people. Uncle Will said Come on and ride over to Ocean City with him, so I did. SueAnne fixed him a drink—one for the road she called it—and we went out and got in the old pickup truck.

Uncle Will had trouble getting it started and then didn't seem like he could drive it so good. He said Cooter had trained the damn pickup not to let anybody else drive it, specially if your hand was white. I held his drink for him so he could mess around with the knobs and things you mess around with when you drive a car. Every now and then he'd slow down a little bit and reach his hand over and I'd give him his drink and he'd take a couple of swallows and hand it back to me. It don't take but about fifteen minutes to get to Ocean City and Uncle Will talked pretty much the whole time. Talking about What in hell was Ray Poole thinking about arresting Uncle Benny. And stuff like that.

When we got to the Ocean City Police Station, Uncle Will made me stay in the pickup while he went inside. I was sitting there real bored with nothing to do, and wishing I hadn't come along with Uncle Will, then all of a sudden he was back, mad and cussing. Uncle Benny was there in jail all right, but that dumb Sergeant What's-his-name wouldn't let Uncle Benny out unless Sheriff Poole said it was all right and Sheriff Poole had gone home. And he wasn't answering his phone. So me and Uncle Will drove over to Sheriff Poole's house on the chance that they were out in the yard and didn't hear the phone ringing. But a lady from next door called over to us and said that the Sheriff and Mrs. Poole had drove down to Mount Pleasant to visit Mrs. Poole's sister.

Uncle Will told her "Thanks" and him and me got back in the pickup and Uncle Will said that that was just too bad for Uncle Benny because we weren't about to chase all over Charleston County looking for Sheriff Poole. So we drove back to Ruffins Inlet.

On the way I asked "Uncle Will how come they put Uncle Benny in jail?"

"I don't know for sure, son," he said. "Sue Anne thinks it was because of them damn cock fights Benny was havin' there for a while. One of the guys tol' her that. But hell, Benny hasn't had a cock fight in a long time."

"Wha's wrong with cock fights?"

"It's against th' law."

"Oh."

"Anymore booze in that glass?"

"No suh." I picked the glass up off the dashboard and held it up for Uncle Will to see.

"Well, le's step on it," he said. "Yo' Uncle Will needs a drink!" We were home in no time.

I thought about Uncle Benny some more later. But you know, it didn't really matter much what they put him in jail for. Uncle Will got him let out the next day.

XXXIV

In the afternoons now, I go read to Aunt Sissy. I been doing that for a pretty good while. It started when I was staying at the Manor when Mama was in the Hospital, after Sweetpea went away. Aunt Sissy got me to read to her one afternoon. To calm her nerves, she said. Then the next afternoon she wanted me to read to her some more. And then some more the next afternoon, and some more the next. Finally I just got used to going by her room every afternoon before supper to read to her for a while. Aunt Sissy likes murder stories, and she likes to try and figure out who did the murdering. So halfway through the book she gets me to read the ending to myself and find out who the murderer is. Then she tries to guess who it is. She's always wrong. But I go easy telling her she's wrong because she gets so mad when she guesses wrong. And then she has to take some pills to settle down her nerves.

And when I tell her she's wrong, she calls me names—mainly "liar." And she claims I'm not giving her the right ending. So then I give her some hints and she guesses some more. If you want to know the truth, she's not a very good guesser. But that's the way she likes to do it. When we first started doing this guessing-the-murderer, I used to give her big hints to make it easier for her to guess. And she guessed two of them right. The trouble with that was that after she knew who the murderer was, she wasn't interested in reading the rest of the book and finding out *how* the murderer did it. And that's a very interesting part that I like to know. So I quit giving her hints. And she don't ever guess right any more. I just decided to let her yell at me if she wanted to.

And you know what? I'm not scared of Aunt Sissy any more. Used to be every time I was around her I'd get this funny feeling, like there were a zillion wiggly worms in my stomach. But it doesn't do that anymore. And I think Aunt Sissy likes me. Almost as much as she used to like Sweetpea.

She don't like Sweetpea so much any more. In fact she won't even let you call his name around her. If you say anything about Sweetpea you're supposed to call him the "former tenant." That way she knows who you're talking about, but you don't call his name so she doesn't get mad. I kind of don't blame Aunt Sissy for being mad at Sweetpea, because Sweetpea said some real bad things about her. And after she'd been so good to him and sent him to that college up in the North that costs a lot of money. And Sweetpea wrecking her big Cadillac car nine hundred dollars worth. That wasn't very nice, I don't think. And him calling her a bag of shit. You shouldn't call your aunt names, especially when she's done a lot of nice things for you.

Aunt Sissy explained to me one time what all she'd done for Sweetpea. "I gave that boy the bes' of everything," she told me right in the middle of *Chicken Murders* by Sir Helmut Delany. "An' look how he paid me back." I never know what to say when Aunt Sissy gets to talking like that. So I just quit reading and listen and try to see whether she wants to talk some more or whether she wants me to read some more. Sometimes she wants one thing and sometimes the other.

One special day I remember good.

She said to me "Ches-boy. Ain't gonna be long before you're fifteen. You know that?"

"Pretty long, Aunt Sissy," I said back. I folded down the corner of the page so I wouldn't lose the place in the book. "I ain't but 'leven now."

"You know what I been thinkin'?"

"No ma'am."

"I been thinkin' maybe I'll get that ol' red jeep fixed up for you. Y'know th' one?"

"Yes'm," I said. "I know th' one." Just thinking about that red jeep belonging to me got me all excited. "Only I still got four years to go b'fore I can get my license."

"Oh don't worry 'bout a license," Aunt Sissy laughed. "Sheriff Poole ain't gonna bother you. I pay th' son-of-a-bitch too much money. Wait'll you're twelve an' your Uncle Will'll teach you how to drive that jeep."

I got so excited that I jumped up out of the chair I was sitting in and leaned way over the bed and put my arms around Aunt Sissy's neck and kissed her good, on the cheek. She liked that.

"Ches-boy you *do* love your ol' Aunt, don'tcha?" she laughed when she said it.

"Yes'm I do," I said. I felt kind of dumb after kissing her like that and went and sat back down in my chair. I waited a little bit to see if she was going to say anything else, but she didn't. So I picked the *Chicken Murders* up off the floor where I'd dropped it and turned to the folded down page and started reading again. I couldn't hardly read for thinking about me driving Sweetpea's red jeep. Only now it wasn't going to be Sweetpea's jeep anymore. It was going to be mine. I was having a hard time reading, but it didn't make no difference because Aunt Sissy wasn't listening anyhow. She was thinking other things, too.

"Ches-honey get me my blue an' yellow butterfly pumps out th' armoire," she said. "I feel very festive today."

I got her the butterfly pumps out the armoire and she poked her little feet over the side of the bed and I put them on for her. Then she wanted Flossie and Myrtle, and I got them out of their pen and put them on the bed so she could play with them. I ain't scared of them dogs like I used to be when we first come to Ruffins Inlet. And they don't bark at me like they used to. Cooter was the one that showed me how to do it. You look them straight in the eye, and hold your hand out and let them sniff it real good. And the whole time they're sniffing your hand you look stern at them, and you think to yourself "Bite me, you damn dog, and I'll bust your Goddamn neck." And it works. Flossie and Myrtle sniff your hand for a second or two, and then you can pick them up and do anything you want to with them.

Talking about Cooter makes me think of something else. That's another name you ain't supposed to say around Aunt Sissy. Cooter. It makes her sad when you call his name. But every now and then *she'll* start talking about him, though. And that's okay. She'll talk about how good-looking he was even with his glass eye that didn't match. And she'll tell me again how she sent Cooter to this big Hospital in Baltimore that's the best Hospital in the world to see if they could fix up his eye. There was some kind of worm got in it when he was a baby and I guess the worm et his eye or something. Anyway, them Baltimore doctors knew all about what the worm did, but they didn't know how to fix Cooter's eye. And they had to operate on him and take his bad eye out and give him a glass one. Aunt Sissy told me how Cooter wanted a blue glass eye on account of Sweetpea's got blue eyes. And the doctors said No, that Cooter should have a brown one to match his other eye. Then comes the part that tickled Aunt Sissy so much.

"I tol' 'em, 'Hell, it's his eye, ain't it?'" Aunt Sissy laughed and slapped her leg. She'd laugh every time she told me that about Cooter's blue eye. "I tol' 'em he could have a red and white polka-dot one if he wanted it. Them doctors didn't much like that. But I was th' one payin' th' bills, so they give Cooter th' blue eye like he wanted."

And another time Aunt Sissy'll tell me again about how Cooter could make hushpuppies like nobody else in the whole world. About how Cooter had figured out this secret stuff he put in with the corn meal and other junk. And he wouldn't tell nobody what was in it, or let nobody watch him when he was mixing up a batch.

"He probably made it outa nigger sweat an' toenails an' ground-up fish eyes, an' stuff that'd make you sick," Aunt Sissy would say, and laugh her big man laugh. "But Goddamn, it was *good*! I ain't never tasted nothin' like it."

She was sure right about that. The hushpuppies that Ramona

taught LeRoy how to make don't taste nowhere near as good as the ones Cooter used to make.

When Aunt Sissy talks about Cooter, she says things like "He died *so* young," or "God took him away too soon." It's like Cooter got some bad sickness and died. Never nothing about Cooter choking hisself dead with coat hangers. One time I said something about how Cooter'd kilt hisself and Aunt Sissy started crying and threw her hairbrush at me. So now I'm real careful not to say anything like that no more.

Most of the time I just read to her. And when she talks I just listen and nod my head Yes, or shake my head No, to whatever she says.

There's another reason I know Aunt Sissy likes me. That day when she told me she was going to fix up Sweetpea's red jeep for me when I got to be twelve, she asked me Didn't I want to come live with her and Uncle Will at the Manor, and have the former tenant's room for my very own. She really asked me that.

I told her "No ma'am, Aunt Sissy. I can't leave my Mama. I gotta stay home with my Mama."

Then she said "I mean *after*."

"After what Aunt Sissy?"

"Oh I didn't mean after anything, Ches-baby," she said. "I jus' meant maybe *sometime*."

"That's mighty nice of you to ask me Aunt Sissy," I told her. "But I always want to stay with Mama."

XXXV

This last time when the Senator, Aunt Sissy's Bow, come to Inlet Manor he brung his whole family with him. And something bad happened. Old Booze hauled off and bit the biggest one. He'd have bit another one too, if Catlin hadn't grabbed him by the collar and hung on and made him quiet down. Catlin said that the Senator's boys were teasing Booze and poking him with sticks. The Senator's boys said they wasn't poking Booze neither, that they'd just been walking along and Booze jumped them. Booze didn't bite him so bad. Broke the skin and there was only a little bit of blood. But wow! how that boy yelled. I thought he'd never shut up.

Some doctor from Mullins was on the dining porch eating dinner, and he stopped eating long enough to look at the boy's leg where Booze had bit him. All he did was put some Merthiolate on it and a band-aid. That made the boy yell louder than ever.

The only one yelling louder than the boy was his Daddy. The Senator was carrying on like a crazy guy, throwing his arms up in the air and making a whole lot of racket. He may be Aunt Sissy's Bow, but he's sure a big pain in the neck. "I demand that that dog be put away," he said, and "This is outrageous," and he called Booze a "Vicious animal." Those are the only things I remember. He said a lot more that I don't remember. And he said it all very loud.

Aunt Sissy was carrying on pretty good too. Much worse than Mrs. Senator was. Aunt Sissy was saying stuff like "A person ain't safe with *that animal* loose," and "I just knew something awful was going to happen with that dog around."

Catlin was trying to tell them what had really happened and why Booze had bit the boy, but nobody could hear her because they were all talking so loud. So she pulled Booze away and took him off under the house.

I hung around a little while because I was waiting for Ramona to give me a plate of supper to take home to Mama. It stayed noisy on the front porch for a long time with that boy whining and crying, and his Daddy talking loud and big-shot. When I grow up I'm sure not going to vote for *that* guy. And I'm not going to be a Senator, either.

Finally him and his family got in their car and drove off and took the racket with them. Aunt Sissy went back upstairs. And everything got quiet again.

XXXVI

It happened in the afternoon the very next day when I was reading to Aunt Sissy. It was *Camera, Action, Murder* by C.K. Carrington. We were at the part where the movie star lady that's been doing all the murdering takes off all her clothes and tells Sgt. Nail that he can have anything he wants. She's got a real pretty body because she's a movie star, but Sgt. Nail shoots her right in her naked belly. Aunt Sissy liked that part so much I had to read it to her three times.

Then's when the bad thing happened.

The door to Aunt Sissy's bedroom opened up real fast, like a TV cop was kicking it open. And there's Catlin standing in the doorway with Sweetpea's twenty-two rifle. "Why'd you do it?" she screamed at Aunt Sissy. It scared Flossie and Myrtle so bad they started barking and running round and round their play-pen. Catlin's crying to beat the band.

Aunt Sissy was maybe too surprised to say anything. Or could be she was too scared. Anyway she didn't say nothing. She just looked at Catlin, big-eyed, with her mouth part-the-way open.

"You rotten ol' turd face. Answer me!" Catlin screamed even louder. "Why'd you do that awful thing?"

Aunt Sissy sat herself up straight in bed. You could tell she'd got herself together again. "Catlin Flanigan you stop that foul language this minute," she said. "What do you mean prancing in here like that, scarin' th' daylights outa me? You jus' turn yourself around and march right back out that door. Why, you liked to give me a heart attack!"

Catlin didn't move a hair. "You ain't got no heart, you mean ol' bitch," she said.

"You get yourself right . . ." Aunt Sissy started saying something but Catlin wouldn't let her finish.

"I got a gun," she said, holding up Sweetpea's twenty-two rifle.

Her bottom lip was poked way out and her face was all wet from crying. "I'm gonna do to you jus' what you done to po'r Booze, you hateful ol' cow's ass."

"What *I* done to Booze?" Aunt Sissy said. I have to give the old lady credit. After she got over her scare she didn't back down one little bit. "I ain't done nothin' to that dog."

"Shut your lyin' mouth, ol' lady. You know what you done. You got LeRoy to take Booze out in the woods an' shoot him. LeRoy tol' me you did. So don't try lyin' your way outa it. You didn't have no right doin' that awful thing to po'r Booze. Booze never hurt you. Booze never hurt nobody." She started crying hard again. "You believed what them lyin' kids tol' you."

"That damn dog bit Lloyd-Junior bad."

"An' you know how come? You know how come Booze bit him? 'Cause he was pokin' sticks up Booze's asshole. Tha's how come Booze bit him. You'd have bit him too, if he'd been pokin' a stick up you." Then she looked at me. "Tell her Ches, tell her. Ain't that right? That shit-faced kid was pokin' po'r Booze in the ass!"

I wasn't expecting Catlin to ask me that. "I ain't sure Aunt Sissy," I said. "Maybe he was, but I ain't sure. It was kind of dark an' I couldn't see so good." That wasn't very fair of Catlin asking me a question like that and getting me in bad with Aunt Sissy.

"You're makin' that up," Aunt Sissy said to Catlin. "Th' Senator's children don't do things like that."

"Well, tha's what they did. An' tha's why Booze bit him. An' on account of that *you* killed Booze, you hateful ol' bag of shit." Catlin backed off a little ways from the bed and raised Sweetpea's rifle to her shoulder. "An' now *you're* gonna get it. I'm gonna shoot you jus' like you done to po'r Booze."

Then's when Ramona came in. She said "Wha's all th' racket? I can hear you from downstairs."

"Back off, Ramona," Catlin told her.

"What you doin' wid that gun, chile?" Ramona asked. She started walking toward Catlin.

"She's gonna kill me, Ramona." Aunt Sissy broke down and got a little wild sounding now that Ramona was there to take care of her.

"Chile gimme that gun," Ramona said. "You ain't gonna shoot

nobody. Don't you know they'll put you in the Reform School for doin' that?"

"You know what this pig-face bitch done, Ramona? She kilt my dog. She kilt Booze." Catlin started crying again. She wasn't making any noise, but water was pouring out of her eyes like a leaky spigot. "My Booze. I loved that ol' dog so much. An' she kilt him."

"The dog was dangerous. . . ."Aunt Sissy started to say.

"*Now* I'm gonna fix her." Catlin hoisted the gun back up to her shoulder. Ramona had stopped midway, listening to what Catlin was telling her. Now she jumped the rest of the way and tried to grab the gun. At the same time Catlin backed away and shot. Pow! Shot Aunt Sissy in the left foot and ruined her pink and white polka-dot-high-heeled shoe. Then Catlin handed the gun to Ramona and walked out the door, leaving Aunt Sissy screaming and cussing and bleeding like a stuck pig.

XXXVII

I found Catlin where I figured I'd find her. Back in the woods behind old man Sawyer's house. It took me a while to search her out because she wouldn't answer me when I called to her. But I found her anyway. Behind a big clump of Myrtle bushes back where them real tall pine trees are. She'd found Booze, and she was squatting down by him and stroking his head, and telling him what a good dog he was and how much she loved him.

I stood there for a long time behind the Myrtle bushes, just watching and listening. Then I walked over slow, and sat down with her and Booze in the pine needles, and stroked my hand down

Booze's furry side. He was lying there just like he was sleeping, only one side of his head was all bloody.

"Take your han' offa my dog, pig-fucker," Catlin said, real nasty. She didn't even look at me when she said it.

I knew what she was mad about. She was mad because I didn't stick up for her with Aunt Sissy.

"Catlin, I'm gonna tell her th' truth," I told her.

"How're you gonna tell her th' truth when she's dead?"

"She ain't dead."

"She ain't?"

"You jus' hit her in th' foot."

"Shit!" Catlin said under her breath. "I meant to kill th' ol' bitch." She spit in the pine needles, off to one side. "I was cryin' so hard I couldn't aim good." She thought a minute and then she raised her head up and looked me in the eye. "You *swear* she ain't dead?"

"Swear t' God."

Catlin didn't say nothing for a while. Just went on smoothing Booze's fur. Then she said "I don't know whether I'm glad or not. Maybe if I didn't kill her they won't send me to Reform School. But look what she done to my Booze." She was crying again, and sniffling to keep her nose from running. But it ran down her lip a little ways anyhow. And when she wiped it with the back of her hand, it left a dirty smudge across her cheek. But I didn't bother to tell her. It didn't seem important.

"If you don't see th' bloody part you'd think he was jus' sleepin', wouldn't you?" Catlin put her hand over Booze's ear so you couldn't see the blood.

"Yeah," I said. I couldn't keep from crying a little bit too. For a long time we didn't talk. Just thought. Then finally, I asked her "Where we gonna bury him?"

Catlin shook her head. "I dunno."

"How 'bout down th' creek where we caught all them crabs that time. You 'member how Booze liked lyin' up under that ol' bent-over cedar tree?"

"I know where we gonna bury him." Catlin stood up and looked down at me squatting by Booze. "We gonna bury Booze in th' 'Piscopal Cemetery."

"How come you want to bury him there?"

"Tha's where my Mama's buried."

"Suits me," I said. "How we gonna get him over there?"

Catlin thought a minute. "Skippy Mercer's got that blue wagon. Remember?"

"Mrs. Mercer would have a fit if she knew we were puttin' a dead dog in Skippy's wagon."

"What she don't know won't hurt her."

I got up off the ground and brushed the sand off the seat of my pants. "I'll go get it. You stay here with Booze." Catlin said "Okay" and sat back down in the pine needles by Booze, and commenced stroking him again and singing to him. "Jesus loves you, this I know. For the Bible tells me so."

I went and got Skippy's wagon out the Mercer's garage. They were eating supper, so I didn't bother asking. Just took the wagon. And while I was there I borrowed a shovel too. You got to dig a hole when you're going to bury somebody, you know.

We buried Booze next to Catlin's Mama in the Episcopal Cemetery. It was getting pretty dark by the time we got there, so nobody saw us. Catlin knew where her Mama's grave was and there was room beside it for Booze. It took us a while to dig the hole right. The first time we didn't dig it deep enough. Booze is bigger than we figured he was. And when we covered him up, his head was left out. So we had to do it all over again. The second time we dug the hole extra deep. Ain't nothing but sand, so the digging was easy except for one root that got in the way.

We filched some flowers from Reverend Hazelton's flower garden. Lots of them. And we sang "Jesus Loves You" again. And Catlin said a prayer for Booze and I said one. There were a zillion lightening bugs out, sparkling all over the place. It was kind of pretty. But real sad.

We had just took Skippy Mercer's wagon and his Daddy's shovel back to his house and were walking down the road to Inlet Manor when this car came from behind and stopped alongside of us. It was Sheriff Poole and a lady policeman.

"Git in," they said.

XXXVIII

Ramona was right. They took Catlin off to Reform School.
Uncle Will was real upset about it. He came busting into Aunt
Sissy's bedroom saying "Sissy you ain't gonna let 'em do it, are
you?" He walked over to the big brass bed and stood there looking
down at her. "I ain't gonna letcha do it. You can't let 'em take that
chile off to Reform School." Uncle Will is very tall and Aunt Sissy
had to hold her head so straight-up to look at him that she didn't
have double chins.

"Will, look at this pretty bed jacket Ethel Lazenby sent over.
Isn't it lovely?" Aunt Sissy held the bottom corners of her pink bed
jacket out on each side of her so Uncle Will could see it. "I jus' *love*
these little blue flowers. It was so sweet of Ethel to think of me,
don't you think?" Aunt Sissy was sitting in the middle of the big
bed like always, except her hurt foot was all bandaged-up and
resting on a big white pillow. Like it was a prize or something.
Uncle Will didn't say nothing about her new bed jacket, so she
dropped the corners and picked up the brown cigarette she'd left
resting in the ash tray beside her on the bed and took a draw on it.

"Why you doin' this Sissy? I don't understand why." Uncle Will
was kind of rocking back and forth like he was standing on the deck
of the *Inlet Queen*. And the way he smelled, I think SueAnne had
fixed him an early drink of Bourbon. "I don't understand why
you'd wanta do this to that p'or orphan chile."

"Don't let's talk about it in front of the boy, Will." Aunt Sissy
pointed her brown cigarette at me, sitting there beside the bed
with a mystery book in my lap. Then she checked the little blue
bow-ribbons that tied her bed jacket closed, and sort of tidied-up
herself. "An' Will, take your hat off, please. I never saw you
wearin' your hat in th' house before."

Uncle Will pulled his captain's hat off his head and sailed it
backhand across the room like a frisbee. "I'm upset, Sissy," he
said. "Can'tcha see that? This damn thing's got me all upset!"

Aunt Sissy held her hand out at me and wiggled her fingers like an upside-down bye-bye. "Ches-honey," she said, "Git up an' let your Uncle Will sit down." I said "Yes'm," and got up and moved down to the foot of the bed and leaned across the shiny brass rail and folded my arms to get myself comfortable. Uncle Will was carrying on so, it got me a little upset. I'd never seen him like this before. He was always the coolest guy in Ruffins Inlet. Like he was the boss of everything. You knew that Aunt Sissy was running things, but you felt like she was doing it all for him.

Uncle Will never once looked at me. He just dropped down into the chair I'd got out of and laid his head down in his arms on the bed. "Oh Sissy. Why?...Why?" he said. His voice was smothered by his arms so the words sounded far away. Aunt Sissy stroked the back of his gray head like he was Myrtle or Flossie. Uncle Will pushed her hand away and raised up his head and looked straight at Aunt Sissy. "That chile never done nothin' to you."

"What are you talkin 'bout? Never done nothin' to me!" Aunt Sissy shuffled her behind in the bed and sat herself straight up and pointed at her hurt foot. "Will Ruffin, that chile tried to *kill* me. She took a gun an' tried to *kill* me. Don'tcha understand *that*?"

"Aw Sissy," Uncle Will said. "You can't tell me she really meant to hurt you. Anyway, all she did was shoot you in th' toe."

Aunt Sissy started to say something back to Uncle Will but then she changed her mind and looked down at me, hanging over the foot of the bed. "Ches-honey run along an' play. Uncle Will an' me got some talkin' to do."

I said "Yes'm," and ran across the room and out the door quickly. But as soon as I closed the door, I stopped dead in my tracks. And put my ear back close to the door to hear what they had to talk about. If it was about Catlin I wanted to hear it. I had to almost touch my ear to the door on account of Shirley Mae had her stereo cut up so loud I could hardly hear.

Aunt Sissy was talking real sweet, but what she was saying wasn't sweet at all. "Will-honey, I'm getting damn tired of you takin' up for that girl all th' time. Really I am. Here she got a gun an' tried to kill me. Kill me! Do you hear? Kill me—God knows what woulda happened if Ramona hadn't been there to save me!

An' all you can say is 'She didn't mean to'. You always take her part. An' I'm damn sick an' tired of it."

"I don't *always* take her part."

"Th' hell you don't. Every damn time somethin' happens an' Catlin's in it you take her part."

"But sweetheart," Uncle Will said, "she's a little orphan chile. If I take her part it's only 'cause she's got nobody else."

"There's a helluva lot more to it than that."

"No ma'am there's not. Not one bit more." Uncle Will's voice was a little mad-sounding. I put my eye down to the key hole to see what they were doing. Uncle Will was on his feet, leaning way over the bed with his arms straight up and down, like the start of a race. His head poked close to Aunt Sissy's. "How many times do I have to tell you, Sissy? There ain't no truth to what you're thinking. It ain't possible. There ain't no way *possible* I could be Daddy to that chile."

I stood up straight from leaning over the keyhole and thought. Whose Daddy? Which child? Was he still talking about Catlin? Was Uncle Will Catlin's Daddy?

"Can't you turn nothin' loose?" Uncle Will's voice came even louder through the door. I ducked my head down to the keyhole again. "God Sissy!" Uncle Will stood up and threw his arms around in the air. "You git somethin' in your head and it stays there forever." He walked away from the bed over toward the window, to where I couldn't see him. "That was ten years ago."

"Twelve" Aunt Sissy corrected him.

"Maureen Flanigan was pregnant when she got to Ruffins Inlet. You oughta know that for a fact—you hired her. I never laid eyes on th' girl till you hired her. She was pregnant. An' her no-good husband had run off an' left her."

"Husband. Huh!"

"Sissy we been over this an' over this!" Uncle Will was getting madder and madder.

"No need to raise your voice Will," Aunt Sissy said. "My hearin's perfectly good." She lit another brown cigarette and blew a stream of smoke toward where Uncle Will must have been standing. "You're gettin' too upset," she said. "Git yourself a drink."

I still couldn't see Uncle Will, but I could hear him messing around in his whiskey cabinet. And then the gurgling sound of something getting poured in a glass. Uncle Will sort of grunted and sighed and it sounded like he sat down in the big wing chair by the front window. "Maybe if it hadn't been for us, Maureen would be alive today."

"You'd like that wouldn't you?" Aunt Sissy can really make her voice sound nasty when she wants to.

"You bet I would, baby." Uncle Will let out a big sigh when he said it. "I don't need this thing on my conscience."

Aunt Sissy took another long drag on her cigarette. While she was blowing the smoke out, she took the ashtray in her lap and poked the cigarette against the bottom till it was out. "You blame me," she said. Uncle Will didn't say anything. "You blame me, admit it. It's like I was drivin' that Exxon truck myself. How'd I know th' damn girl was goin' to get drunk an' take a stroll down th' Highway in th' middle of th' night?"

"Godamighty, Sissy," Uncle Will said real loud. "Le's don't *talk* about it anymore. It's been *years*! It's all *over*!" I could hear something clanking like ice in a glass again, like Uncle Will was pouring hisself some more whiskey.

"But you *do* blame me, don't you?" Aunt Sissy had a funny sound in her voice, like she was getting ready to cry.

"I'm not th' one to blame anybody." Uncle Will said. "But you gotta admit you didn't have to do what you did. Now did you?"

"I had to protect our business, Will."

"You had to, huh? You *had to* blackball Maureen? You *had to* fix it up with all your buddies—all them people you do business with—so nobody would sell her anything?" Uncle Will started coughing like he'd swallowed his drink the wrong way. When he got through coughing, he said "After she'd sunk every penny she'd saved into that place. And was up to her ass in debt."

"Will! . . ."

"How th' hell was she s'pose to run a restaurant without food?" Two more coughs. "There's room for mor'n one restaurant in Ruffins Inlet. An' you know it."

"That's exactly what I don't know." Aunt Sissy barked at Uncle Will like a little dog. "Listen to me, Will Ruffin. When you got as many mouths to feed as I got, you can't *give* your business away. That's just what I'd've been doin' if I'da let Maureen Flanigan open up her damn restaurant."

"All right Sissy. Have it your way." More glass clanking and whiskey pouring. "Ain't no sense arguin'. You got it set in your head an' Godamighty himself couldn't change that."

Aunt Sissy started crying. "What was I gonna do, Will? Let you run off with her?"

"Run off with her?" Uncle Will's voice was getting hoarse from talking so loud. "Goddamn it, you *still* believe that, don'tcha? Sissy, I *never* was gonna run off with Maureen Flanigan. Never! Seems like after all these years you'd believe me. God knows, I've told you enough times."

"You liked her a lot, Will Ruffin. Don't deny it. You liked her a lot."

"I liked her a hell of a lot. That I did. But I never had any idea of runnin' off with her." Uncle Will walked over next to Aunt Sissy's bed, and I could see him through the keyhole again. He was sipping from his glass, and when he finished he put one elbow on the shiny bedstead and leaned over real close to Aunt Sissy. "Maureen was a po'r girl with a little baby to take care of. She needed help, Sissy."

Then another voice I wasn't expecting came from right beside me and scared the daylights out of me. "Chester St. Clair, what're you doin' listenin' at Mama's door." It was Shirley Mae, looking like a big jack-in-the-box the way her head was stuck out her bedroom door with her hair all up in big pink plastic curlers. I'd been listening so hard I hadn't heard her open her door.

"I jus' come up to read to Aunt Sissy," I whispered.

"No such a thing." Shirley Mae shook her head, and all the pink curlers went wobble, wobble. "You're listenin' to somethin' you ain't s'pose to listen to. Tha's what you're doin'." Shirley Mae ain't supposed to be very smart, but sometimes she's *very* smart. She opened her door wider and came out partways into the hall. She wasn't wearing nothing but old white overalls with the legs cut off and her boobs were coming out on both sides. "Who's Mama talkin' to?" she wanted to know.

"I don't know." I shrugged my shoulders and tried to pretend like I didn't know and I didn't care either. "I jus' come up to read to her. But sounds like she's busy talkin' to somebody, so I'll come back later." I turned around and started down the creaking stairs. I didn't look back until I got to the landing. Out of the corner of my eye, I watched Shirley Mae lean her ear over and listen at Aunt Sissy's door for a minute. Then she turned back around and went into her room. I waited a minute or two before I sneaked back up the stairs, scared that every creaky step would bring Shirley Mae back out again. But it didn't. Her stereo was making more noise than the creaky steps.

When I got back to the door, I could hear Aunt Sissy say "How'd I know she'd get herself killed because of it? How was I s'pose to know that?" I put my eye down to the keyhole. Uncle Will was sitting in my chair by the bed again. All I could see was the back of his head. He seemed to be just looking at Aunt Sissy. Not talking, just looking. Everything was quiet for a minute. Then Aunt Sissy said, "Will honey, please don't cry. Will, I can't stand it, seein' you cry like that. Pour yourself another drink. It'll make you feel better."

Then all at once Shirley Mae was back in the hall again, standing behind me with her hands on her hips. "I caught you Chester St. Clair. I caught you. You were lyin' to me before."

There wasn't no way out, so I told her the truth. "Shhhhh," I said. "Your Mama and Daddy are in there talkin' 'bout Catlin."

"What about Catlin?" She didn't whisper, but talked loud as usual.

"Shhhhh, Shirley Mae. They'll hear you," I whispered. Then I explained to her "Uncle Will don't want Catlin to go to Reform School."

"She's already gone." She whispered this time.

"I know. But maybe Uncle Will can talk Aunt Sissy into gettin' her out." I pulled Shirley Mae away from the door, and into her room so Aunt Sissy and Uncle Will couldn't hear us talking.

"Sweetpea's gonna do that," Shirley Mae said.

"Gonna do what?"

"Get Catlin outa Reform School."

"How's he gonna do that?"

"I don't know. But Catlin tol' me he was gonna do it."

"When'd she tell you that?"

"Las' night," Shirley Mae said. "I was helpin' pack her clothes in a suitcase. I was cryin' 'cause I didn't want her to go an' she said Don't worry Shirley Mae, that Sweetpea was gonna come get her. That ol' ugly Police-lady was there watchin' us an' listenin' to everything we said. So we had to whisper real soft."

"Catlin tol' you *that*?"

Shirley Mae nodded her head up and down.

"How you reckon she knew?" I asked. "How you reckon she knew Sweetpea was comin' to get her?"

Shirley Mae shrugged her shoulders and shook her head that she didn't know.

"D'you think maybe Catlin's *seen* Sweetpea?"

"Naw. She'd've tol' me."

We didn't get to talk about Sweetpea and Catlin anymore because about then is when we heard Aunt Sissy calling "Shirley Mae, Shirley Mae" real soft, like when somebody's asleep and you don't want to wake him up. Shirley Mae stepped past me and opened her Mama's door. Inside somebody *was* asleep. Uncle Will. He was sitting in my chair by Aunt Sissy's bed, but only halfway in the chair. Most of him was lying over on the bed. He was sleeping like a baby.

XXXIX

And then Ramona left.

We found that out when me and Shirley Mae went downstairs to get a Coke like Aunt Sissy told us we could. Ramona wasn't in the kitchen. Only Christine and Blossom.

"Where's Ramona?" Shirley Mae asked them. "Ain't she here?"

"Ramona gone," Blossom said. I looked at Blossom close

because her and Christine are always joking around and I thought she might be funning with us. But she wasn't. You could tell because there wasn't no sparkle in her eyes. And not a piece of smile on her face. Christine was the same way.

"She lef' that letter on th' table there," Christine said without looking up from the lettuce she was washing in the big sink.

"Wha's it for?" Shirley Mae wanted to know.

I picked up the white envelope and read out loud "Mary Eloise." It was written in pencil in big shaky letters. "Who's Mary Eloise?"

"Tha's Mama's name, dummy," Shirley Mae said. "You didn't know that?"

"Tha's her real name?"

Shirley Mae nodded her head up and down.

"I reckon we oughta take it up to her," I said.

"Le's get our Cokes first," Shirley Mae said.

The whole time we were getting our Cokes and drinking them, Christine and Blossom didn't say a word. Not to each other and not to me or Shirley Mae. That's very different from how they usually are, joking and teasing all the time. The only time one of them said anything was when I asked "Where's LeRoy?" and Christine said "He gone wid Ramona," and that was all. She didn't say where they went or how come.

After we'd drunk our Cokes, me and Shirley Mae took Ramona's letter upstairs and gave it to Aunt Sissy. Uncle Will was stretched out sound asleep on the side of the bed nearest the door, where me and Shirley Mae had rolled and pushed and shoved him, getting him out of the chair onto the bed. Aunt Sissy was on the other side, nearest the window, propped up on her pillows, working on her ledger Books, with her hurt foot sitting up high on another pillow at the bottom of the bed. When we came in the room, she moved her hurt foot a little bit to get comfortable, made a face, and said "Owwwww, that damn thing hurts." When Shirley Mae gave her Ramona's letter, she looked at "Mary Eloise" written on the front and raised her eyebrows and poked out her bottom lip, like you do sometimes when you shrug your shoulders, only Aunt Sissy didn't move her shoulders.

She opened the letter, and while she was reading it I watched her face do different things. First her eyebrows squinched down like she was having a hard time understanding what she was reading, then they went back up on her forehead like she was thinking about crying, and then her eyebrows went down over her eyes and she looked real mad. "Damnit," she said, "she can't do that to me." She crumpled the letter up and threw it across the room. "Who th' hell does she think she is?"

"What's it say, Mama?" Shirley Mae wanted to know.

"What?" Aunt Sissy said, almost like she didn't know she was talking. Then she looked up and saw me and Shirley Mae standing there by the bed looking at her. "Oh," she said, "it's Ramona." She took a deep breath and blew it back out like a snort. "She's gone."

"You mean she's gone on a trip or something like that?" I asked.

"No, I don't mean she's gone on no damn trip." Aunt Sissy spit the words out. "I mean she's *gone*! Gone away! Left!" She reached over and caught Uncle Will's shoulder and gave it a shake. Uncle Will rocked back and forth without opening an eye. He was breathing through his mouth and his nose at the same time and making a snoring racket. "Will!" Aunt Sissy said, "Wake up! We gotta get over to Ramona's house quick." She shook Uncle Will some more. "Will, Ramona's leavin'." More shakes. "Will, you gotta wake up. I swear t'God I don't know what I'm gonna do without Ramona." Now she was rocking Uncle Will real hard, back and forth like a rowboat that you're standing up in and pushing down with your left foot on one side and your right on the other. Even with all that rolling, Uncle Will never even started to wake up. Directly, Aunt Sissy decided there wasn't no use trying to wake him up and she gave him a final hard push like she was mad at him and then she stopped shaking him. She turned her head and looked out the window a minute, like she was thinking, figuring out what to do.

"Tha's *all* Ramona said in th' letter, Mama?" Shirley Mae asked her Mama.

Aunt Sissy didn't answer her for a second and then she nodded her head Yes. She sat there looking big-eyed, like a little girl, sort of. We waited, but she didn't tell us anymore about what Ramona said.

"How come she lef', Aunt Sissy?" I asked. I figured maybe if I asked her straight out she'd tell me.

Aunt Sissy didn't answer me back for a long time. Then she said, "Ramona's got a cousin in Orangeburg tha's real sick. An' Ramona's gone to take care of her."

"Tha's too bad," I said.

"Crappola," Aunt Sissy said. "Ain't a word of it true. Oh, she's got a cousin in Orangeburg okay. But I betcha a quarter th' cousin ain't sick. Betcha th' cousin ain't even got a runny nose."

"How come she'd tell you that if it ain't th' truth?" I asked. "You think Ramona'd lie to you, Aunt Sissy?"

"Oh hell, it aint' exactly lyin'," Aunt Sissy said. "She made up that story 'cause she didn't want to tell me th' *real* reason she was goin'. As if I didn't know." She looked out the window again. "Lord, I never had any idea Ramona'd walk out on me like this. Without even sayin' Goodbye."

I was trying to understand what Aunt Sissy had meant by the *real* reason Ramona had left. It didn't make sense that she'd say she was leaving for a reason when that wasn't the reason at all.

"I want my Ramona," Shirley Mae said. She started crying, but you could tell she was faking because no tears were coming out. Just noise.

Aunt Sissy reached over and patted Shirley Mae's hand. "Hush up Shirley Mae, that ain't gonna do no good. Cryin' never helps. Ramona's gonna do what she wants to do an' cryin' ain't gonna change it." Then she gave Uncle Will's shoulder another shake. "Will, wake up! Ramona's gone. Will, d'you hear me?" She shook him a couple more times. "Will, we gotta get over to Ramona's house an' talk her out of leavin'." Two more shakes. "Will, Goddamn it. I got a hurt foot. An' I can't drive that damn car anyhow. Will, I need you. Wake up!" She shook his shoulder a few more times. Then she said "Oh hell" and quit shaking.

"What we gonna do, Mama?" Shirley Mae asked.

Aunt Sissy picked up her pink princess telephone and punched some numbers and waited. "What we gotta do right now," she said, "is get help for them girls downstairs. Hello. Adelaide?" Aunt Adelaide must have asked Aunt Sissy how her toe was. "Hurts like hell," Aunt Sissy said. "But that ain't what I called about. I need you over here at th' Manor." Aunt Adelaide must have asked What for? "I ain't got time to talk now, but Ramona

· 204 ·

lef'. Yes, that's what I said. Ramona's gone. It's gonna be hell gettin' all them folks fed this evenin', so get yourself on over here. An' bring Bernadette if you can." She stopped and listened a minute. "Yeah, an' me stuck in bed with this damn foot." Then another minute and Aunt Sissy said "Okay, bye."

Shirley Mae started whining again. "I want Ramona."

Aunt Sissy said "Sweetheart, don't do that. I'm mad, an' my foot hurts like hell. So jus' don't fuss, okay?" She wiggled her pointing finger up and down at the pink telephone, telling me to hand it to her. She took the phone and punched out some more numbers and waited. "Why can't they answer th' damn phone over there?" she asked, looking at me. I didn't know who she was calling, so I couldn't answer her. Then she was talking to somebody on the other end. "Who's that?" Aunt Sissy asked right away without saying "Hello" first. "Chico, put Benny on th' phone quick." Whatever Chico said made Aunt Sissy make a face like she smelled something bad. "He did? What th' hell did he go to Ocean City for?... Never mind. It don't matter. Chico, I'm lookin' for Ramona." Then Chico said something that made her smile. "She is? Okay, now don't you let her get on that damn bus, you hear?" She listened to Chico a minute. Then she said, "I don't give a damn how big she is. You keep her off that bus, y'hear?" Then she handed me the phone to put back in its holder.

Me and Shirley Mae were standing there, waiting for Aunt Sissy to tell us something. But she didin't. She looked at us and said "Don't just stand there. We gotta get movin'. Han' me my damn crutches." Then she started climbing out of bed, cussing the whole time. "Ow-wey. How can one damn toe hurt so Goddamn bad?"

"What crutches you talkin' 'bout Aunt Sissy?" I asked her.

"Th' ones th' Doctor lef', dummy." She pointed under the bed. And sure enough, there were some crutches there.

"How th' hell do you use these damn things?" She asked the question, but she didn't need no answer. She stuck the crutches under her arms and started hobbling toward the door. "Damn rotten time to have a bum toe. Oww!"

"Where we goin' Mama?" Shirley Mae asked her.

"C'mon. I'll tell you in th' car." Aunt Sissy was all the way to the door now. Hobbling pretty good. I jumped over and opened it for her. Shirley Mae and me followed her out the door and then helped her down the steps. That wasn't no easy job. We tried every which-a-way. The best way turned out to be me on one side and Shirley Mae on the other, holding her up going down one step at a time, real slow. All the time Aunt Sissy was cussing and telling us what we were doing wrong. When we got half way down, Christine and Blossom came up from the kitchen and helped Aunt Sissy the rest of the way. They could do it good, and Aunt Sissy didn't cuss so much. When we got down to the bottom step, I remembered the crutches and ran back and got them from the top of the stairs.

"Get me out to th' car," Aunt Sissy told Christine and Blossom, and that's what they did. Shirley Mae was asking her "How come you goin' to th' car, Mama. You can't drive."

"Well, I'm gonna drive." Aunt Sissy was grunting and groaning the whole way across the yard to where the big black car was parked. "Plenty of people dumber'n me can drive. So I can too."

"Mama, how you gonna drive?" Shirley Mae wanted to know. "Yo' foot's hurt. An' it don't reach all th' way to th' floor anyway."

"Honey, you jus' hush up an' watch, okay?" Christine and Blossom had got her all the way in the front seat, behind the wheel. Shirley Mae was wrong, her Mama's feet did touch the floor. They just couldn't reach the pedals. "All right now," Aunt Sissy said. "Chester, get down on th' floor an' work th' gas an' brakes, y'hear? That little one there on th' right side's th' gas. An' th' big wide one's th' brakes. I know *that* much." She looked at the speedometer and all that other stuff that tells you things about the car. Then she looked up and saw us all watching her. "Ches, damnit, get in. We got no time to waste. Christine close th' damn door an' you an' Blossom get on back in the kitchen. You got plenty to do. Miss Adelaide'll be here in a few minutes to help. Now scat!"

I was scared I'd bump Aunt Sissy's toe scrunching in on her side. So I went around to the other side and crawled in. Shirley Mae got in the back seat and hung her head over into the front so she could watch. "Whatcha do first, Mama?"

"Ches, push down on th' brake. No, th' big one, damnit. Tha's right. Now everybody hol' yo' breath. I'm gonna turn th' key. Ready Ches?"

I said "Yes'm," but I wasn't really. Down there on my hands and knees on the floor, I couldn't see nothing and I didn't know what I was doing. I was scared. But I didn't tell her.

"Now, when I turn th' motor on give 'er a little gas with y'other han'." I pointed at the little pedal and looked up for her to nod if it was the right one. But she wasn't looking at me. She was looking out the front window with her eyebrows squinched down over her eyes.

"This one, Aunt Sissy?"

She looked down for a second and nodded her head. "I think tha's th' one. We gonna find out right now." Then she turned the key and the motor started and I pushed down on the gas. The motor went hud-n-n-n-n real fast.

"Don't push down so far Ches, damnit. You gotta push easy. Ease up." I let the gas pedal loose for a second and then pushed it down just a teeny bit. The motor went Hud-n-n-n again, but not so fast. "Good, now take yo' han' off th' brake." So I did, and nothing happened. "Hell, what'd we do wrong?" Aunt Sissy said, looking at the speedometer and other stuff. "Oh, I know." She shifted her fanny in the seat and then she said, "Push down on the brakes again, Ches boy. Okay, you got 'em? Push down hard, now."

"Yes'm."

"Gotta put it in gear. Lemme see." She was pushing the little handle up and down. "I don't know what th' hell that N means, but D must mean *drive*. Okay, Ches, let up on th' brakes. Easy, now. Easy."

I did what she told me and the car started moving.

"Hooray," Shirley Mae said. "Mama can drive, Mama can drive."

"You damn betcha Mama can drive," Aunt Sissy said. "Give 'er a little more gas, Ches." I pushed down a little harder with my right hand. "Brakes! Brakes!" Aunt Sissy yelled. I pushed down on the brakes, but the car didn't stop. It only slowed down. Then we hit something. "Goddamn!"

"You hit a tree, Mama."

"I *know* a damn tree when I see one, Shirley Mae. Now hush up an' lemme drive."

"Yes'm."

"Ches, you ready?"

"Yes'm," I lied.

"Now next time when I yell 'Brakes' you turn loose th' gas an' push th' brakes with both hands, y'hear? Real hard."

"Yes'm."

"Lemme see. We gotta back this damn thing up, don't we? Push on the brakes, Ches." Aunt Sissy pushed the little gear handle up and down some more. "Ain't no damn B on here for *back-up*. Le's try R for *reverse*. Okay, Ches. Easy now. Turn loose th' brakes an' give 'er some gas." I was pretty scared now, but I did like she told me. I hardly pushed on the gas at all. "More gas," she said. So I pushed harder.

"Brakes! Brakes!" I quick put both hands on the brakes and pushed hard as I could, but I was too late. Bam! We'd hit something else and on top of that I'd bumped Aunt Sissy's bad foot. "Oww-w-wey."

"We hit th' porch, Mama."

"Goddamnit, I know it, Shirley Mae." Aunt Sissy's face was all squeezed up like her toe was hurting bad.

"I'm sorry, Aunt Sissy."

"Okay, but don't do it again. Now Shirley Mae, hush yo' mouth or we gonna leave you home. Y'hear?"

"Yes'm"

"O-o-ey. This po' damn toe," Aunt Sissy said. "We ain't got time to wait for it to quit hurtin'!" She wiggled her fanny in the seat again, shifted the gear handle and said, "Give 'er some gas." I pushed down easy on the gas. "Little more." I pushed a little bit harder and we were moving. "Good boy, Chester." We went on a little ways and I could tell we were going across the front yard from all the bumps we were getting from the big tree roots. Then we were on the road and it got smooth. "Give 'er more gas, Ches. We gotta get to th' fillin' station before th' damn Greyhound leaves."

"Yes'm." I pushed a little harder on the gas. But not much. I kept feeling like we were going to run into something else any minute. A loud honking horn passed by one side and a voice yelled out "Stupid idiot . . . My Lord, it's Sissy St. Clair."

"Watch who you call names, Bud Mercer," Aunt Sissy yelled back over her shoulder.

"Mama, you ain't s'pose to drive down the middle," Shirley Mae said. "You're s'pose to stay on one side."

"Give 'er a little more gas, Ches. We gonna miss that damn bus if we don't get there soon." I pushed down on the gas pedal just a teeny bit more. I knew we were almost to the Highway and I knew with all them cars zipping by I had to be ready to push on the brakes. I was praying to the Lord we wouldn't get killed. Then we turned, and I knew we were on the Highway because all these horns were blowing. Soft when they started, then real loud as they passed on one side or the other, and then dying away.

"Mama! Th' Greyhound's there," Shirley Mae yelled. "Looks like it's pullin' out." Then I heard the loud bus horn real near. And felt the bump. "There," Aunt Sissy said.

That's when we hit the Greyhound bus. I didn't know till afterwards what it was, because I couldn't see anything. And I got bumped up against the brake pedal, but not bad. It didn't hardly hurt at all because we were going pretty slow. I got up off the floor just when the bus driver was coming up to Aunt Sissy's car. He was real mad.

"Lady, are you out of your damn mind?" he asked Aunt Sissy. "If I hadn't stopped the bus we'd have all. . . . " His cussing didn't bother Aunt Sissy a bit.

"Driver you've got Ramona Wilcox on that bus," she said. "I wanta talk to her."

"You wanta *talk* to her?" the bus driver yelled. He looked a little bit crazy. "You wanta talk to her, so you run into my bus? What're you, crazy?"

"Driver, my foot is hurtin' bad. I don't know how much longer I can put up with you."

"Put up with me?" The driver was screaming now. I was scared he was going to maybe hit Aunt Sissy.

Along about then Chico came up pulling Ramona along, with LeRoy tagging behind. "Here she eees," he said. "Here Ramona, Aunt Seesee."

"Ramona, I come to take you home," Aunt Sissy said.

"Ain't goin' home wid you, Miss Sissy," Ramona said. "Goin' to Orangeburg to look after my cousin."

"Crappola," Aunt Sissy said. "Yo' cousin ain't sick."

"What th' hell's goin' on?" the driver wanted to know.

"Don't butt in, boy," Aunt Sissy told him. "Ramona, yo' cousin ain't sick an' you damn well know it. You goin' up to Orangeburg to take care of that kid."

"I goin' to look after my cousin," Ramona said. The look on her face stayed the same. No smile, no frown, no nothing. Lots of people had got off the bus and were standing around watching.

"Lady," the bus driver screamed. "Will you get your damn car out of the way so this bus can leave?" Some of the bus people said "Yeah, lady," and "Le's get goin'" and things like that.

"Reach me my crutches," Aunt Sissy said over her shoulder to Shirley Mae. Then she opened the car door to get out.

"Crutches? Oh, my God," the bus driver said. Me and Shirley Mae helped Aunt Sissy out of the car and onto her crutches. The bus people moved back to make a path for her.

"Chico, move th' Caddie so these people can go," Aunt Sissy said while she hobbled toward the Filling Station. Chico got in Aunt Sissy's car and slowly eased it away from the bus and over by the Station. The bus driver looked over the front of his bus, but we hadn't hardly dented it so he shook his head and yelled "All aboard." The bus people started climbing back onto the bus.

"Ramona, we been together all our lives," Aunt Sissy said. She was really begging Ramona. "Please don't go. I don't know how I'm gonna do without you."

"You'll get along," Ramona said.

"But damnit Ramona, I need you."

"That chile needs me mo'."

"There! See? You admit it." Aunt Sissy stopped her hobbling and turned so she was looking straight at Ramona. "You *are* goin' up there to look out for that chile."

Ramona didn't answer her. She looked at her a minute, then she took LeRoy by the arm and headed for the bus. The last few people were getting on, and the driver was trying to get them to hustle. "That chile needs me," Ramona called back over her shoulder.

"Oh, Ramona. . . ." Aunt Sissy held out her hand and slowly slipped down on the ground. Like she was fainting, but she was careful when she fell not to hurt herself. Me and Shirley Mae tried to catch her, but she was too heavy. And when we stooped to help her up Aunt Sissy hissed at us, "Get away."

"Ain't no use, Mary Eloise," Ramona called from the bus door. "You can't fool me. I know you too long."

Aunt Sissy raised up on her elbows and then pushed herself to sitting up again. "Ramona, damnit," she yelled.

"Bye, Miss Sissy," Ramona called back at the same time the bus door closed. And then the bus pulled off.

"They got me over a damn barrel," Aunt Sissy groaned.

XL

Everybody keeps telling me that Ramona and Catlin will be home soon. But it sure ain't happened yet. Mama says them things take time. And she says a little bit of Reform School won't hurt Catlin anyway. It will teach her to be a good and decent human being, that's what Mama says. She says Catlin needs a strong hand to show her right from wrong, so she won't end up being a bad criminal when she grows up. Maybe Mama's right. I sure don't want Catlin to be a bad criminal when she grows up.

"Mama, you really think Catlin's bad?"

"Well, honey. That wasn't exactly *good*, was it? Shooting your Aunt Sissy with a gun?"

I reckon Catlin shouldn't have shot Aunt Sissy's toe off like she did. Now Aunt Sissy's got to use a walking stick to even stand up, on account of she ain't got her big toe to help balance her. I didn't know it before, but your big toe does a lot of balancing for you. If it wasn't for your big toe, you'd fall down all the time because you couldn't balance yourself.

Aunt Sissy don't like to talk about Catlin coming home. But I had to ask her about it. Because when you ask anybody else they always tell you they don't know. So when I was reading the murder book to Aunt Sissy yesterday afternoon, I just plain asked her "Aunt Sissy when's Catlin an' Ramona comin' home?"

Aunt Sissy didn't answer me at first, or look at me either. She sat there in her big bed and puffed on one of her long, brown cigarettes, like I hadn't asked her anything. Then she blew out a bunch of smoke and said "Catlin don't want to come home."

"She don't?" I was really surprised.

"Yo' Uncle Will's been up there twice to coax her back. Catlin says she'd rather stay at Reform School than come back here." Aunt Sissy laughed a silly laugh and gave a little shrug. "Tha's what she says. She'd rather be there than here. In Reform School, for Christ's sake. I don't understand that at all."

"She's still mad 'cause you got Booze killed."

Aunt Sissy turned herself around so she was looking straight at me, and snarled at me "I'm sick of hearin' 'bout that damn dog. Y'hear? Damn vicious animal."

"Yes'm." She got so upset, I was scared to tell her about the Senator's boys poking sticks at Booze.

She turned back and took a last puff on her cigarette and poked it out in the ashtray. I thought that was all the talking we were going to do, so I opened the book and was looking for the page from the day before. All at once Aunt Sissy said, "Ches-boy, you just gave me an idea."

I looked up from the murder book. "I did?"

"Frank Jenkins' ol' hunting bitch had puppies here a while back." Aunt Sissy was smiling a funny way. "If he ain't got rid of 'em all, I'm gonna get one from him. I'm sure gonna do that."

"An give it to Catlin?" I put my finger in between the pages so I wouldn't lose the place.

"Next time yo' Uncle Will goes up to Orangeburg he'll take along a little present from me. That just might work."

That made me feel good and I told Aunt Sissy so.

"Well, I can't wait for Ramona to get back," Aunt Sissy allowed. "But I gotta tell you, I don't know what th' hell I'm gonna do with Catlin when she gets home. She hates me. An' I admit, I ain't too crazy about her either."

"Catlin don't hate you, Aunt Sissy," I told her. "She's took up for you when people said things."

"She has?"

"Lotsa times." I really couldn't remember but one time, but it sounded like a good thing to say.

Aunt Sissy thought about that a minute. Then she sighed and shook her head. "It sho ain't gonna be easy," she said. "I mean, th' way that kid talks back burns me up. Makes me madder'n hell. It's like she's all the time got a chip on her shoulder. And when you say anything to her, she thinks you're trying to push her around."

"Mama says you and her are a lot alike."

"Who? You mean Catlin an' me?" Aunt Sissy gave one of her snorting laughs. "You gotta be kiddin'. We ain't a damn bit alike."

"Mama said Catlin copies th' way you do things. Th' way you talk. Th' way you kinda strut when you walk. Things like that."

"Lucille said that, did she?"

"Yes'm."

"Mmmmmm. Catlin's like me, huh?"

"Tha's what Mama says."

"Well, I'll be damned." Aunt Sissy thought a minute. She slipped another cigarette out of the package beside her on the bed, and I struck a kitchen match for her to light it by. She took a puff and blew the smoke out and watched it float off in the air. "Well, I'll tell you. That's one chile you can't push around."

"No'm."

"I mean, she don't take nothin' off nobody." Aunt Sissy shook her head back and forth and smiled. "Tha's like me." She said the words soft, like she wasn't really saying them to me.

Then the whole time I was reading to her she was only halfway listening. She kept stopping me every now and then and saying "Catlin's like me, huh?" and I'd say "Yes'm" and then go on back to reading again. I'll probably have to read that part all over again because she won't remember a bit of what I read.

Mama said something else that I wanted to talk to Aunt Sissy about. But it was about Sweetpea. And you can't talk to her about Sweetpea. What Mama said was that she bets Sweetpea will be coming home one of these days. She said that him and Aunt Sissy are tied by too much love to stay away from each other for long.

"Lordy, Mama!" I said. "All that screaming and yelling sho didn't sound like love to me. Sounded more like they hated each other."

"Ches-honey," Mama said. "You, most times, can't tell by the noise people make what's going on inside them. You have to look beneath the surface. And you can take my word for it. Your Aunt Sissy and Sweetpea have a lot of love for each other. One of these days Sweetpea'll be back home again."

"You really think so?"

"I almost guarantee it."

That got me to thinking. I want Sweetpea to come home, but maybe it'd be better if he didn't. If he comes home, I won't be able to use his room anymore. And Aunt Sissy sure wouldn't give me the red jeep then, I don't think.

But I'll be glad when Catlin gets home. There ain't nobody around here that's fun to play with like her. Nobody to go shrimping with, or fishing with, or do anything fun with. Right now I'd give anything to go crabbing with Catlin over on Palmetto Causeway.

And I sure hope she gets back before next Thursday. That's when school starts and I'm kind of worried about it. There ain't no school here in Ruffins Inlet, you know. We have to catch a school bus and ride all the way up to Ocean City to go to school. I get a little bit scared thinking about going to a school I don't know, in a different town that I don't know anything about. I try not to think about it. But if Catlin gets home before then, it'll be a lot easier. I'll have somebody to go with and tell me where things are. She knows all that stuff.

I got plenty to do till school starts. Aunt Sissy keeps me busy reading murder books to her every afternoon. And I help look after Shirley Mae in the mornings. And I sweep out the Laundrymat and wipe off the machines every day. And take care of Mama. She still ain't got her strength back. But she's getting better every day. And she's real pleased with me. I haven't said "shit" in a long time.